PINTAIL

THE CODE

G.B. JOYCE is the author of six books of sports non-fiction, most recently *The Devil and Bobby Hull*. He has worked for ESPN since 2003 and before that was a sports columnist at *The Globe and Mail*. Gare worked for a year as a scout for the Columbus Blue Jackets while researching a previous book.

THE CODE

G.B. JOYCE

PINTAIL

PINTAIL
a member of Penguin Group (USA)

Published by the Penguin Group
Penguin Group (Canada), 90 Eglinton Avenue East, Suite 700, Toronto, Ontario, Canada M4P 2Y3
(a division of Pearson Canada Inc.)

Penguin Group (USA) Inc., 375 Hudson Street, New York, New York 10014, U.S.A.
Penguin Books Ltd, 80 Strand, London WC2R 0RL, England
Penguin Ireland, 25 St Stephen's Green, Dublin 2, Ireland (a division of Penguin Books Ltd)
Penguin Group (Australia), 250 Camberwell Road, Camberwell, Victoria 3124, Australia
(a division of Pearson Australia Group Pty Ltd)
Penguin Books India Pvt Ltd, 11 Community Centre, Panchsheel Park, New Delhi – 110 017, India
Penguin Group (NZ), 67 Apollo Drive, Rosedale, Auckland 0632, New Zealand
(a division of Pearson New Zealand Ltd)
Penguin Books (South Africa) (Pty) Ltd, 24 Sturdee Avenue, Rosebank,
Johannesburg 2196, South Africa

Penguin Books Ltd, Registered Offices: 80 Strand, London WC2R 0RL, England

First published in Viking hardcover by Penguin Canada,
a division of Pearson Canada Inc., 2012
Published in this edition, 2012

2 3 4 5 6 7 8 9 10 (RRD)

Copyright © Penguin Group (Canada), 2012

Manufactured in the U.S.A.

ISBN: 978-0-670-06690-2

Visit the Penguin US website at **www.penguin.com**

PEARSON

For Nick Garrison

Year	Team	Games	Goals	Assists	Points	PIM
1985-86	Boston College	43	11	12	23	26
1986-87	Boston College	43	20	19	39	48
1987-88	Minnesota	4	1	0	1	4
1987-88	Kalamazoo	61	17	25	42	67
1988-89	Los Angeles	13	2	4	6	11
1988-89	New Haven	59	19	30	49	78
1989-90	Los Angeles	45	7	15	22	63
1989-90	New Haven	30	15	11	26	33
1990-91	Los Angeles	65	13	20	33	88
1991-92	Los Angeles	61	11	21	32	101
1992-93	Los Angeles	32	4	9	13	28
1992-93	Montreal	22	4	11	15	10
1993-94	Montreal	36	7	9	16	45
1993-94	Vancouver	20	6	10	16	14
1994-95	Vancouver	70	21	26	47	27
1995-96	Vancouver	6	0	2	2	7
1996-97	Vancouver	12	2	5	7	4
1996-97	Toronto	18	3	3	6	10
1996-97	Pittsburgh	7	1	2	3	6
1996-97	Syracuse	15	3	2	5	29
1996-97	Wilkes-Barre	3	0	2	2	4
1997-98	Pittsburgh	34	5	7	12	11
1997-98	New York	21	4	5	9	16
1997-98	Wilkes-Barre	5	0	3	3	2
1997-98	Hartford	13	4	3	7	25
League Career		**458**	**91**	**149**	**240**	**445**
League Playoffs						
1989-90	Los Angeles	6	1	0	1	4
1990-91	Los Angeles	8	2	1	3	6
1991-92	Los Angeles	6	2	2	4	2
1992-93	Montreal	17	7	6	13	8
1993-94	Vancouver	14	3	5	8	10
1996-97	Pittsburgh	5	1	1	2	4
League Career Playoff		**56**	**16**	**15**	**31**	**34**

Brad Shade

Center
6'1"
195 lbs
Sept 25, 1967
Toronto, Ont.

Drafted by Minnesota
(2nd round, 30th overall
in 1986)

Understand that the league is a systemic organization of hatreds. You might know a lot about the game but you'll know nothing about the league until you accept this. It's true of all of them: the players, the coaches, the general managers, the executives, the agents, and the owners. It goes from the high and mighty, the commissioner and his ilk in their plush Madison Avenue offices, right down to the lowest ranks, the scouts who sit next to me in arenas great and small.

No man is above the blackest animus. Could be a ref you jawed with. Could be your linemate who maybe knows your girlfriend better than he says. Could be the agent who rounds up his cut every time he thinks you're not looking. Could be the massage therapist who rubbed you the wrong way. Could be the goalie farting in the whirlpool when you're next in. If you are or were in the league in any capacity, even for the briefest time, somewhere somebody hopes that the next breath you draw will be your last. And guys won't give up hating you when you're dead. At that point the hate crosses over and they'll draw the same exquisite satisfaction from your demise that they'd take from raising the Cup.

Hated and Hated By: They should be listed on a hockey card, right below the height, weight, position, and hometown. They're a lot more important than your hometown, that's for sure.

I've got my hates, too—not many, but deeply felt. The number-one slot is reserved for Lavery, the guy who kneed me and shredded my ACL. I think of him when it rains. That's my Arthur, which has me popping Celebrex in the A.M. and hobbling whenever I have to climb two flights of stairs. I'll probably end up with plastic where there's bone, but for now I'll put off the repair work. Once I seize my chance to run Lavery off the road I'll see the surgeon and my conscience will be clear.

Lavery edges out, barely, the agent who somehow managed my finances into complete ruin and gave me nothing more than a well-practised what-can-you-do shrug. He parked my money and all his clients' in blocks of commercial buildings in downtown Pittsburgh, in what he said was a sure winner. Upon the subprime crash, tenants fled in the dark of night, and soon our investments couldn't have been deeper underwater than if we'd thrown our money into a parking lot in suburban Atlantis. Did I mention that my trusted rep bought these properties on "our behalf" from his brother-in-law? I had hopes that the criminal justice system would look after him for screwing me and two dozen other clients, but the courts spat him out. I guess the judge figured that millions earned playing hockey isn't like money socked away from honest toil.

I played with a bunch of names you'd recognize: Gretz, Mess, Mario. I played against all the others who mattered. I didn't last long in the league: 457 career games. One year near the end I got called up from Hartford for a single game and was told I was being sent back down before I untied my skates. You can buy my rookie card for a nickel. For every league game I played, I played two in the bus leagues. My last four seasons I spent on a European tour—Germany, Switzerland, Russia, and Finland.

One sportswriter tagged me "the Journeyman's Journeyman," a pejorative squared. They always said I was "good in the room." I was just being pragmatic. I wasn't good enough on the ice to have an attitude. Gifted, I wasn't. I had to think my way around the ice, and I took the same approach off it. I played in the minors with and against dozens of guys who were better than me but who never played a game in the league or landed a job there after hanging up their skates. Funny how in the minors I felt like a guy apart, like I got inside the league's door only far enough to get it slammed on the instep of my skate.

2

Whoever said no man is an island has never stood in front of a customs officer at Frankfurt International and tried to explain that he lost his passport and his ticket. At that moment I felt as lonely and desolate as a shipwreck-strewn shoal off the Bikini Atoll, and twice as radioactive.

The customs officer, a guy who reads Nietzsche for laughs, took one look at me and pressed a button on his console, presumably reserving the lead-off spot working the waterboard in the EU's interrogation playroom. He didn't need to shine a light in my eyes—he just let it reflect off his shaven pate. The Plexiglas he sat behind muffled his questions. I could barely make out his words, and those behind me could hear only me desperately pleading my case.

"I'm sorry ... I lost it and my ticket too," I told him.

"Canadian," I told him.

"In the Czech Republic," I told him.

"Someone took my computer bag," I told him.

"I'm a scout ... a hockey scout ... not a player, a scout. I work for a professional team, Los Angeles," I told him.

"No, I'm not American. I'm Canadian. I live in Canada and work for an American company," I told him.

"I'm a scout ... someone who looks for players," I told him.

"I went to Stockholm and Prague. No other countries. Eight days. I arrived March 7," I told him.

"Yes, I know I'm in Germany now. I arrived an hour ago," I told him.

"I haven't contacted the Canadian consulate ... This just happened in the airport here, maybe an hour ago," I told him.

Saint Peter would roll out the red carpet for a war criminal (probably the customs officer's grandfather) before I'd be allowed to move from Terminal 4 to Terminal 3. Smiling security guards used to hold open the back door at the arenas, never bothering to ask for my league credentials and chasing away any autograph seekers. In those days I was somebody. Now I was being held up while everyone else was asked a couple of questions, quickly checked out, and instantly cleared by the Interpol database.

The officer spoke into a microphone in his lapel and his superior immediately entered the booth through a back door. They talked, turning the volume down lest I pick up a word. If only I'd taken German instead of Spanish in high school—then again, the looks they gave me made me think I was better off not being forewarned of my fate.

I cast a backwards glance despite the risk of fuelling the customs officers' suspicion that I was out in front of a vast global conspiracy. I saw four scouts from other teams standing in line, but in this, my moment of greatest need, I could take no comfort from the company of my peers. They were glaring at me for the holdup, not that I had any hope that they'd vouch for me and run the risk of getting dragged into this mess.

Maybe if I'd been a well-known, well-respected veteran hockey man, a scout who was one of the boys, they'd have spoken up for me. That wasn't the case. At the end of my playing days, I'd been the object of ridicule when my life's belongings, my Cup ring even, were put on the auction block. My second life in the game was still an unlikely experiment, a reclamation project. I'd been a scout for not quite two full seasons and this was my first trip to Europe. I was still a few years away from acceptance by the open-minded, and many, maybe most, would never have the time of day for me. My work with the players' association's assistance program for its troubled alums should have helped my standing with the scouts, but it didn't. The guys who have clout in scouting circles generally didn't need help when they were playing or afterward.

I'm not sure who could have bailed me out of this jam in Frankfurt. As my problem escalated into a full-blown international crisis, the guys behind me shuffled over to another customs officer. I knew their faces and names. Anderson was the leader of the little pack. Back in my first week in the league he'd jumped me. I didn't appreciate it, but then again it wasn't me who had to get sewn up in the dressing room. You might still be able to lift my knuckle prints from his formerly fractured orbital bone. Anderson learned the hard way that you should always find out if the rookie you're going to chirp and run is a left-hander.

From the other line Anderson panned the room, but he really only wanted to look at me without drawing attention to himself. For the split second that our eyes made contact, he registered exaggerated amusement and unexaggerated condescension. On the ice, Anderson and two of the others had made more in one contract than I did in my whole career. His look said: Winners' line over here. What's that make your line?

I stood there for a few awful minutes as the others moved through customs with nary a snag. Anderson even offered a smirk and then said, just loud enough for me to hear but not draw attention to himself, "School's out." My blood pressure shot up and my hands started to shake. In the first-class lounge they were messaging contractors about progress on the additions to their Muskoka estates. Me, I was still standing there, worried that, among other things, my child-support payments might not clear. And, worse, I worried that they'd hook me up to a polygraph and ask me again what I did for a living. Would the arm swing way across the page, catching me not in a lie but in self-doubt about a job I'd been handed unexpectedly? Does it show up as telling the truth if you're talking about living a lie?

Never in my playing days had I been so nervous that I couldn't think straight. I could be counted on to make the right play, the smart play. At this point, though, I made an error that would be replayed forever in *The Worst Plays in Hockey History* should the Frankfurt security video ever land in the hands of a mean-spirited sports-network producer. I reached to my hip and slipped my BlackBerry out of its case.

"Maybe if I call ...," I said and nothing more. At that point red lights started flashing, a buzzer deafened with a white noise, soldiers with guns drawn rushed me, and the area went into lockdown. The BlackBerry was ripped from my hands and I was knocked to the floor, the barrel of an automatic weapon pressed to the back of my head and the heel of a boot cracking my spine.

Before I'd been handed an L.A. clipboard and a windbreaker with the team logo on it, I heard a lot about the fraternity of scouts. I was looking forward to working beside men who shared my love of the game and hoped to be part of a winning team off the ice. Prostrate on the floor of Frankfurt International, I had my epiphany. I went from disappointment that none of the other scouts had backed me up to anger that Anderson would tell this story over beers on the scouting circuit. And I had plenty of reason to believe that Anderson knew exactly where my passport and ticket were. He was a strong number two to Lavery on my hate list and rising.

I WAS DETAINED for forty-eight hours, but thankfully my plight didn't make the national news or the sports pages. My ticket was likely floating in the Frankfurt sewage system and my passport had probably already moved on the black market. The Canadian consulate sent over temporary letters of transit, which were stamped and handed to me without ceremony. No apologies from my captors. They gave me back my BlackBerry, pointed me to the door, and turned their backs. I felt vaguely disappointed that I couldn't sustain their suspicions, that they viewed me as too pathetic to pose even a minimal threat.

I called Hunts from a payphone at the terminal. He told me that he'd been trying to get hold of me and feared the worst—that I was out on a bender or was banging some Czech talent. "If only," I said. I gave him the cursory details, my passport, ticket, and computer bag lifted when I dozed off on my stopover, leaving out the flashing lights and automatic weapons. Told him that the power wound down on my BlackBerry and I had a short in my adapter. Even downplaying it this way I looked like a screw-up, but at least it was Hunts. He let me off with a "you effin' dope." I deserved worse since I was sticking the team with a hefty premium to change my flight home.

"Never again," I told him.

"Same thing occurred to me," he said.

This mocking forgiveness was a shining example of the

flipside to Ubiquitous and Undying Hate: loyalties. You build them as a player if there's a brain inside your helmet, and you hope they'll keep you in the game at the end of your career.

The loyalties are built around a moment, something that passes between two guys, unnoticed by everyone else but deeply appreciated by one of the principals. It might be jumping into a fight to bail out the guy on the losing end, or covering for a roommate on night manoeuvres when his wife calls. You hope that the guy whose loyalty you've won will become a big deal in the league and you'll be part of his crew. You see it all the time. A team hires a veteran general manager and he gives jobs to the guys who worked for him before. They'll follow him from one organization to another and then on to the next. Or a team will hire a big name, giving him his first executive job, and he puts a bunch of former teammates on the payroll.

It doesn't matter if it's a GM who's in the Hall of Fame or someone who's sitting behind the desk for the first time. He'll presume that the members of his posse will have his back. They usually do, though often with knives in their hands. That is to say, loyalties are forever except when they're just memories.

Yeah, the game is played on ice but the league is like an iceberg. If you're not on the inside, you don't see five-sixths of what's going on. People think of hockey as a cold-weather game, but it's tropical compared to the league. The league is a business as cold as the dark side of Pluto.

I have a job thanks to a loyalty forged, as usual, with generosity in awful circumstances. Chad Hunt, the GM who hired me, slept on my couch in Los Angeles when his wife threw him out. Her mistake.

Nobody thought that much of Hunts at the time—he was just some kid from Morden, Manitoba, a goaltender, making the league minimum. Hunts looked like a career backup or even a minor-leaguer. But once the divorce was final you wouldn't have recognized him. He lifted his chin off his chest and angled it upwards. His back straightened out of a depressed stoop. His demeanour went from all-is-lost to eff you. He turned into the Masked Marvel. Three times he landed on the league's second all-star team and he parlayed that into a five-year contract, that, for a season anyway, made him the highest-paid goaltender in the game and one of the ten highest paid at any position. When he signed that deal I'd played my last game in the league and was playing out the string for sixty grand tax-free in Europe.

People outside the league thought his breakthrough was a matter of him getting her off his mind. It was really him getting off the bottle. His drinking was common knowledge around the league, but I was the one who stayed awake with him when he had the DTs. He's been forever loyal to me. I'm loyal to him, but if he had to go, well, draw your own conclusions. Like I say, I'm pragmatic.

I THOUGHT the worst part of this trip was behind me. Not quite.

I had a six-hour wait for a seat in the last row of a Lufthansa flight to Toronto, one that was held up for three hours on the runway for unspecified mechanical malfunctions. While the mechanics were counting and tightening the bolts, I hoped they'd get around to patching the air seal around the washroom directly behind me. Assaulted by the constant fragrance of methane, I tried in vain to figure out how to get my oxygen mask to drop down without tripping an alarm.

Wedged into a seat that would cramp a lithe schoolgirl, I remembered those too-brief salad days when I had flown on team charters joyous after victories. My career on the ice is safely behind me but so, unfortunately, are my oversized glutes and quads that make it impossible to buy jeans off the rack. The charters accommodated our extreme lower-body development with first-class seats stem to stern. Other organizations recognize that a scout, inevitably a former player, doesn't revert to your average Joe's physique upon announcement of his retirement or, as was the case with me, the morning-after realization that the phone won't ring again with his agent delivering the happy news of a contract offer.

Kind-hearted GMs will make sure that their scouts, the guys who travel offshore and cross-continent, can park their battle-swollen glutes in first class. It's not just considerate. It's humanitarian. No such luck this trip. The team had to pay a premium to rebook my ticket. Asking for first class would be really pushing my luck, especially with my tainted rep. Anyway, I was originally booked in economy, as I always am.

Don't imagine that I'm a whiner. With so many guys on the outside looking in, I'm grateful to have and desperate to keep my job in the league, more grateful still on many counts that I work for L.A. While the Edmonton scouts are freezing their asses going to mid-winter meetings in their team's offices at the arena, our staff gathers in SoCal for our draft-prep war rooms. The Edmonton guys pack their parkas and our crew brings golf clubs.

Climate, though, is just about the only perk our franchise offers the scouting staffers. Our owner, Mark Galvin, made his wad in high-tech but can't get his mind around the idea that a hockey team lives or dies with its R&D. He believes scouting can be done on the cheap and should be if that enables him to stock higher-grade caviar in his plush, nay garish, box at the arena. So while struggling starlets roll out a Trumpian spread for Billionaire 4.0 and his guests at games, we go about our business as Spartans, sustained many nights by steamed tube steaks dispensed by acne-scarred teenagers at the snack bars in Chicoutimi, Sudbury, and Swift Current. While Software

Scrooge gets his publicist to plant fact-free stories about his philanthropy in the Sunday papers, our salaries have been frozen for two years and counting. Pensions remain something this Nerd in the Clover vows to get around to someday. And while the Proprietor is air-lifted to New York in his Learjet to inspect the Broadway show he's underwriting for the amusement of his fourth diamond-encrusted wife, my sorry ass is jammed in economy.

I dropped down my tray, grabbed a napkin, and borrowed a pen from the fat lady spilling out of the seat next to me. As others might do crossword puzzles to the point of obsession, I'm forever writing down the names of teenage future millionaires and those who'll fall short. My job is to sort the former from the latter, to get the names in the right order. To compile a shopping list that, over the course of the draft and across the span of years, will keep our team in the playoffs, keep my GM's nameplate on his door, and keep me on the payroll.

Galbraith
Dailey
Mays
Sorensen
Meyers
Popov
Thomas
Kotsopolous

I had been in Hradec Králové to see Dailey play for the U.S., Sorensen for the Swedes, and Popov for the Russians at the Five Nations under-18 tournament. The Canadians don't send a team to the tournament, only to the world under-18s in April. Six hours in the arena every day, three hours commuting from Prague to Hradec and back, and at least three more hours working up thumbnail reviews on forty players, and I'd seen absolutely nothing of the Czech Republic.

But what the trip lacked in glamour it made up in substance. Dailey had been a force, the leading scorer for the Americans, who won the gold. He was a Bloomfield Hills kid who probably would have been playing football ten or fifteen years ago before hockey established real traction in Detroit's tony exurbs. Dailey was in the top two of the draft, a coin flip with Galbraith, and thus off the board for us unless our Ping-Pong ball dropped first in the lottery. My entry in our team's database: *Best player on the ice any game here. Prototypical power forward, upside is first-line franchise player and 40 goals. Physically dangerous. Will play in league at 19.*

I liked Sorensen a lot. And I had liked him more in March than in December. He showed a great stick in the two games I saw in Stockholm and you had to wonder what he'd become when he physically matured. But he was sometimes a highly skilled enigma, going from an A game to a C minus the next night, from first line to benched. *Creative but inconsistent. Benching a strange one. Coach assured Sven it wasn't illness or injury. Some noise in the background about him being "difficult."* That "noise": Sven, our Swedish scout, usually a fierce advocate for young Tre Kronors, wasn't a fan of Sorensen. I suspected it had something to do with Sorensen's agent being a hated rival of Sven back in their playing days.

Popov was a high-risk, high-reward proposition with Moscow Spartak. Any team that drafts a Russian invites the hassle of coaxing the kid to come West and offering dough that competes with the tax-free coin he makes in the Kontinental Hockey League. Compared to other teams, though, we've done pretty well landing Russian kids—they'd rather be parked poolside with the cocoa butter than fitting their Lamborghinis with snow tires.

Popov had spent all season lighting up the K against veteran pros and making seven figures tax-free. No wonder he looked bored. (*Amazing dangle and finish, can't find his own end with a GPS.*) I had him listed purely on talent. We weren't going to draft him in the first round. Hunts didn't need the headaches. If Popov were already playing junior in Canada, okay, you at least know that he wants to play in the league rather than the KHL. Popov didn't even talk to the Quebec junior team that owned his rights.

I know what you're thinking about those thumbnail evaluations, but I'm not sent traipsing across two continents to file deathless prose. I'm sent to make dead-accurate evaluations of future pros. When you're dealing with eighteen-year-olds, dead accuracy is an occasional thing and certainty is for fools. I'm like all the other scouts sitting in the corner seats—just out there taking notes and making educated guesses.

I had drawn up my reports and patched them into the team database right after the games in Hradec, while impressions were still fresh and before jet lag made me incoherent. I started to go down the rest of the list and strategize. Who to go see and where I'd have to go to see them.

I didn't really need to do a workup on Galbraith in Vancouver. I'd seen all I needed to at the world juniors and, like I said, he was off the board. We wouldn't be picking that high. That left Mays, Meyers, and Thomas—Peterborough, Halifax, and Saskatoon, respectively. Peterborough: I'd be able to commute from Toronto and sleep in my own bed, but Mays was knocked out of the lineup a couple of weeks before I left for the Czech Republic. Halifax: Okay, I could see flight delays with the fog but, again, a decent place to work out of. Saskatoon: I'd catch up with Chief, our main guy out west. Not a garden spot in March and it could be a lot harder to get to, plus a helluva lot worse when you get there. But better than the next name on the list: Vachon.

Freakin' Baie-Comeau. You have to hit the brakes or you'll fall off the edge of the map. That's why my list went only eight deep. Avoidance.

How glamorous does the job sound so far?

3

Despite the unexpected extra cost of my Lufthansa ticket, I'm a real value to my still-sober GM. A lot of guys on the L.A. scouting staff can't write an intelligible report. That's not the worst of it, though, just a sore point for me. At the start of my second full year, Hunts began sending me to check out the players flagged by scouts who work the regions or Europe. I was designated as the de facto amateur scouting director, the cross-checker, a role that's usually reserved for a veteran. I had taken on a job more complicated than the average scout's: assessing the players and assessing the assessors.

My promotion after a year and a half on the L.A. staff put some noses out of joint, and I can understand why someone who has put in five or even ten years would feel that way. I had a job they coveted. Still, Hunts figured I'm a quick study, and by nature I'm suited to the job. A lot of things I just do by intuition. I'm a fly on the wall outside the dressing rooms in arenas hither and yon. I listen in on conversations in the media rooms at tournaments, floating a little disinformation out there.

The scouts in other organizations know when I'm in the arena—any scout worth his salt can survey a crowd of ten thousand and pick out the competition. Still, I try to be cagey about exactly what I'm doing there. I'll leave a notebook on a table in the scouts' room and make sure it's open to a page where I've made bogus notes about a player I'm not interested in, circling his number just to make it all the more obvious to rubberneckers. I keep my cards close to my vest.

You'd think that everyone in the business would maintain a similar embargo on advertising his intentions, but such is not the case. A sizable contingent of hopelessly insecure and underqualified guys in similar positions can't resist the urge to share their work. Either they want to look like they're a big deal to their peers or they're fishing for some sort of confirmation of their flimsy opinions.

I come by the stealth honestly. I grew up in a none-of-your-business culture. My father's approach to parenting, as with all aspects of his life, was of a piece with his work. I grew up watching him asking questions but fielding none while he took notes. He retired from Metro Toronto's force after more than thirty years and had high hopes that I'd go the same route.

He wasn't a detective, never got on that career track on the force, though I don't doubt that he could have. He ended up as the staff sergeant of the mounted division, but his other role made him something of a legend, known by everyone from the greenest rookie right up to the commissioner: He was the coach of the cop hockey team. He was a player-coach, on the ice right up until his fiftieth birthday, when he made it clear that he felt he could still play but could no longer tune out my mother's ever more vocal protests.

I was in grade school when he brought me to practices to work as a stick boy and play deaf when the guys swore a blue streak. By the time I was fourteen, he was letting me skate with the team in Saturday-night pickup games. He convinced me that I should go to college rather than to major junior when I was in my teens. Sarge figured a college man with some sort of useful specialty could make officer in a hurry. He never said a word to me about my major until I declared it: criminal and social justice.

When Minnesota drafted me in the third round back in '86 after my freshman year at Boston College, things became complicated in ways I'd never imagined. Minnesota had a big fat contract waiting for me after my sophomore season. It was impressed on me that the contract might not be there after I graduated or even in a year's time. My agent gave me the song and dance about finishing my degree by correspondence, but truth was always the first casualty of his commissions. It turned out criminology just wasn't going to fly as my major if I was doing courses by mail, so I had to switch to history, to my regret and my father's. Not that it mattered. Before my pro career passed me by, the window for joining the force slammed shut on my fingers.

I eventually did finish my degree, six years after signing away my life to Minnesota, but I've never really had a chance to put my knowledge of pre-Confederation Canada and Elizabethan England to good use. My two years of criminology eventually did help out, though.

After I hung up my skates, my cash flow vanished and my net worth vaporized. I had to watch as the receiver catalogued each and every thing I owned and threw it up on the internet to attract bidders and amuse those in the league who had me on their hate lists. I was thoroughly destitute and wouldn't have had a car but for the old Beemer that my father lent me.

Starting your life again in your mid-thirties: I don't recommend it, especially when you're starting in a hole up to your hairline. I had to work a square job to make my child support payments, so my father made a call to an old friend who had taken early retirement from the force and established a private-investigation business. I was qualified to snoop around gathering intelligence for divorces and other miseries. I had been through my own and knew what to look for. I picked up insurance work. My favourite: I was a one-man tree-hidden gallery for a guy with a debilitating back injury who shot five-over for thirty-six holes.

I spent four years in the mire and developed a deeper appreciation for just how awful people are. I worried that I was becoming one of them, that mid-life crisis was an infectious condition. At my lowest point, Hunts threw me a life preserver. Supposedly the owner was impressed that he had a real-life detective on the payroll, though that billing vastly overstated the case.

4

Canadian customs was a walk in the park. I dropped my bags in the hall of my tight little apartment on the Danforth and checked my voicemail. My absence hadn't sparked an international manhunt. Ten calls in five days.

Five of them were someone trying to get me to switch banks or phone services.

Three were where-are-yous from Sandy. She understands the scouting dodge, plans made, plans torn up, new plans made again. With each call her concern escalated minutely.

One was a thought-you-were-coming-back from Lanny, my daughter, calling from her boarding school in Wisconsin. She wanted to talk about a tournament her team won in upstate New York. She had a stack of hockey scholarship offers from schools in the States, so her boarding school tuition was sort of a front-loaded education. She wanted me to further front-load it by wiring her spending money. Which I was fine with, so long as it kept her a distance from her mother, who could better afford tens of thousands than I could C-notes.

The last call, from two days ago, was an invitation to an old-timers game in Peterborough. It was being organized by Vis Hockey Enterprises, an outfit that had started with the purchase of a kids' hockey organization in Woodbridge and grown into a multi-million-dollar business with teams and arenas across the province. Like everything else out of Woodbridge, Vis was as Italian as grandma's ziti. And like a lot of things in Woodbridge, it was a family business, with gobs of money from sources unknown, suspect, or shady. Vis was founded and run by Giuseppe Visicale, ostensibly for his sons, four tanks who never won a sportsmanship trophy, tough enough to play pros but with less than half the skills to pull it off.

I was advised that Vis Hockey was organizing this charity old-timers tilt to raise funds for a hospital. I suspect that Vis was looking to get a piece of the publicly owned Peterborough arena. And once Vis Hockey Enterprises got a piece of something, it generally ended up with all the pieces.

Before I checked in with the women in my life, I got back to the organizers of the game. Yeah, I was free the next evening, St. Patrick's Day. Sure I'd come out.

FAMOUS STORY: About twenty years after they last played the game, Rocket Richard and Teeder Kennedy wobbled down the red carpet to do a ceremonial puck drop one night at the Gardens. They didn't make eye contact and didn't shake hands the whole time they were out there. That's how it is. With guys who play in the league, hate's always there. Even after their playing days are over, it doesn't pass. It ages like Scotch.

I'm the last guy they call for old-timers games, and the first to jump at the chance. Most people didn't notice that I was in the league, never mind that I'm gone. Still, I'm as public-spirited as the next guy, more than most who pass through the league.

I'm young enough and my Arthur isn't bad enough that I can't get through a bunch of half-speed shifts with fifty-year-old men whose knees are ten years younger than mine.

Truth is, it's a voyeuristic deal for me. When I accept that invitation I am witness to a secret spectacle. Yeah, at any intersection of twenty former players in a dressing room you're bound to find four- or five-decades-old hatreds, and I get a kick out of watching them try to set aside blood grudges, rub scars the other guys left, and smile through gritted teeth, all for a good cause. Accept an invitation? I'd pay for hockey entertainment like that. For me, it's like watching the war from a Swiss mountaintop.

As for the other crap that goes with old-timers games, well, I'm up for shaking the hands of people I'll never see again and signing autographs for kids who have no idea who I am. I'm game to meet people who might help me in my working days at the arenas. I'm not a people person but I can fake it.

It's easier for me to get out to these games than it is for a lot of guys. I'm not bound by family. My girlfriend, Sandy, is no ingenue. Hitting forty. Married once. Through the wringer variously. Scrapbooks that haven't been opened for years. Kids nearly grown. Spooked. We're meant for each other. She accepts me for who I am precisely because she sees all that when she looks in the bathroom mirror.

Sandy signs off on my taking a few nights over the course of the winter because she wants me to feel young for a little bit and she can use a girls' night too. She also knows that, on the next opportunity, the make-good is her choice of dinner, her choice of movie. Yup, she'll trade a night away from me for future considerations.

Reliable, relatively unencumbered, and absolutely incapable of commanding a dollar for an appearance: That's why I'm on a list of numbers to call if the league alumni group needs a spare body or two to fill out a roster on short notice in Ontario. That's how I ended up in a dressing room in Peterborough on a Wednesday night in March, surrounded by a lot of guys who are famous names and regulars on the old-timers circuit.

5

I was the last of the old-timers to make it to the arena that night.
The others had all landed in P'boro the day before and been put
up at the best joint in town so they could sit at the head table
of a sports celebrity rubber-chicken shakedown, uh, I mean,
fundraiser. They were already dressed and waiting to lace up
when I was pulling into the parking lot and getting my bag and
sticks out of the trunk.

I scanned the lot for Norm Pembleton, the veteran GM from
the London juniors who was the honorary coach of the all-stars
and me. I wanted to at least introduce myself, maybe work him
up as a source. He had one draft-eligible kid who was a mild
prospect-of-interest to me.

I figured Pembleton would be outside chain-smoking in
advance of three twenty-minute withdrawal sessions. Sure
enough, I spotted him in an undesignated smoking area, ankle-
deep in the butts of unfiltered Exports. He stamped out a bare
stub and before lighting another took a long hit from a silver
flask.

Just hours before, he'd been in a hearing with the league's commissioner. This had become an almost weekly meeting. Pembleton had been involved in several incidents this season. After a disallowed goal he'd emptied a stick rack onto the ice and would have gone over the boards and after the refs if he hadn't been restrained by one of his players. That was eight games. He'd grabbed a player by the neck at a practice. Six more. In the most recent brouhaha, Pembleton had narrowly avoided suspension for a profane and slightly physical encounter with a fan in a hallway at the London arena. By the most believable eyewitness account, the fan had slandered Mrs. Pembleton and then spat on this coach.

The latest episode was just another reason to restart the debate about Pembleton's fitness to coach teenagers, a debate that played out in newspaper columns, on talk radio, and across panels in television studios. His judges and juries were guys who'd never darkened the door of a junior hockey arena. The highest and mightiest said he should be booted out for life for the next merest transgression. I thought that was extreme, and I'd bet his players would too. I'd rather have the Mean Old Bastard Who Knew Hockey as my coach than A Builder of Character Who Couldn't Match Lines.

I was about to wave or introduce myself or even voice my support for Pembleton when I thought better of it. Mr. Misery was muttering. He stalked a short path, back and forth, step for step, like a caged tiger. He seemed lost in some terrible memory pulled from a thick bank of what-might-have-beens.

I did see Ollie Buckhold, leaning against the hood of a gold Mercedes. He was like a chameleon, his sunbed-acquired tan blending in with the paint job. His V-shaped physique was draped in a seven-thousand-dollar hand-tailored suit.

Ollie was on his Bluetooth talking to a GM in disbelief and

dudgeon. "Two-point-four? We're thinking three-point-two," he shouted, more amused than angered. His surgically unwrinkled face broke into a smile. This was the sight and sound of millions being harvested.

Ollie had been involved in seven- and eight-figure dealings all his adult life. He'd been a director and producer of football and hockey telecasts and ended up in New York, assigned to the Super Bowl and World Series. People thought of him as a technical genius, the best in the television sports biz. Before his thirty-fifth birthday he walked away from it all and launched a hockey agency with a single client. That his single client went to the Hall of Fame helped his cause. That his single client made ten times as much money off the ice as he did on it had top players flocking to the Buckhold Sports Agency.

At one point, Ollie had tried to steal me away from my shyster agent. Nothing untoward about it, every player is eventually targeted and no agent is above trying. Looking back, I wish he'd tried harder, and I wish I hadn't considered myself a principled guy, a bad phase I left behind when my liabilities exceeded my assets. My Thanks But No Thanks to Ollie is way up my list of what-might-have-beens.

"Hi, Bradley," he said, dropping fifty decibels and affecting a voice soothing enough to get parents to give up their fifteen-year-old sons in their living rooms over cupcakes and promises. I just waved. I feared that Ollie was on the phone to Hunts and the boss would take it as some sort of omen if the contract talks went sideways, like I was a black cat crossing through their negotiations.

I waited out the call. Three minutes. I wanted a quick word with Ollie about Billy Mays Jr., who was one of a dozen Buckhold Sports clients likely to be selected in the first round of the draft. Ollie did his best to keep the contract talks short and civil and mostly succeeded. As soon as the call ended, he turned to me. "That no-good bastard," he said.

"Ollie, is there any way I can sit down with Mays the next few days?"

"He's a wonderful young man. Brad, my friend, of course, anything for you. We'll work something out."

Every Buckhold client was "a wonderful young man." Everybody in the business was "my friend" to Ollie, including "that no-good bastard" the next time Ollie saw him. The single exception to this was Mays's coach in Peterborough, who'd made life tough on all agents, and especially Ollie. Red Hanratty bad-mouthed Buckhold to all his young charges, calling him "that effin' nancy agent" and "that bucktooth fairy." He alluded to Ollie's life away from the arena, one that Ollie managed to conceal fully. That Hanratty had said this to Mays was a cause of some strife over at Buckhold Sports, enough so that Ollie was commuting to Peterborough seemingly every other night to make sure that no agent was trying to scalp his prized client aided and abetted by the homophobic coach.

I WAS EN ROUTE to the dressing room when I heard a desperate "Brad, Brad, Brad!" behind me. I turned to see an old guy in a brown corduroy jacket with elbow patches and well-worn brown Oxfords struggling to make his way through the fans crowding the hallway. Though I was walking with my bag over my shoulder and an armful of sticks, the old-timer was on a dead run (emphasis: dead) and losing ground to me. Predictable, I guess, as he was packing about 270 pounds on his five-foot-seven-inch frame.

"B-bbb-brad, Harley Hackenbush of *The Peterborough Times*," he said, as if I should have recognized his name. I did but hadn't heard it for years. Back in the '80s, he used to write the Ontario

junior league column for *The Hockey News*. The headshot they ran
with his column looked like something you'd see in the house
of mirrors: a half-inch of forehead and cheeks the size of canta-
loupes. His blood pressure was probably along the lines of a
properly inflated bicycle tire. "C-ccc-can I get a minute with
you, Brad? Just a c-cccc-couple of questions?"

I stopped in my tracks. Not that I like doing interviews. I
don't, never have. The next intelligent question I hear from a
reporter will be my first. But I figured if I didn't stop and this
guy kept chasing me, he was going to need CPR and his blood
would be on my hands.

"Sure, I got a minute."

"Brad, we got all these great players coming here tonight for
this game. W-www-what do you think Coach Hanratty means
to the game of hockey?"

My career-long streak of dumb questions was intact. Oh well,
flick the bullshit switch.

"The game is only as good as the kids who come up through
the system. And they're only as good as the coaching they get.
Numbers don't lie. No one has won more than your coach here,
and I don't know that anybody turns out all-stars and Cup
winners like he does."

(Of course, a thoroughly mangled version of my words was
going to show up in the morning *Times*. Something about stars at
this game not making it to the league without the sage mentoring
of Coach Hanratty, blah, blah, blah.)

Hackenbush wrote furiously in a tattered, ketchup-stained
notebook. It was hieroglyphic shorthand. He seemed to get
three or four scrawled symbols on each page. At that pace the
notebook shouldn't last even one decent interview.

He managed to spit out a few more questions, panting like
a bulldog in a heat wave. I would have begged off, but I feared

he'd go into cardiac arrest if he had to chase any more quotes. He hemmed and hawed, scratching around for something that would fill out his story for the paper. I mean, what can you really say about an old-timers game? I tried to throw this mutt a bone, but when I got to the part about the debt we former pros owe the game, coaches like Hanratty, and the fans, Hackenbush's pen had run dry and he was trying to shake ink out to the tip. He was so preoccupied he didn't hear a word I said.

I checked my watch. I had to get moving but worried that I hadn't been much help to him. He looked disheartened, and his "Th-thanks" sounded soaked in a healthy scratch's defeat. So I offered up a bit of sunshine.

"Harley Hackenbush ... I used to read you in *The Hockey News* when I was growing up."

He lit up like he'd won the lottery. And then it was as if he realized he'd been looking like last week's numbers.

"Yeah, everyone used to. Been f-ff-four, no, f-fff-fifteen years since I wrote those columns."

"Why'd you stop?"

"I g-ggg-got yanked off the junior beat and moved to the night sports desk at the *Times*. F-fff-fifteen years working 5:00 to 12:30. Kept me s-sss-sober, mostly, and in c-cc-clothes."

The broken blood vessels in his nose and the frayed and ill-fitting thirty-year-old jacket said otherwise.

Behind him I saw a fan pointing at him and talking out of the side of his mouth to a friend. I couldn't make out exactly what it was he was saying, but I could imagine it: "That used to be Harley Hackenbush," or something like that. My guess was more accurate than anything Hackenbush attributed to me, I'd bet.

"HEY, UH, Shadow? Is that you?" Grant Tomlin said when I walked into the visiting team's dressing room. It wasn't a greeting so much as an anal probing. Every hockey fan recognized Tomlin. These days he's the Outspoken Conscience of the Game, jumping in front of television cameras harder than he ever went into the corners. Yeah, he put me in my place when I walked in. Millions recognize him, him with his frosted tips and gel, and he traded on the idea that guys who'd played with and against me don't recognize me. Is he ever out of character?

"Geez, Toms, any way you could make me your heart-and-soul guy tonight?" I said. This was strictly my shot at one of his on-air tropes, which, as everyone in the room recognized, bestows honour upon a player who possesses qualities that Tomlin himself never did.

I don't hate Tomlin. *Hate* would be too strong a word. I just imagine that there's a special place in hell where they'll apply fire-retardant foundation on his scarless mug, enabling him to do his stand-ups. This, of course, was consensus sentiment in the room. Tomlin was the only one who'd played fewer games in the league than me—one season and part of another for Ottawa in their expansion year. Yup, I was taking a shot from the Ultimate Media Whore, an imposter who, to the torment of the great talents in the room, was making bigger coin running his mouth these days than they had in the best seasons of their Hall of Fame careers. Tomlin is irrefutable evidence that the systemic organization of hatreds is utterly devoid of proportion and justice.

Tomlin smiled his studio smile like it had been punched in by a producer in the control room. There were no buddy-buddy bygones, et cetera, in this for me. A month back he'd told viewers that Hunts was in over his head as a GM. "Chad Hunt knew the problems with his team last summer and he has done nothing to address them. It's not like he doesn't have the answers. It's like he doesn't understand the questions."

He pulled this line out of his ass on the U.S. national broadcast on a Sunday afternoon. This pithy observation wasn't intended for the millions who'd tuned in to a game on a Saturday night. The executive workings of our front office wouldn't have resonated with our fan base, never mind a national audience. This was a direct appeal to The Guy Who Signs Our Cheques. Hunts told me that Tomlin had been chatting up Our Perpetually Tanned Titan of E-Business outside the executive boxes during intermission a week before in Vancouver. They hadn't been talking about the price of real estate in Beverly Hills. By the accounts of neutral eavesdroppers, Tomlin was carving Hunts and, of course, positioning himself first as the owner's newest BFF and eventually as Hunts's successor.

I looked around the room, at a bunch of heaps of gristle and bones and scar tissue left over from the abuse of themselves, each other, and the game. The game doesn't discriminate and doesn't reward. Some of the constantly cautious emerge from it crippled, some reckless bastards come out of it pristine. I was probably the most banged up in here and there were a couple of guys who'd played 1200 games in the league. The others in the room were wearing numbers that were retired and today hang from the rafters in the arenas where they won Cups. Me, I was assigned a sweater, number twenty-eight, a number I'd never worn before, and there was no name on it, just a fresh coffee stain when I stepped on the ice. Perfect. That's me, generic old-timer. Retired but still a call-up.

The Peterborough minor-hockey program had a cute idea, getting each old-timer to skate out with a kid from the atom house league. The kid who drew my name could scarcely conceal his disappointment and, after the handshake, never said a word or made eye contact. If I ever needed a reminder about my very small place in this universe, the pre-game would have provided it. You've heard players say that they don't hear the crowd during the game—me, I listened hard when they introduced me before the game.

"He played nine seasons in the league ..."

Technically true but misleading: parts of ten seasons would be more accurate. Better: parts of seven seasons playing in the boonies and Europe.

"... and played on a Canadian team that won a world junior championship ..."

True as far as it goes: On that team I wasn't one of the ten best pro prospects. They show highlights from the gold-medal game and I've never been able to find myself except at the bottom of the pile of teenagers celebrating. I was nearly smothered by the backup goalie's chest protector.

"... you know him best for the unforgettable shutdown job he did on the Great One for the Montreal Cup winner back in '93 ..."

Yeah, Grant Tomlin, that would be the ring you never wore. The one I had to buy back from a good-hearted collector when I got back on my feet. The one I was wearing inside my glove.

" ... ladies and gentlemen, 'the Shadow,' Brad Shade."

I stepped off the blueline and waved. I think I heard a guy in the last row crack his knuckles.

6

It was league alums versus Peterborough alums, a date to raise funds for a bunch of local charities. The usual. Sign some sticks and sweaters. Silent auctions. Fifty-fifty draw. (I bought a ticket. Do I have to tell you how that turned out?)

You might wonder if there would be enough Peterborough alums around to ice a team. Rest assured, you practically have to have played ten years in the league and salted away eight figures to afford a place on a lake up there. Dozens of famous guys have settled in Peterborough and have nothing better to do than drive up the price of real estate. Those who played junior there, even guys who originally came from Toronto or Ottawa or Kingston or wherever, end up settling there. Twelve league scouts, all former players, live within ten minutes of the arena. I went to a minor midget game there one time and the two teams were both coached by guys who'd played in the league all-star game, and four sons of players scored in the tilt. I read somewhere that there are more league alums per capita in Peterborough than any place in the world, and I believe it. They could have iced two

Peterborough alumni teams that Wednesday night, but then who would the fans root for?

Because this was Peterborough, it meant a turn by Red Hanratty, the coach of the Peterborough juniors since they used to play with a rover. Okay, not quite that long, but he played in the Original Six. At seventy-something he was still getting on the ice with the junior team in practice most days when his shingles weren't acting up. He had worked thirty-plus seasons and missed only five games—four with suspensions and one because of the death of his wife.

Back in '84 Hanratty had picked me in the junior draft in the fourteenth round coming out of minor midget and talked to my parents about sending me to Peterborough. A few junior teams had called my folks before the junior draft, and my father let them know long and loud that I was going to college. Hanratty drafted me anyway. He came over to our house and made his pitch. Hard-ass versus hard-ass.

"No," my father said. "He's going to be the first in our family to get a college degree. It wouldn't have mattered if you took him in the first round. What round did you have him, first or second?"

"Sarge, I hate to break it to you," Hanratty said. "We had him in the fourteenth. I didn't even know about this college thing until I walked in here."

My father was offended. He figured Hanratty was a sore loser. In retrospect, I'm sure Hanratty was telling the truth. Direct, yup. Blunt, you betcha. Trying to con my father? Nope. With his history, if he didn't have a parent at a handshake, he'd have said to hell with you. I'm glad my father didn't ask Hanratty to show him his scouts' list because I would have quit the game right then and there if I'd seen the names of 260 Ontario sixteen-year-olds ahead of mine.

I mustn't have made any impression on Hanratty. In the

warm-ups before the old-timers game, I skated by him and gave him a "Hey, coach." He had no idea who I was. If I told him I was the one who got away, he would have called security.

If you think I ever hated Red Hanratty, you've got it all wrong. I never regretted going to college instead of Peterborough, but I probably would have liked playing for him. He won a helluva lot more than he lost and turned out more pros than any junior coach. More wins in the juniors than anyone else ... check that, than any two guys else. Some have thought that his position these last few years was ceremonial—you hit seventy and leave it to your assistant coaches to be on the ice and take on the lion's share of the work. So the thinking went. Not the case at all. He ran every practice, his voice echoing through the arena, every last profanity. He was the one who identified the talent, and he was the one who put them in the position to succeed, first in junior, then in the league. He was the one with the clearest read on opposing teams. His players didn't panic because he did. They played their bags off for him.

If you went by the stories in the sports sections you'd have assumed that Hanratty was the exception to the Rule of Ubiquitous and Everlasting Hate. Yeah, Norm Pembleton's teams had played Hanratty's for thirty-plus years and Pembleton was the ultimate hard-ass—never shook the hand of another coach, not even Hanratty. Still, Pembleton's enmity seemed a little theatrical—the bad moustache bought second-hand from a '40s B-movie villain. And at some level, he and Hanratty knew each other's life and work better than anyone else could.

With this one exception, Hanratty seemed like the Beloved Icon. He always smiled, always cracked wise, always perched a cheap stogie in his pie-hole. (You had an open invitation to enforce a no-smoking bylaw on him and have hockey fans stone you. Fact is, he mostly gnawed at an unlit cigar that lasted from his morning coffee to last call.) He evoked a time when men were men and helmets were for soldiers. You just sort of imagined that his home looked like a wing of the Hockey Hall of Fame. If you loved this game, you loved Red Hanratty. This was the flipside of the Rocket Richard—Teeder Kennedy vignette: Red Hanratty was the Beating Heart of Oldetime Hockey.

Hanratty was coach of the Peterborough alums that night. His former players, the guys who went on to fame and millions in the league, came out to the old-timers show just to pay homage to the Ol' Redhead. As soon as they heard him bark they were sixteen all over again. When they posed with him for a team photo that would appear in the local rag the next morning, they all beamed like they had just won the Cup. The Peterborough alums lineup had three Hall of Famers: Bobby Reagan, Reggie Hofferman, and Eddie Talbot. All had dropped Hanratty's name in their acceptance speeches at their induction ceremonies, putting him at the top of the list of Those Who Made It All Possible. Talbot, in fact, a three-time fifty-goal scorer but in a lot of ways a social misfit, went into great detail about his indebtedness to Hanratty twice in his incoherent ramble and forgot to mention his own wife and parents.

Whatever Hanratty did to make these guys players is at best mysterious and to my mind debatable. I always say genetics is destiny. Hanratty turned out the most players because he was around the longest and he did less to hold them back. That's not a knock. Hanratty himself admitted that he always believed the worst thing you can do is overcoach talent. Self-deprecation was the perfect coaching philosophy for Hanratty to bring to this old-timers game. Hanratty's chief responsibility this night—check that, his only responsibility—was something he had a lot of practice at. He had to make sure the beer was cold.

At the end of the game the beer was cold. At the end of the night, so was Red Hanratty.

7

The old-timers game ended up 12–10, and when the goaltenders went down you would have needed a crane to get them back up on their skates. I pulled off the impossible and went scoreless, pointless, again. Most of the time I was the youngest guy on the ice, too.

The Peterborough alums won, natch, while Hanratty and Pembleton jawed at each other. Thankfully, the cheers and hoots drowned out a bunch of f-bombs that were attached to aspersions about manhood, character, heritage, and intelligence or lack thereof. The two old pros invoked incidents, most of them Pembleton's embarrassments, that were league lore. They made it look like it was real. Or maybe made it look like an act. I couldn't really tell which and Pembleton was right standing behind me, reeking of vodka.

I had a beer in the dressing room after the game. A chamber of commerce type came by to thank me and hand me an envelope with gas money and a gift certificate good for seventy dollars toward a dinner for two, drinks extra, at the Falling Water Café.

Who knew Frank Lloyd Wright worked in Peterborough? (I was going to drop that line on receipt of the comp but already had my fill of blank stares.)

All in all, a night well passed. Nobody who played got hurt, though everyone was going to be sore as hell the next morning. Small blessings. For me it didn't even take that long. Arthur had my knee pulsing like the windshield wipers on the ninety-minute drive back to the Big Smoke. By the next day, Arthur was the only one who would remember that I played in the charity game.

I sent a text to Hunts on the drive back—fear not, I did it while sitting in the full-service lane at a gas station just outside the city limits.

> *No sick leave necessary. Hurtin', chronic but not terminal.*

It was about midnight but he was on the West Coast. He knew about the game in Peterborough.

> *Chek fine print of yer contract: old-timers injury gets unpaid leave only.*

One beer in the showers hadn't fully rehydrated me, so I parked trusty Rusty Beemer in the underground lot and limped over to the Merry Widow for a pint or three and a quick update on the league's late games from Nick the barkeep, father of the next phenom, sez he. Hearing the latest exploits of young Pericles was a small price to pay for good company and a seemingly endless stream of jokes. I've never had the heart to tell Nick that a kid in bantam double-A, not his team's best player or even its fourth best, should look to the game for a good time and nothing more. I've always suspected that Perry will follow his father into the biz and become the hole-in-the-wall's proprietor. I told Nick that he missed his calling—any guy who can watch four games simultaneously at 7:30 and four more at 10:00 and give you eight game summaries from memory while keeping the regulars' orders straight would make a hell of an air-traffic controller. Then again, air-traffic controllers don't bet on the planes landing safely.

"Your company won tonight," Nick said. It was always easy to tell if Nick had put a check mark or an X beside the L.A. game, and it was plain that tonight my team had cost his kids new shoes. He knew that, given my team's favourable outcome, he wouldn't have to pull out the Bushmills and pour me a double. Sure enough, the score came up in the news scroll below the highlights: L.A. 5, Calgary 3. My ragged colleagues on our patchwork staff would sleep the sleep of scouts knowing that their jobs were safe, which was ever a night-to-night proposition. I already knew the score before I walked in. I was listening to updates on satellite radio sports.

"My company needed a win," I said. "It was starting to feel like we hadn't won in a month."

"You guys took two of three on the road, what, ten days ago. It's not that bad."

"That's how it looks to you, not me. If you had a bunch of rich guys in here ..."

"I wish," Nick said, looking down the bar at the unwashed and broken men staring at the last inch of their drinks and rooting around their pockets for elusive change. In some bars they'd be called regulars. Nick called his sorry lot the Irregulars.

Some had names. Polo had just one, a two-syllable handle instead of the three names he was given at birth that totalled over forty letters. Polo was on his BlackBerry, looking at game summaries, counting goals and assists for his all-Czech team in the Merry Widow hockey pool. Some had jobs. A bunch of paramedics anaesthetized themselves after twelve-hour shifts delivering fallen seniors, stabbed wannabe gangstas, and all-thumbs home handymen to the emerg at East Gen. They had their own cachet, separate from those who wore hospital blues and mostly pushed brooms or delivered food trays to patients. A lot more were familiar faces whose stories went untold and whose source of drinking money was unknown and uncertain.

It was comforting that none ever bothered me with questions about the game or players I knew. They weren't the least bit impressed. The worst cases didn't go there to be social. Exactly the opposite. They went there to forget themselves.

I ignored Nick ignoring me and carried on with my rant. "... those rich guys would be asking you to turn off the game and put on a business channel where they can watch the stock ticker to see if Apple is down a nickel. You could drop a bomb beside them and they wouldn't hear it. That's human nature. Every loss is a kick in the nuts. Some are worse than others, but there's no upside to having your whole living threatened. A kick in the nuts is a kick in the nuts ..."

My diatribe was gathering from stage four to five, but Nick drifted off into his thoughts, some graduate-level calculus, a formula factoring the night's handle at the bar plus sales he didn't ring in, less his lost wagers and the vigorish. The last line of these complicated equations would be his stake for an all-night poker game in the basement of a souvlaki palace in Greektown. Little did his countrymen suspect that they were regularly cleaned out by a high school dropout Pythagoras.

My BlackBerry pinged. Another text from Hunts. He must have been channelling me. Did he know I was in a bar? We're tight. As soon as the draft hit my lips, he probably broke out in a cold sweat.

Did you ask Red about Mays?????

Billy Mays Jr. was seventeen going on two point five million. In four months' time he was going to be selected in the top ten of the league's draft, quite possibly top five. As a result of a pretty wizardly shell game orchestrated by Hunts on the trading floor the previous June, we owned Columbus's first-rounder, a dead-sure lottery pick. Mays was way up on our list, even though his left arm had been in a sling a few days back, the result of a hit from behind a couple of weeks earlier. He was Red Hanratty's leading scorer this year. He'd shattered a Peterborough rookie scoring record that had stood for twenty years. He was six feet three and two hundred pounds as lean as a slice of deli turkey, and blond with a jaw borrowed from an actor on the soaps. With his arm now out of the sling, he had nothing but open ice and a league owner's open wallet to look forward to.

Scouting reports from the L.A. crew read like mash notes to *Tiger Beat*. The last and representative entry in our database was filed by Kapps, our impossible-to-impress septuagenarian part-time bird dog in Sudbury: *Upside is franchise forward, all-star.* That passed for a discouraging word among the twenty game reports on Billy Jr. this season.

Red Hanratty said that Billy Mays was the best pro prospect he'd ever coached, and, though the coach was a famous BSer and hype artist, no one doubted it. That meant Hanratty rated Mays a better pro prospect than two guys who wear Cs in the league right now: Floody in Phoenix and Rox in Edmonchuk, who just happened to be the youngest captain in the league. Better than the three Hall of Famers who came out for the old-timers game. Better than two other guys in the lineup that night who would have plaques in the Hall of Very Good: Mel Malinowski (394 career goals, including a Cup winner) and Kevin O'Brien (a.k.a. K.O. the Destroyer).

My GM figured that if I was in Peterborough I might as well get the goods on Baby Jesus from the Grand Old Man. It was something the GM and I had talked about, but I had decided to wait until the next time I saw Peterborough play. Red probably had a jar going and was being pulled in every direction all night long. Better to handle it when I could buttonhole him privately (and introduce myself if necessary), I thought.

Just asked around.

A white lie. A lot of guys freeze when you pump them. Sometimes, maybe most of the time, you have to keep your radar on if you want the Juice Not from Concentrate. Especially if you want the Juice with Lots of Pulp. I was listening hard (and not just for someone to cheer for me in the pre-game introductions). You have to scope things out like a security camera, replaying the significant moments, the character tells after the fact. Life as a scout is a stakeout, chum.

Golden Boy came into the room before the game to shake hands with the legends. He introduced them to Markov, the Russian import who was his linemate, his roommate, and his special project. A lot of Russian kids are phlegmatic, but not the one Mays had in tow. Markov was engaged, pretending to recognize names and understand what was going on around him. The one thing he did know was that his friend owned the room.

Seventeen-year-old Billy Mays Jr., the Peterborough mayor, and Giuseppe Visicale were going to be dropping the puck for the photo-op opening faceoff, and it was the ironing-board-stiff Waspy mayor and the glowering, gold-chained Sicilian who looked star-struck. On the sidelines applauding were the mayor's enablers, the geriatric town councillors, and Visicale's posse, a couple of thumb-breakers and his *consigliere*. The applause for the mayor and the hockey boss was polite. A thunderous roar went up for Mays, and he gave a wave that made it seem like he'd done this all his life.

Standing on the blueline while they rolled out the red carpet, I got a laugh out of Hank Royden, a scout for Montreal. "What's wrong with this kid that he can't sing the anthem?" In the folds of scar tissue under his visor Royden rolled his eyes. "Too pretty to play this game," quoth he. The gods of the game won't punish Royden, for he knew not what he was saying.

Those teenagers who are destined for a big place in the game get it. They do the right things. They say the right things. They know the dressing-room etiquette like they wrote it. Polite. Deferential. Comfortable in their own skin. Well turned out in appearance. Social. So it was with this kid. Meeting the legends pre-game, he didn't walk around the room so much as glide. Tomlin buddy-buddied him, acting like he'd been the kid's best friend going back to kindergarten, and the kid suffered it— *nota bene*, this high school kid wasn't impressed by Tomlin and knew that he shouldn't be. That's genius-level social intelligence needed to handle all the crap that's inevitable when you convene a couple dozen egos on a daily basis with millions at stake.

He was accompanied on the tour of the room by his father, William Mays Sr., who had once been a player in Peterborough and was now a player of a different sort: a guy who wore ten-thousand-dollar suits and stared out smugly from the cover of business magazines that promised to reveal the secrets of his investment successes. On this count they failed, but they did manage to fully portray his vanity (dramatic changes in appearance that might be traced back to a plastic surgeon's office, a syringe full of testosterone, and a bottle of Grecian Formula), his ostentatious lifestyle (an over-the-top mansion on Post Road that had riled powerful neighbours enough that it ended up as a landmark city bylaw case), and his love of the usual expensive

toys (a collection of vintage sports cars and a Rolls to run house-
hold errands in).

William Mays knew how one company could swallow up
another for fun and profit and, if his critics were to be believed,
how a CEO could raid a pension fund. I don't know about that,
but he did know hockey. He had gone around the room, knew
our names. It seemed like millions and billions demanded that
work never stop—he had fumbled a file folder and a vibrating
iPhone, spilling his coffee on my sweater, when he extended a
thick right mitt for a vise-like handshake. He posed for pictures
standing beside each of us: He was being tailed by a photog-
rapher and an authorized biographer for what was sure to be the
bestselling business book of the coming season. He went up on
his tiptoes just before the flash.

I find it hard to be impressed by a kid who grows up with
all the advantages, but I was by Billy Jr. He was snagged by the
local radio reporter for an interview and sounded more professional than the guy asking the questions (and, it goes almost
without saying, than Harley Hackenbush). He went into great
detail about his shoulder, sprained and bruised "but no damage
to the rotator cuff. This sling is strictly precautionary. I could
be out of it this week after I go in for an assessment." He won
the league's academic award last season and was a lock to win it
again. Carrying a full load of math and science. Story goes that
he finished in the top ten of the provincial high school math
competition. Fluently bilingual. Christ, why don't we just make
the kid the commissioner and be done with it? (A: overqualified.)

His father had played for Red Hanratty and scored fifteen
goals in his one season in junior. The old man did get full marks
for turning out a kid like this, though. Maybe the mother was a
player—happens more than you know. Either way, I figured, you
had to give sire and mare a lot of credit for turning out this colt.

After the game I snagged Spike, the long-time Peterborough trainer, for an icepack for the road and dropped Mays's name. If you ever want the unvarnished truth, the most likely source, the one without an agenda, is a team's trainer. This, however, was a testimonial. I swear, Spike's tears flowed as a rivulet along an eighty-four-stitch scar where he caught a skate blade in his playing days. "As good as he's been for us, it'll be hard to see him move on, but there's nothing more we can do for him here," he said. I figure I could spend two lifetimes in the game and never meet another trainer going wistful on me.

"When that kid came down with mono last fall he wanted to be on the ice the next day," Spike said. "We had to fight 'im to get 'im to rest like he was supposed to. When he came back, he played as hard as any two kids in the league. Just an unlucky break, him doing up his shoulder and all. Maybe it was for the best. He was working real hard—skating, the bike, lower-body work that no kid would get through—to get ready for the playoffs, and I guess he wasn't really over the mono when he came back in November. They had to shut him down cold the other day. I dunno when he's back."

Work ethic, three check marks. I asked Spike what the downside was, because there always had to be one. "Meddling father and a divorced mother who's a piece of work," he said. It meant nothing to me. Every coach or trainer thinks a kid has meddling parents unless he's an orphan. As for the mother being a piece of work, Spike would never be up to the job with any skirt. Given his trade, days pass without a woman speaking to him unless she's asking him, "More coffee?" His bosses were old men, his charges teenage boys, and women were on the other side of the Plexiglas. Alas, a lot like the found-ins at the Muddy Waters.

Barside, I tried to encapsulate the background check in 140

characters or less. I looked at the draft taps and saw the handle of the Irish brew that's my private stock at my local.

I heard the kid fart and it sounded like a harp.

I hit Send and looked up at the widescreen. A fight between two knuckleheads in the league. Oh yet again, the elemental soul of the game, I thought. Just at that point my eyes drifted down to the news scroll at the bottom of the screen. I wanted to see who'd scored for us against Calgary. The scroll of game scores and goal scorers gave way to a news flash.

BREAKING NEWS: JR. COACH RED HANRATTY
RUSHED TO HOSPITAL.

I didn't think much of it, really. The old guy overcome by a toxic level of nostalgia, I figured. Maybe he was laughing so hard at some old joke that he choked on his cigar and needed his stomach pumped.

I'VE NEVER been a good sleeper. Guys in the league generally play, eat, chase skirts, and sleep, that being in ascending order. They can nod off on command, like a volunteer drawn up to the stage by a hypnotist. A snap of the fingers and they're out like a light. I've seen guys grab a quick zees on a ten-minute bus ride from the team hotel to the arena. Guys might be able to play without skate laces but not without an afternoon nap.

I have no idea how they do it. In the bus leagues I couldn't sleep on overnight rides. On red-eyes there's only one light on in the cabin and I'm sitting there hoping in vain that a historical bio will help me nod off. I know guys in the league who've struggled every once in a while but eventually straighten it out in a day or two. I'm a disaster when it comes to sleep. I guess it's some rogue gene that prevents me from ever getting my circadian rhythms back in beat. Some people have vivid memories of great views they've seen in their travels. Me, I bring back indelible images of smoke detectors and sprinklers on the ceilings above the hotel room beds.

Three pints brought me down only so far after the old-timers game and the ninety-minute drive back to Toronto. I knew there was no point going straight to bed. I knew there'd be a couple of messages on the phone but they would have to wait. Nothing I'd hear would help me sleep any better. I went to my laptop and opened my sked for games to scout over the last weeks of March.

Given my GM's interest in Mays, it seemed incumbent on me to book a couple of extra viewings of the wunderkind when he made it back from an injured shoulder, preferably not back in Peterpatch. Nothing against the town, mind you, just that I prefer to see a player of interest on the road, where his team won't have last change so he'll face a tougher matchup. In that situation you're more likely to see best on best—any coach, Red Hanratty included, will want his best against some poor, hopelessly overmatched sixteen-year-old. And I prefer to see a player of interest in back-to-back games, even in the third game in three nights, situations that are a physical challenge. It's a good measure of their toughness, physically and psychologically.

I checked Peterborough's next ten games and saw three dates that worked for me—the first was the coming weekend, a Saturday-afternoon tilt in Oshawa (nice rivalry game on the heels of Ottawa in P'boro Friday night). The other two I logged in, but to tell you the truth I can't remember what they were. I didn't go to them the way things panned out. Things went sideways with my plans.

My phone rang. Hunts. It was 3 A.M., but our last text exchange had been about half an hour before.

He never bothered with the Hi-how-are-yous. When he called you it was always like he'd been sitting beside you for four hours on the team bus. Short and disgruntled.

"I know it's late but I knew you'd be up and even if you weren't I'm your boss."

"That's yes, yes, and yes," I said. It didn't register. Like so much of my side in our conversations. But the GM knew me well enough not to slow down to parse it.

"So what happened?"

"How far do you want me to go back? To the big bang theory?"

"Asshole. What happened tonight?"

"I was the youngest guy on the ice and I'm hurting worse than any of them right now. I'm ready to upgrade to Tylenol 3."

"Not you, asshole. What the fuck happened with Red Hanratty?"

"You got me."

Pause. I heard guys shouting in the background and then realized it was the chatter of his car radio. Hunts always listened to the hockey station on satellite radio on the drive home.

Then my memory kicked in to the bulletin on the scroll.

"I guess they took him to hospital."

"They just said Red Hanratty died."

I gave my head a shake. Cobwebs off.

"Who is 'they'?"

"The *HockeyCentre* guys. Didn't say the cause. It's already out there on Twitter."

"You're shitting me."

"I'm not shitting you. You didn't know?"

"I just left after the game. Drove home."

"Makes me wonder what else you miss in your reports." He paused, like he was waiting for the rimshot.

"What's the big shock. He's seventy-something ..."

I continued in the present tense because this didn't sound like a done deal. It might have been a bad rumour in a business rife with them.

"... and his diet has been fortified by cigars, kegs of beer, and ten thousand bags from Rotten Ronnie's after-game dining. It's a miracle he was breathing, never mind coaching."

Another pause. That's the GM's business-conversation style.

I kept going. "Maybe it was something that they knew was coming. Maybe that's why they had that game, knowing he had some health deal ..."

"Hold on, gotta take this."

Since he landed the corner office in L.A. we've never had a conversation that wasn't interrupted by an incoming call, a message from the field, whatever. I heard my refrigerator gurgle. That's not good, I thought.

A minute later he came back on the line.

"You might have to rethink, sleuth," he said.

"How's that?" I said.

"The natural causes thing. They found him on the asphalt beside his car in the parking lot. Supposedly beaten up. Likewise the team doctor. Dead as doornails, too. That doesn't exactly sound like some health deal, Sherlock."

Key word, I thought: *supposedly*. I had nothing to say at this point. Hadn't really processed this. I should have seen where the conversation was going.

"Look, if Hanratty is dead, this is gonna be a big deal and every team in the league will be sending somebody to the funeral to represent them ..."

Yeah, I know the drill. I didn't get it at first but it's a professional courtesy that guys in the game notice. If you want your team to get respect, you have to show it sometimes. If you're a GM or an AGM of a team, you don't want to do business with another outfit that is a herd of asses. No, you want to do business with guys who are good citizens of the game. I did a mental inventory of the L.A. staff and none of us had played for Hanratty. About half our staff came up in the Western league— our Prairie GM looking after his own. In fact, my small connection to Hanratty was more direct than anyone else's.

"... I'm up to my asshole in alligators out here and I'm not sure the owner would want me missing one of our games. I gotta get you to go to the funeral."

"Yeah, yeah," I said. I had no great enthusiasm and didn't bother pretending. I have to drive an hour and a half each way so that I could mourn a guy who didn't even recognize me. But I have to admit that my antennae were twitching: Who would have iced the Grand Old Man of the Game?

8

A stick is all sharp edges. A skate creases your flesh and you're at the hospital getting 137 stitches. (The skates that Spike sharpens in Peterborough are sharper than the one that left a seam in his grill thirty years ago.) Hockey has a lot of things but there's a surfeit of blunt objects. And a blunt object is what the Peterborough police said brought about Hanratty's demise. A blunt object that added a part to the then-living legend's trademark brushcut. The same blunt object that the perp used to open up the old doctor's scalp right down to the medulla oblongata. The blunt object being a cinder block that provided a low stool for the jockey-sized maintenance man on smoke breaks. These tidbits I picked up at the funeral home a couple of days after the grisly fact. Not what I pumped out of anybody, just what I picked up while I was being politely ignored and while Grant Tomlin rubbed shoulders with league executives who to a man knew that he was a complete fraud. Effin' ghoul. Oh well, his preoccupation with dredging up rumours for his trade-deadline show spared me another of his "Shadow?" routines.

I panned the room, looking for my fellow C-listers. I made a beeline for the cheapest suit I recognized: Double J, Jackie Jameson, a Florida scout who grew up in Peterborough and played one season for Hanratty, the only season he played in major junior. Short but squarely built, Double J had been a legend in lacrosse, his main game back in his day. He became a pretty good scout, a decent judge of talent, and, more importantly, an excellent cultivator of useful friendships. This last skill has enabled him to stay employed for almost twenty years. Every time there was a front-office housecleaning, he had a marker he was able to call in.

Double J was not above stating the obvious just to fill the silence.

"This is unbelievable," he said.

"At best," I said.

"If his wife were still alive it would be enough to kill her." Double J worked a variation on a line he heard so long ago that he couldn't remember the source.

"What do they know about what happened?" I asked. I presumed not a hell of a lot or it would be all over the news. It wasn't.

"My brother-in-law works the desk downtown ..."

I had heard this before. Because of that connection, Double J had the 100 Percent Real Juice when any of the Peterborough kids had scrapes with the local peace officers. This happened with alarming frequency, a fact that was tied to the very loose reins Hanratty had kept on his youthful charges, another reason for their love of the old coot.

"... and he says they've questioned pretty much everybody who was around that night and don't have any real leads. Security got what they think was a car leaving the scene. Got the make of car, not the plates. A Caliber, I think."

I hadn't been contacted, but I figured the investigators would get around to me eventually—the last guy to call, just like the old-timers game's organizers. "They didn't question me and I was there ... but I'm alibied up."

"Shadow, you've got no history of violence."

"I beat myself up but that's about it."

Double J stifled a laugh, as was appropriate. As soon as he composed himself he carried on. He looked over at those passing and pausing beside the open casket. The funeral home director buried his chin in his chest, not because he was moved, though. The Great Man's teenage soldiers had walked in out of the freshly fallen snow and were tracking salt on the freshly shampooed carpet.

"Is he gonna be buried, cremated, or just stuffed and mounted in the Hall of Fame?" I asked Double J.

"I thought the boys in the backroom here did a real good job putting him presentable and everything."

"Well, he probably wouldn't look as good if it had come down after a loss."

If this had spilled from the lips of someone in any other trade, Double J would have shot me a dirty look. With me, he just smirked. In case you haven't picked up on it yet, irreverence is the stuff that keeps a scout sensible, if not sane. Besides, this had the ring of truth. The blackest thing in hockey was the Ol' Redhead's mood after a loss, and the players' best worst stories would always feature a bus ride home after a loss on the road with not a word spoken for hours at a time. Hanratty didn't allow music or even whispered conversation in the back of the bus while he and the assistants drained flasks in the front.

There are infinite variations on the story. Reagan has always related the account of the longest night of his life: the

Peterborough bus getting held up at a border crossing after a loss in Michigan because a Slovak import, a decent defenceman, didn't have his papers in order. According to Reagan, the bus idled in silence for five hours. The best worst story of all I take with a grain of salt: After a loss in Owen Sound, the Peterborough driver managed to take the bus into a ditch, and even with a crashing thud the players were as mute as the cheerleading squad at Gallaudet U.

My chest tingled. The BlackBerry was muted. I was gonna change the ring tone but I couldn't find "Taps."

It was Hunts shooting me a message.

> *Sit on Mays. If he's back playing do the games. If not, just do the background.*

Serendipity. The Local Hero was standing the length of a stick away from me. I knew that Hunts had liked him when he caught a couple of views of him in the early fall. He was thinking he'd still be on the board at number four or maybe number five in the June draft. And a pick in that slot or better would be ours if Columbus kept going sideways. By February before the draft, scouting staffs draw up their targets. You want to know enough about everyone but everything about anyone who's in the mix where you're likely to land in the draft order.

When Hunts said "sit" he was telling me to get the comprehensive workup on Mays. The Large Pitcher of Fresh Squeezed. A stretch of games, five or six. Something well beyond thumbnails of family. First rule of drafting is that you don't draft a prospect—you draft the whole family. Sitting on a kid is in a lot of ways the best assignment you can hope for. You can get fooled on a single viewing—fooled into writing off a kid with talent, fooled into thinking a kid will show up for every game when really he's there one game in five.

Interviews are pro forma. Likewise, comprehensive background checks. The previous administration in L.A. wasted a top-five pick by drafting a kid whose father was a complete grifter, a guy with a criminal record who somehow flew under the radar. Dad ended up with the son's platinum card, and $175,000 in online gambling debts and hookers later, the kid didn't know whether he was coming or going. He never made it through his second contract. Happens more than you'd expect, but it wouldn't have happened if they'd known the father's "issues."

My sitting on Mays was complicated by several factors. The least of them was the cancellation of Peterborough's three upcoming games out of respect for the Dearly Departed Legend. More problematic: In an important stretch of the season, the Peterborough kids would be under the direction of a hopelessly overmatched old-timer, Hanratty's long-time second banana. No assistant in hockey was asked to do less assisting than the unfortunately named Harold Bush. It was always Hanratty's show, and he was widely considered the master of line matching and game management. Bush wouldn't have had any problems if he'd just tried to do what Hanratty did in similar situations, but I'm not sure poor Harry was paying attention all those years, and he sure as hell wasn't taking notes.

I didn't anticipate this being much of an assignment. I guess I'm a Freudian at heart, thinking about character only when I suspect something is wrong. My intuition isn't foolproof but it's pretty solid, and it told me that Mays would be above reproach. Hunts isn't a Freudian, though. He suspects everybody who might cost him a dime.

Double J saw me check the message. I shook my head.

"Hell of a time for Sandy to tell me to pick up milk and eggs on the way home," I said. "So what's on tap for you the next couple of weeks?"

"Same thing as you," Double J said.

My dumb luck to be playing poker with another hustler. Yeah, everybody was going to be sitting on him.

9

The phone rang through to messaging. Sandy is one of those who don't bother personalizing the greeting. In fact, she doesn't even give her name. It's just the automated recitation of her phone number. Making things impersonal is an occupational consideration. I tell her that, at some level, we're in the same business: She works with troubled teens. The difference: She helps those who can't help themselves, while I'm looking for those we'll help ourselves to so that they might help our team down the line. Hers is a calling, mine a dodge. She sleeps more soundly than me but, then again, that's true of most anybody, I guess.

I left a message that was succinct but not quite as offhand as it might seem at face value.

"Hey, my little chou chou, it's me. I'm in Peterborough. Hunts wants me to sit on this kid up here ..."

I pretended to stammer.

"... well, I thought if you wanted to, we could make a weekend of it ..."

I was planning on using that gift certificate to the Falling Water Café and getting a receipt for the full amount for my expenses.

"... Hunts won't mind if we got something plush like the spa up here ..."

I had to play this one up while seeming matter of fact. Hunts *would* mind if he knew the story, but if I'm ever called on it I'll tell him that everything was booked up and the roads were bad. He'll know I'm lying and he'll let it go. I had already made a mental note: Ask for spa charges to be billed separately.

"... I gotta do some door knocking but there's no game skedded ..."

Cancelled out of respect, et cetera. That's what team officials will say, but that's not the whole story. The board of directors just didn't have a clue what to do and had to buy time, because Red Hanratty was Hockey's Longest-Running One-Man Show. Coach and general manager. He had no handpicked successor. No one he was grooming for the job. He just had a coterie of old cronies too intimidated to even say "yes"—they just bobble-headedly nodded in agreement. Who could run the show? Who could even run a practice?

"... You could do a mud bath and get cucumbers over your eyes while I go to the rink and rattle some cages for a couple of hours ..."

Okay, I was officially rambling. She's smart. In fact, I figured it was better than even money that she was going to figure out an unstated motivation for this invitation to a weekend getaway in Peterborough: cover. With Sandy along for the ride, I had good reason to separate myself from other organizations' scouts who'd landed in town. I didn't want them to know what I was doing. It was bad enough that Double J made me.

"... Call me. I love you ..."

I had already checked to make sure no scout was within earshot in the funeral home's parking lot.

"... bye."

I dialed Lanny. The call rang through to her voicemail. I left a message. I told her that I was sorry I missed her tournament in upstate New York. I told her I'd been in Europe, just in case she forgot. I don't think she did. There would probably come a time when she would start to forget things like that or not care to know in the first place. She was old enough to roll her eyes when she overheard someone call me Shadow. It was her mother's idea that she should go to the boarding school, not mine. It made her mother's life easier and mine harder. I was going to be a shadow to her someday.

10

At the funeral home the Hanratty sons and daughters, all sort of florid in a hard-living way, let everyone know that the town was staging a memorial service at the arena the next day. The funeral was skedded for the day after that. I told Double J that I was driving back to Toronto. I didn't want to tip him on L.A.'s intense interest in Mays, and my cover would be blown if, a half-hour after the fact, he saw me pulling into a hotel parking lot on Water Street. I actually checked to see if he was tailing me—paranoid, I know, but I err on the side of caution as a default mode. I drove out to the highway and pulled over at the first coffee shop on the route back to the Big Smoke. The only open table was beside a bunch of guys off the town's garbage trucks, and they were comparing notes, as I imagine they do daily, about their latest finds salvaged from their routes—"like working and shopping at the same time," one said. Thank God the open table was upwind.

I grabbed a coffee and picked up a copy of the national newspaper while I waited for her callback. I skipped sports.

Almost every scout I know reads only the sports section, but I already know all the scores from the league and in junior. And, truth be told, I don't follow any other sport. I couldn't tell you who won the World Series last year, hard as that is to believe. I cared only about hockey when I was growing up. I played it and, during the time that I wasn't playing, I followed it.

I flipped right through the sports section until I found the obituary page. That's normal for me. Obits put a notable life's work into perspective. Maybe this sounds strange, but I've always wondered if I'll be obit worthy. I'd guess yes—a guy who plays one game in the league might not clear the bar for the obit page, but I figure getting invited to an old-timers game is a fair measure of my valueless notoriety. I wouldn't be the main obit but I'd probably get three paragraphs, the minimum for the trivial. Still, I'm not sure I'd get even that. I hope I die on a slow day for death.

An obit written by a reporter from the sports department spelled out the Ol' Redhead's life and lore.

> Edward "Red" Hanratty, who won more games than any other coach in junior-hockey history, died of injuries suffered in an assault in Peterborough Wednesday. He was seventy-two.

Yup, he looked it.

> Mr. Hanratty began his coaching career with the Peterborough juniors in 1973 and, after leading his team to a national championship in 1975, assumed the duties of general manager.

The late Shakey Summers had been the GM who hired the Then-Young Redhead with the hopes that Hanratty was going to be in for the long haul. Shakey's only worry was that a couple

of owners in the league might get into a bidding war to have
him move up to the pros. After Hanratty's second season and
the championship, Summers, well past the best-before date for
any working hockey man, gave in to the inevitable—though
Hanratty greased the Batpole from Summers's corner office by
burying him with the Peterborough board of directors. Some of
Hanratty's gripes were even valid, to my understanding.

*Over his thirty-seven-year career, he coached two Hall of
Famers ...*

Who the hell fact-checks this stuff? Three.

... and more than fifty players who made it to the NHL.

Well, again, technically true but misleading. A few of those
fifty dropped in for a very short stint—guys picked up late in the
season when Hanratty was loading up his team for a deep run in
the playoffs.

*"I know I never would have made the league if it hadn't been for
Red," said Bobby Reagan, the former Peterborough captain who
played for three Cup winners in Detroit during his twenty-year
career. "He made me a player and I was lucky enough that he
coached me at the most important point in my development. Any
young man who played for Red was lucky that way. Red got the
most out of his teams, and he helped his players get the most out
of themselves."*

Schmaltz. One: Bobby Reagan would have made the league
and been an all-star and Hall of Famer if he'd been coached by
Oprah. He was never, never, a marginal player. Two: He wasn't a

finished product at age sixteen when he landed in Peterborough. Hanratty was lucky to get him and smart enough not to screw him up. And that was true of all the pros who came out of the Peterborough program. Reagan was simply reinforcing the Myth of the Coaching Making the Player, the notion that attaching your son to the right coach for four years will make him (and you) a millionaire. I guess Reagan felt obliged to do the faithful son routine, honouring his former coach by repeating the sales pitch he gave hundreds of parents.

> *Mr. Hanratty recorded 1485 regular-season wins in leading Peterborough to seven Ontario league titles.*

A matter of record. He had about six hundred more wins than Norm Pembleton, who started around the same time but did a couple of seasons in the pro bus leagues and four more on the sidelines out of work. Pembleton had been saddled with some dog teams, too.

> *"He was the heart and ..."*

It couldn't be ...

> *"... soul of junior hockey," says television and radio commentator Grant Tomlin. "I've known Red for twenty years and for him every day was a great day of hockey."*

So said a guy who never played a shift for Hanratty. Or, for that matter, against Peterborough in the Ontario league. Until Tomlin landed his television gig eight years ago, he'd never met him. Hanratty might as well have been the Red-Headed Stranger. Grant Tomlin didn't even play junior hockey. He played in the NCAA, just like I did. He was an effing walk-on. He didn't even get a ride. I can't imagine why the Gelled Blowhard felt qualified to offer his opinion. Then again, I'm just a naïf on media matters. I'm sure he solicited the paper rather than vice versa. He'd call them on a daily basis, trying to get his name into print.

I lost my enthusiasm for this brief voyage through the Late Lamented Mentor's life five words into Tomlin's banal hearsay testimonial. Thankfully, at that very point my heart vibrated. Sandy calling.

Conceptually, Sandy thinks of my work as an adventure. Whenever she looks behind the curtain, though, she attaches quotation marks to "job." Her best line: "When I was in school you could improve your mark 5 percent with perfect attendance, but with you guys 100 percent of it is just showing up."

The vagaries of my working dodge were lost on her.

"Sugar," she said, "are you really stuck in Peterborough? It would be one thing in April or May when the courses are open."

She golfs. I don't. Not anymore. No fun for Arthur. Yeah, it's that bad. I drive the cart and tell her how beautiful her swing is.

"I guess you'll just have to relax and be treated like a queen and lose yourself in some fine dining," I said.

"Sugar, it's small-town Ontario, not the south of France," she said. "You'd be more believable pitching me on roughing it."

"Okay, let's rough it."

This well-practised routine continued for a couple of minutes, mostly for our own amusement and, I think, for an eavesdrop-ping garbageman's. Eventually she acquiesced.

"Pack your bags and then pack mine," I said.

That got her. "So it's legit," she said. "You were really ambushed."

I pushed the sympathy button. She has always been a sucker

for helping out and has thrown me a life preserver I don't know how many times. She probably figured I had ulterior motives. Close. I was still trying to figure them out. No matter. The road trip was on.

II

I checked into the Best Available Bunkhouse Offering Points.
Staying in Peterborough would spare me three hours of driving,
and the price of a room was about a wash with the mileage. I
thought it was a more effective use of my time. Being on the
ground in Peterpatch would give me a chance to small-talk my
way to wisdom re Billy Mays Jr. Go around town. Go to the gym.
A coffee here. A beer there. Watch a game in a sports bar. Act like
just another fan. Mention that I was in town for the Hanratty
funeral. If pushed, I could say that Hanratty was a friend of my
father's. Next stop I could say that the old doctor used to snap on
the rubber glove when my father walked into the office. I could
have fun with that stuff and then mention Mays. There'd be no
more than two degrees of separation in Peterborough. It would
be more like squeezing tangerines than oranges, but squeeze
enough of them and you'd still get a Pitcher of Real Juice.

First stop: the local gym, the House of Pain where the
Peterborough juniors lift and where buff young puck bunnies
and not a few cougars window shop. Ten-dollar guest pass with

receipt for wishful expense filing. I threw a couple of plates on a bar at the bench and asked a likely offensive tackle from the local high school team to spot for me. The kid was three bills, soft as a pillow, painfully red-headed, and speckled with freckles. Beef struck me as the type of jock who'd envy the local heroes and resent their trespassing on these two thousand square feet of rubber mats, what he would have considered holy ground and his rightful domain. And, of course, they would get the girls and Beef would be left behind. I tossed 225 like a salad—I didn't remotely need the spot. I just wanted to make sure that I had his attention and respect.

"Pretty good," he said.

"You gotta be doing that with three plates," I said with a straight face.

"Oh yeah, for sets," he lied.

After the second set I mentioned that I was in town for the funeral and that I used to be Red Hanratty's accountant. With a teenager there'd be no follow-up to that line—he wasn't going to ask me for a business card. I told Beef that Hanratty used to send his stuff to our offices in Toronto but felt that he needed a CA closer to home. I kept going until I made sure he was fully tuning me out and would talk just to hear me shut up. A teenager is too easy to flim-flam this way. Pretty soon he was singing.

"They come in all the time ... they're really loud. Shitheads. And they've got nothing. They're not that strong and they're not serious about it ..."

The resentment flowed, as I'd fully expected. Message to self: Factor in Beef's animus with any intel he volunteered.

"... They walk around school like they own it ..."

Perfect fit. Beef knew the whole story.

"They make trouble at all? I hear those kids get into all kinds of trouble."

"There's always something going on. I know Christie, the guy who was captain last year, was banging the mother of the family he was staying with."

Poor Beef. So young. I didn't have the heart to tell him that every team has at least one or that the truly ambitious managed the mother-daughter exactor.

"That's disgusting ..."

Better to be sympathetic than didactic.

"... Bet the girls fall over the stars and everything for that ... what's his name, the really good kid, shit, what's his name?"

"You mean Mays. He's in my history class ..."

Bingo.

"... No, he's a good guy. He was always in here but I haven't seen him the last couple of days. He's real serious about things. He isn't bulky or anything but he's strong. If he was lifting or not, he'd be on the stationary bike, just sweatin' buckets ..."

Beef went on to offer a testimonial that reinforced the stuff I'd read in the media. Billy Mays Jr. was an Eagle Scout who provided an example to the rabble. No problem with girls. No problem with kids at school. He got along with everybody. I started to get the idea that Beef might be a little less forthcoming about his classmate's foibles, so when I moved over to the incline bench, I tried tapping him about other kids on the Peterborough roster. He was only too willing to dish the dirt on them. First stop: no worse than a rave.

12

Next stop: Tim Hortons beside the arena. I could have sprung for a decent meal on the company, but I'd save that and the gift certificate for the Falling Water Café until Sandy arrived. Besides, the guys who work at the arena wouldn't know how to read the menu at any place offering near-haute cuisine. I figured they'd only have time to duck into Tim's for a coffee and a doughnut after doing a flood for the girls' figure-skating practice.

I'd prepared myself to be made by the Zamboni driver and a member of his pit crew, a guy who wore his maintenance all-browns like a team sweater—after all, I'd played in the old-timers game at the rink less than forty-eight hours before.

"Excuse me, but weren't you at the visitation today?" I asked.

"Yeah, we were," the Guy Who Turns Right for a Living said. "You a friend of the family?"

Not a clue that I was in the game or ever had been. I was wounded only slightly by the idea that my celebrity was even more fleeting than I'd imagined.

"I had a brother who was drafted by Peterborough but didn't

end up playing here," I said. "He didn't want to go away to play, and he was a low, low draft choice anyway."

"Too bad," the Broom Pusher said. "There's nothing in hockey like playing for Red Hanratty, God rest his soul."

"Yeah, God rest his soul," Lord Flood said.

I figured three-part harmony wasn't going to get me anywhere, so I tried to strike a different note.

"What's gonna happen now with these kids and the team?"

"They were a playoff team with Mays, but I suspect he's done for the year," Mr. Maintenance said. "I mean, they're gonna have games cancelled, but I guess Mays's shoulder's a little worse than they originally thought."

Bruised and sprained shoulder and out for the season with more than six weeks left? Red flag.

The Zamboni driver took this as a challenge to impress with the dirt he gleaned from being on the deep inside. "I guess the kid wants to come back and he could get clearance to play, but his agent is worried about him getting injured again."

Okay, a lighter shade of red for that flag.

"I feel sorry for the kid," the driver said. "He comes out to every practice with that injury, even though Red would have let him get away for a while and concentrate on school. He was getting on the bike and holding on with one hand until Red chased him off. Just tries to do everything right. He helps out the headcase that's his roommate like he's a little lost brother or somethin'. God knows why. I'm surprised Red didn't run that kid or at least put Mays with a more regular kid. Why?"

"We'll probably never know," Arena Sweeper said.

"Well, Busher doesn't know ... wouldn't know," said Slow Oval Fellow. "What's he gonna do now? He had to ask Red the combination for his lock every day."

At that point the arena workers were joined by the security guard who was working the parking lot the night the Ol' Redhead and Bones crushed their last beer cans. The guard wore thick glasses, not the type for the average near- or far-sighted Joe, but the ones with convex lenses that the near-blind need to make their way through the haze. The boys yelled his name and he turned his head, not to look at them but to hear better and figure out the general direction of their seats. He paid for a bowl of soup at the counter with what he thought was a twenty but was in fact a five-dollar bill. First he couldn't find the spoons on the counter. After he was handed a plastic one by the young girl who made his change, he sat down with us and couldn't find it on his tray. It was a white spoon sitting on a white napkin.

"How did it go?" the Zamboni driver asked.

I wasn't sure what "it" was. Then it was clear.

"They asked me a lot of questions. I told them what I knew."

"Which was nothing," Mr. Maintenance said.

"No, no, I told them that nobody came in the lot from outside. The only people who were in that lot had to come from the arena. Nobody got by me. It's pretty closed off, right."

"Someone could get by you if you were left to guard an open manhole," the driver said.

"Naw, couldn't have. I told them that all the cars left the lot by 11:30 except for a white Caliber, which left at 11:45, and Red's old Cadillac, which didn't leave at all. I couldn't leave until Red's car was gone. I was there right up to when the police got there. Muzz, the night maintenance guy, went on break for a smoke and when he went out the back door he saw the bodies."

"If you don't mind me asking ..."

I was going to double back and, actually, it wouldn't have mattered to me if he did mind me asking.

"... how do you know it was a white Caliber?"

"In the first period I went around the lot, counted the cars, checked to make sure that they had their tickets on the dashboard. I counted the cars on the way out after the game. There were two left and then the Caliber went belting out of there. It was the only white car parked there that night."

The boys didn't look up from their Timbits and the guard spilled soup on his shirt.

"They asked you if you got the licence plate number? Did you have it copied down on a slip when it came in?"

"He'd have been lucky to see a car, never mind the number. He couldn't have read the plate if you held it six inches from his nose."

"Yeah, I just ask for passes. I don't ask for the licence plates 'cause I check the lot after. I don't want anybody to get towed unless they're by a fire exit or something."

This repartee quickly lost its appeal. I bade farewell. In search of a Box of Jelly-Filled Deep Background, I came away with crumbs.

13

Next stop: O'Murphy's. As if Murphy's wouldn't have been Irish enough for a faux Irish bar. O'Murphy's was a favourite haunt of scouts and former players who lived in Peterborough. It was just pricey enough to scare off Joe Fan, and any working hockey man could seek sanctuary in the testosterone-charged backroom, where only the members of the Legion of Alpha-Male Rink Warriors and the affiliated Sisterhood of Deeply Invested Cougars dared tread. A half-dozen Peterborough junior alumni were there when I checked in. About as many scouts who, like me, would be their teams' designated mourners. Among them was Anderson, who decided to put words to that smirk he'd directed at me at customs three days before.

"Shadow, you better file those expenses daily," Anderson said. "You don't know who's going to be around to approve them. I hear Hunts is in trouble. Take a tip from me—I've never been fired before but I heard it from old guys who had. When they start talking about successors for your GM, go get all your dental work done and make a date to get new glasses."

"Andy, thing is, we're going to be in the lottery by trade but you guys are in it the old-fashioned way," I said. "You guys were mathematically eliminated before New Year's."

If you had walked in at that point, you would never have guessed that I wrote my economic history essay on seventeenth-century Dutch mercantilism. No, you would have presumed that the last paper I handed in was written in crayon. *À la recherche du playgrounds perdu*: None of us are exempt from reverting to such juvenilia and some, like Anderson, know nothing else.

F-bombs were exchanged and there followed a giddy delight that made the room tingle, like everyone had forgotten to use Static Guard. I was embarrassed by my behaviour, less so when Anderson shoved me, even less so when he did it again, and not at all when he took a swing at me. And then he said it once more: "School's out, eh. Isn't it, Shadow? School's out."

That's as low as it is unoriginal. That's always a go for me.

"SCHOOL'S OUT." It might seem like an innocuous saying to you and may be Alice Cooper's greatest song. To me, however, those two words, ten letters and an apostrophe, push my button. Too many memories of better times and my worst.

I was twenty-one when I met S, a tall, leggy blonde, in an L.A. club during training camp of my second season. She struck me as earnest and not very smart, but I found her more endearing than those calculating beauty queens who were preying on my teammates at our usual watering hole. Our first conversation was a strange one. She came up to me and just stared. "Hi, there," I said. "I'm Brad. I play hockey."

She continued to stare. It was sort of amusing. I was young enough to think that my celebrity had hypnotized her.

"Cat got your tongue?" I asked her, trying to settle down the poor star-struck thing.

She took a big swallow, a big windup for an autograph request, I figured.

"Friend," she said, "you got some set of wrists."

I wasn't quite prepared for this type of dialogue, even though our reading list in English Lit 101 included Samuel Beckett.

I could have traded non sequiturs with her all night but it was all easily explained. S grew up in Petaluma, California, site of the world wrist-wrestling championships. Her father was a former middleweight champion and a long-time referee. S could judge wrists at a glance more wisely than railbirds can rate thoroughbreds with hours of hard study of *The Daily Racing Form*. S had a formidable set of wrists too, though she was so cute you were likely to miss them. She waited tables forty hours a week, squeezed in acting classes and auditions.

We dated. It was all kinds of fun. G, PG, and X.

We shacked up. S could give up waiting tables. She took more acting classes and auditioned once or twice a week, but nothing came of it. I figured her future might be in arm wrestling.

And we got married. Her father almost put me on the IR when he shook my hand.

We were two days into our honeymoon and she got word that she had landed a part on a Saturday-morning show, a regular gig playing the fifteen-year-old girl next door. She was twenty-one but could pass. On day three of our vacation in Hawaii we headed back to L.A. I guess I should have taken this as a sign of troubles to come. But a few weeks later when Episode 1 aired, there she was at the end of the opening sequence, shrieking what would become her trademark line: "School's out." Nothing in hockey had me as happy as I was for her at that time. For me the thrill wore off around the ten-thousandth time someone yelled "School's out" at her when we'd be having a quiet dinner at an upscale restaurant, but she never tired of it.

Flash forward a few years. We were a couple regularly featured on the front page of the rags they sell at supermarket checkout counters. It was a small sensation when S's pregnancy was written into the show's script. The tabs and Hollywood gossip shows couldn't get enough of her. I was in the supporting role, the "rugged bohunk ice warrior," her Knight in Shining Shoulder and Shin Pads. We were squarely in the middle of the B list, which is way up there for a hockey player in L.A. I was downgraded to a B-minus when I was traded out of L.A. to Montreal, but no matter.

Flash forward two years after that. There she was on the cover of the tabs once again. Clubbing with the guy who played her boyfriend on the series that was soon to be cancelled. He had wrists like the junkie he was, but S was too stoned to notice. He was landing roles, the flavour of the month, and they were the It Couple, never mind that, in the eyes of the law and our team media guide, S and I were Mrs. and Mr. I was in Montreal with our infant daughter—thank God it was late-summer. S called her divorce lawyer, her agent, and her publicist, in what order I'm not really sure. I was calling on my sister to come up to Montreal to help me with Lanny when training camp started. The day the divorce was handed down, I went blind with all the camera flashes when I exited the L.A. courthouse. And that day S found out that she had landed the role of a mermaid in a superhero movie starring a neophyte actor who'd been an Olympic swimmer.

A couple of years later, when the sequel was in production, they were the It Couple.

I suppose if you're underwater you can't hear people shouting "School's out" at you.

THE SUMMER after my bantam season I started training with the martial-arts instructor who worked with cadets at the police academy. It wasn't too useful in a hockey fight, but that wasn't what I wanted out of it anyway. Karate was a pretty decent aerobic workout and good for improving my very limited flexibility. A roundhouse kick to the head is a thing of beauty, something like an end-to-end rush and a great deke and wired shot, a highlight-reel move.

I wish I could say that I knocked out Anderson with a round-house to his thick skull, but such was not the case. No, I aimed low, a sweeping kick with my shin hitting his quad at forty-five degrees with downward force. This doesn't sound like much and might not scare you, but the pain is instantaneous and the charley horse is good for a season. Anderson was one-legged after the kick and it was easy to take him to the mat. I sat on him and didn't bother trying to punch him at first. I opted to choke, crossing the lapels of his blazer over his windpipe, like you would the heavy collar of a judo *gi*. I squeezed until all the air went out of him.

"Is your fuckin' insurance paid up? You want to know who was banging your wife on road trips? You think they're going to enjoy spending your money? You ..."

I had only just started my interrogation when Lee tried to bail out his buddy and wrestle me off him. No third-man-in rule, no worries about suspensions and fines. Others put their drinks down and pretty soon it was a pie fight, like the third act of a Three Stooges short. Lee bounced a punch off my left temple and I realized that I was in this alone, like jumping into the other team's bench to start a brawl. At that point I felt an immense and sudden pressure hit my back, driving me down so that I was face-to-reddening-face with Anderson and unmoving bodies were piled on top of me. It felt like the ceiling had dropped on us. In fact, an angel had descended from heaven to restore order and save me from an even uglier situation. I had to struggle to turn my head to see what had happened. There on top of the pile was an angel. Beef.

Beef wasn't the doorman. He was a busboy. The mammoth cherub was making the minimum wage and all he could eat, which made him, on an adjusted basis, one of the highest-paid citizens in Peterborough. He had jumped into the man-pile like he would have dropped on a fumble in the mud. With one splash he managed to wind five former pro jocks. He then stood up and started to peel everyone off. The doormen arrived at that point, but the fight had been knocked out of all of us.

I tried to straighten myself out. I was winded and shaking. Lactic acid was surging through me like lava up the shaft of a long-dormant volcano that's waking up. Arthur was molten.

Beef was standing next to me.

"Mister," he said, "you sure get in a lot of trouble for an accountant."

14

The next day's big send-off had a surreal feel to it. The Hanratty family, the Peterborough owners, and the city council decided to stage a public memorial service at the arena. Poster-sized images of the Great Man Himself. A black-and-white shot of him in his unhelmeted playing days. Others captured him in a hundred-decibel plaid jacket swearing at a ref when he should have been reaming out his tailor.

The team attended and moved about as a pack: Twenty-five teenagers with dress shirts and ties under their Peterborough sweaters wandered around like puppies that had lost their master. Yup, Billy Mays Jr. was at the centre of the gathering, alternately looking genuinely inconsolable and standing tall for teammates in shock.

There was the junior league: Every Ontario team sent its coach or general manager and a player who wore a team sweater over his Sunday best. Then there was the league: An assortment of GMs, AGMs, and lesser lights in my category. Hunts would be forgiven for his nonattendance—it's a lot to ask someone to get in from the West Coast, but still the Dallas GM, out of respect for his long-time franchise player, Eddie Talbot, made the trek. Also in attendance were, of course, all the Peterborough alums who were in the lineup for what turned out to be Ol' Redhead's last victory, which came four beers before his swift demise. It wasn't just stars, though. There were a lot of strange faces too, guys who'd played only a couple of games for Hanratty—I figured they came out to keep up appearances, having spent their adult lives exaggerating their accomplishments in the Peterborough arena.

Double J sat next to me in the section reserved for the league VIPs. "I hear I missed a hell of a night," he said.

"I've lived down worse. But not much worse."

"I guess you got nothing to lose."

I thought for a second that Double J was taking a shot at me. Like I had done nothing but lose since the end of my career and had nothing left. But then I figured he wouldn't have been taking a dig at me. Not his way.

"Whaddya mean?"

"The Tomlin thing and everything."

"What about Tomlin?"

"Talking with your owner there. Said the first guy he'd hire for his staff would be Andy as his chief scout or scouting director or whatever."

Gulp. I tried to avoid all tells.

"Yeah, well what can you do?"

"Except choke the life out of your future boss."

"Yeah. Is Andy's contract up this summer or does he have another year left?"

"He's free and clear on July first."

Gulp again. Unbeknownst to me, this was already circu-lating—Tomlin not just coming in but whispering about a wish list of hires, Anderson being at the top of it. This was a lot farther along than I had been led to believe. Thousands came out to remember and mourn Red Hanratty and Doc, but maybe I could have reserved a table for six afterward to gather my friends for a mini-wake, a toast to the imminent passing of my first job in hockey after my playing days. Maybe a table for four would have sufficed. Maybe just a stool at a bar.

THE MAYOR spoke. The commissioner of the Ontario league spoke. The team president spoke. Little Red spoke. (Imagine being almost fifty and still being called Little Red.) That's a partial list of those who paid respects and dragged out their tributes, mostly for their own self-aggrandizement. I could go back to college with the premium meal plan and finish my degree if I had a buck for every old war story that was traded at the arena that day.

The mayor, who had always counted on the *Examiner* running a photo of him shaking the Ol' Redhead's hand right before walking out to centre ice for a ceremonial faceoff during a campaign:

"No one in Peterborough's storied history has ..."

Stifled yawn. The mayor was a Small-Town Machiavelli who always and everywhere thought he ran the show. The Then Living Legend had the mayor in his pocket, somewhere between scissors to snip his cigars and a thirty-year-old ball of lint.

The commissioner of the league who, to keep up appearances, smiled through gritted teeth whenever he and the Ol' Redhead crossed paths in the arena:

"No one in the Ontario league's history has ..."

Big stretch and deep inhale. Unless it was July, the commish would have been only a few days removed from a phone call from Hanratty, usually about some minuscule point but not so small that the coach couldn't stretch a profane tirade out into triple overtime. No one was ever more grateful than the commissioner for the advent of hands-free technology.

The team president who, if Red were an Irish setter, would have been strictly the tail. Or maybe the dutiful walker who must pause on occasion, wait out the hound's exertions, and then stoop and scoop:

"No one in this organization has ..."

Toe tap and fidget. The team president, mocked as "His Presidency" by Hanratty, was a Reliable Rubber Stamp on all things to do with the team's budget. He was well practised in paper shuffling so that, at board meetings, no one made it so far as the third-to-last page of the pile where he neatly hid a considerable honorarium for Little Red, who posed as a scout.

And, yeah, down in the order, Little Red, who had such a tough act to follow that he long ago stopped trying to do anything but fog his rum-drenched breath with the extra-large handful of mints that he no longer had to ask the bartender for upon presentation of the bill. He was the image of his old man, with features that looked like they were sculpted out of mashed potatoes and two beet slices for cheeks:

"No one ..."

He paused to bite his lip and compose himself. Almost believably.

"... cared more about his players. He was my father and I was real lucky that way ... to have a father like him. But he was a father to any young man who walked into his dressing room."

Smirk. Yeah, of all of the speeches, this was the richest, talking about the Hall of Famer as a quality parent when in fact Hanratty had left his kids with father figures who mostly mixed their drinks. When the reading of the will came around I'm sure Little Red would be on the edge of his seat when it came to the assignment of his father's flask.

I mention those four, but more than a dozen got up there to take lead positions on the grief parade. Less would have been more, I figure. The Eskimos had fewer words for snow than the speechifiers had in coming up with ways to say that Red was a credit to the game.

You could have flooded the rink with tears shed by family, friends, team alums, kids who were on the team now. They hauled out a blown-up photo of the Ol' Redhead standing behind the bench in some sort of checkered coat circa '75. He was mid-holler, which is to say it could have been any time, any game. You would have thought that every call had gone against him. Maybe some thought it was inappropriate or undignified to show him this way. Me, I thought it was just about perfect, like he was bitching about this last call. He had been the master bully of refs but, no matter how hard he shouted from the grave, Hanratty was never going to be able to coax a makeup call out of the Big Referee in the Sky.

When you bought a program at the arena, you'd have a hard time finding Bones's name. It appeared in a single line of type, below the names, numbers, and positions of the players, below Hanratty's in bold type as head coach and general manager, below others ostensibly ahead of the team doctor in the organization's pecking order. The bottom line read: *Team doctor ... Dr. Gabe McGarry.* The last name to show up on a long roll of credits, at a point when everyone in the theatre has cleared out.

In death, though, his role had to be writ larger, and in fact it was only fair. The Ol' Redhead held Bones in greater esteem than anybody else involved with the team. He admired his expertise. The organizers of the affair were sensitive to this point and thus made sure to get a mention of Bones in all the speeches. They made sure to get Bones's son up in the middle of the program, likely because they feared that the arena would clear out if they put him last.

"Most don't know it, but my father did all his work for the club on a volunteer basis. When he travelled with the team to championships he insisted on paying his own way. I really think that late in life the team kept him going. He cared about these players, more than wins or losses ..."

Bones II's was a pretty touching speech. Bones II was Dr. Theodore McGarry, who'd played a few games but didn't stick with the Peterborough juniors and wisely headed off to med school. With a gut spilling over his too-tight belt and shirt buttons ready to burst, he didn't look like he'd ever been an athlete at all. His father had been a better player before quitting to study medicine, but Bones II became the better doctor. Bones II was regarded as one of the province's top cardiologists, and he kept his hand in sports, consulting with the Olympics associations and the league and minor-hockey organizations.

Bones II seemed shattered. Here was a guy who had to tell people that the odds of getting out alive were long. Here was a guy who had to tell people that they had no shot at beating it and that they should get their affairs in order. The bedside manner had gone out the window. He was pretty much Code Blue with grief. He soldiered on.

"I was in a unique position," he said. "Some players are lucky enough to play for their fathers. In my time with Peterborough it was like I was playing for both my fathers. Funny thing is, my father wanted me to keep playing. It was Red who encouraged me to go to med school."

It was one of his standard lines and it got a bit of a laugh. Bones II was smart enough to keep it short. That said, when he did get up there many in the crowd seized the chance for a smoke break.

No one took a smoke break near the end when they brought up Billy Mays Jr. to speak for the current team. You couldn't have asked for more grace under pressure than that kid showed. He didn't stutter, not once, though he was choked up and close to losing it. I'd find out later that he'd written the speech on his own. He put in the best shift of all those who took centre stage.

"When I came here Coach told me that he was concerned about me as a person first and a player second and said he took that approach with every player. He told me, 'You're going to play a few years but your life off the ice lasts a heckuva ...'"

Clearly, the kid was cleaning it up for the family audience. Bones had put the Ol' Redhead on a sodium-free diet but the coach's language was as salty as the Dead Sea.

"'... lot longer than your career on it.' He said, 'If you look after your life, if you've got character, if you've got heart, it won't necessarily make you a great player, but it will make you as good a player as you have the ability to be.'"

Pass the Kleenex. Hunts wanted to know about what any GM would have: this kid's character and heart. If I had to file my final report on Mays after he stood up there in the arena that day, Hunts would have thought I'd gone soft. *The kid you want your daughter to bring home. Probably leaving the arena to give blood and then put in a volunteer shift at the Peterborough soup kitchen.*

15

Mays was out with mono back in the fall and missed the first twelve games. When he came back, though, he tore up the league, a point-and-half a game, until he tore his shoulder on a blindside hit. I was a bit troubled by the kid's shoulder but that's barely in my job description.

In late May we bring in the meat for inspection. We fly in all our main players of interest, the kids we're looking at in round one of the draft. We pick them up at LAX and they think they're in for a vacation in the sun. It's a bit of a disappointment to them that we put them through off-ice workouts that must seem to them like variations of challenges on *Survivor*. They're really disappointed when they get leaned into by our team doctor and a sports psychologist in L.A. The former focuses on reported injuries, the latter on unreported psychic wounds. The former only makes sense, but the latter I don't have any time for at all, and neither really does Hunts. The psych's on staff mostly to appease the guy who signs our cheques.

Yeah, our Gyro Gearloose of Beverly Hills never shuts up

about studying psychology in college—to hear him talk you would have thought that Adler had been his thesis adviser. Given that he blows everything up to 400 percent, it's almost certain that his entire background in the field consisted of a one-semester half-credit course with a final made up of true-and-false and multiple-choice questions and sessions with his shrink after each of his failed marriages.

My antennae twitch whenever a kid suffers an injury in junior—pros are bound to get in some train wrecks and, with me as one of the exceptions, most come back from them at no worse than 90 percent. With a kid, though, "once injured" has a way of becoming "always injured." Doctors will tell you that it's a kid getting all screwed up—his growth plates and all—before the body is fully formed.

Some scouts go for the high mystical stuff and think the "always injured" is a kid with a black cloud over his head. I wouldn't discount it. I try to look at it organically: If a kid is getting injured all the time, he's doing something wrong on the ice. He's putting himself in bad places on the ice, taking bad risks, not reading the play. He left himself vulnerable the first time and repeats his mistake. And that adds up to bad hockey sense. The casual fan thinks making a great play is hockey sense, but to me that's just vision. Staying alive and being able to show up for work: That's hockey sense to me. You make a great pass that no one anticipates: vision. You play a thousand games in the league: hockey sense.

At the end of the service, I repaired to the scouts' room, where someone in the team office had thoughtfully placed a few boxes of doughnuts and a couple of stone-cold pizzas to soak up the beer that was on ice in a garbage can in the corner. "Just the way the Ol' Redhead would have wanted it ... if they could take the battery out of the smoke alarm," Double J noted upon entry.

I braced the broadcast play-by-play guy for a bit of fact-finding. Woody McMullin had been the Voice at Radio Free Peterborough since Year Two of King Red's Reign over the bucolic principality. McMullin had career ambitions of bigger arenas and more dough beaten out of him long ago when he sent out tapes to Toronto stations and never got a reply. Understandably, because he had no gift for his chosen occupation—he managed to sing the game out of tune and out of rhythm and frequently couldn't remember the lyrics. He did know hockey, though. He was an assistant coach with the best Peterborough triple-A bantam teams and maybe would have been the head coach and moved up the food chain if he didn't have to spend all his weekends on the job and half of them on the road.

"How are the kids taking all this?" I asked as an icebreaker appropriate to the moment.

"About how you'd expect. They don't know what happened and what's next. The ones that you'd expect are pretty messed up. Others hear from their parents that this is finally their chance to get to play ..."

Oh yeah, there was going to be some of that for sure. The Moulder of Men had been the Nemesis of Many Supposedly Stifled Stars, at least to the minds of their parents.

"... and for the Russian kid it's a vacation," Woody said.

"So long as the cheque clears, he gives you what he has to," I told him.

"Yeah, I guess showing up to the service and the funeral isn't in the deal they did with the KGB to get him over here. It wasn't Red's idea to bring Markov in. He was never big on Euros, y'know ..."

"Shit, he never could figure out how Canada didn't sweep eight games of the Summit Series."

Woody, who worked road games without a colour guy, was used to pausing only for commercials. "... and he didn't like Markov even one little bit. The kid hadn't even played a game and he was bitchin' that he was promised an apartment and a car. He doesn't score a goal in the first month but he's always got his hand out, right in the dressing room, before the game. After the first bag skate the kid packed his bags. I guess he packed them again."

"He's quitting?"

"Well he ain't here. AWOL. Mays said he didn't make it home after the old-timers game. Mays said Markov got a call on his cell during the game—Markov told him that it was his agent and he had to go and that he'd meet him back at the billet's later."

"Does the kid speak English or Mays Russian?"

"Markov's English is pretty good. Found out fast that it's hard to get laid and impossible to order drinks if you don't speak the language."

"Geez, he'd be the first Russian to like to drink."

"Yeah, they tried to track him down but the trail of empties and cigarette butts finally ran out. Maybe he thinks 'Coach die, season over.'"

It was all an interesting if not completely unexpected subtext. Mays's outreach, like Markov was an exchange student, was pretty much for naught. It's hard to get with the program if you don't understand it and weren't raised in the culture. I didn't have any particular interest in Markov, a good skater but too selfish for me. I wanted to know about Mays's game, his bout with mono, and especially his shoulder. Woody gave me the season-in-review, though with a mouthful of maple glazed.

"There's nothing you could fault Mays with, not a thing," McMullin said. "A player you just enjoyed watching, making something happen every shift. When he came back from his mono it looked like he'd never even been away. Seamless it was. He was the best player in the league in December and all these other guys had a two-month head start on him. Still growing."

"How did he go down with the shoulder?"

"A game against Kingston and Markov was in the middle of it. He trades a couple of slashes with Kingston's big Russian defenceman ..."

"Probably some chirpin' about who squeezed more money out of his team," I interrupted with acknowledgment.

"Who knows what it was about. Comes after a whistle. Only time I'd seen any passion out of the Ruskie the whole time. Anyway, big scrum and Mays steps into the middle of it and tries to peel Markov away. Right about this time, Tighe ..."

Tighe being Kingston's Knucklehead No. 1, 210 pounds or roughly 3 pounds for every IQ point.

"... blindsides Mays. Huge cross-check, then like a tackle from the back. Sends him almost headfirst into the boards. Could have been worse. I thought for sure it was a concussion or a neck. Stupid ref. Gives him a double minor when he should have got five games. No review by the league either."

Well, Voice was effectively on the team payroll and had been drinking Hanratty's Kool-Aid for years, so I knew that this would have been the way it all looked to someone waving Peterborough pom-poms. Still, the way McMullin described it, and I had no reason to doubt him, Mays's shoulder had nothing to do with any hockey-sense issue. Fact is, the Boy Wonder was stepping up for a teammate, probably trying to get Markov to buy in. Not a problem with hockey sense, but maybe common sense. Mays was still innocent enough to believe in the basic good in everyone, even in a kid like Markov, who was, in my eyes and every scout's and I guarantee the Ol' Redhead's, a talented dog too lazy to do tricks.

"Any chance that the mono thing is a cover for something wrong with the shoulder, some type of chronic thing?"

McMullin looked offended. "All I can tell you is Red looked ashen when he got word that Mays wasn't gonna be available for the playoffs," he said. "I wanted Red to do an interview that we were gonna put on the sportscast, but he said he wanted to hold off until he knew more and until he had a chance to talk about it with the kid and his father."

"He didn't want to talk to the agent?"

"Red never met an agent that he ever wanted to talk to."

That sounded about right.

16

I really didn't have too many thoughts about the funeral itself, much beyond the fact that the Ol' Redhead's pallbearers would have made a helluva power play. I thought it was a nice touch that the hearse and the cars in line behind it made a detour en route to the cemetery and drove past the arena. I imagined that, inside the arena, the eyes of the Queen were watering and the enduring aroma of Cubans in the coach's office would serve as a reminder of Him Who'll Never Be Truly Replaced.

The team came to the arena the day after the funeral and would do that for the next ten days, until they picked up their schedule again. The league put its entire sked on hold for the Friday night, so that all the coaches and general managers could make it out to the service. Peterborough's upcoming three games were postponed and rescheduled out of respect to the Hanrattys, the Boneses, the organization, the blindsided kids, and the townspeople, dressed in black.

Still, the kids reported to the rink around two in the afternoon on weekdays after school, and about ten on weekends.

The earlier start and daylong sessions on the weekend were a bit much I thought, but those in the organization figured it was an effective deterrent against any of the players partying away their grief. They all came except Markov, but this went generally unnoted in the media. Maybe the team put up lost-dog signs on bulletin boards in supermarkets. No one seemed that concerned about his whereabouts. I thought his absence was curious.

A bunch of parents of players stuck around town for as long as they could get off from their day jobs. For some, the working stiffs, this was hard. They had to use sick days. For the white collars it was a little more manageable. It would have been heartwarming if they were still on the scene out of concern for their sons' emotional well-being, but I've been around enough hockey parents to know that a good number of them were worried about their considerable investments, i.e., the kids whose minor-hockey careers they had underwritten to the tune of ten thousand a year or more in some cases. They had signed their sons on with Peterborough to play for the Ol' Redhead and to have him develop them into pros. Yeah, a lot of them were bitching and moaning all the time about The Leader of Young Men being unfair to their sons, none of them getting the ice time they deserved. Soon as he was gone, though, they were all wet-eyed and worried. I thought it was bogus.

And it seemed like all through this stretch the Ontario league was issuing statements. Every day they had a news release out. One day, the league announced that its most valuable player award was going to be renamed the Red Hanratty Trophy. The next: One of the main league sponsors, a chain of pizza joints, had set up a scholarship program in his name, the best student on each team getting five grand toward his education, which was laughable given that the man himself had a healthy distrust of all manner of higher learning. I was half-expecting that they'd be putting him up for sainthood. Throughout, the league gave assurances that it was doing all in its power to address the emotional needs of these kids, who would forever after be like a Pavlovian kennel, bursting into tears every time they smelled a cigar. I found it all hard to take.

Sandy was on the scene, and I tried to throw anyone from the team off the scent by telling them I was sticking around only to support her with the grief counselling she'd offered the club. This was true, or at least partly true as far as it goes. I dropped her at the arena each day. If she had a question about the hockey end of all this, I did my level best to fill her in. As a professional taking into account patient privilege, she couldn't discuss a whole bunch of things with me.

Like the fact that Mays was the player in the dressing room who took charge when the team met behind closed doors with all adults locked out. Like the kids were shutting out almost all adult help, or at least adult professional help. Like grief-stricken wasn't a way that you'd describe some of the players. Like a few of them were shrugging off the Ol' Redhead's death and just wanted back on the ice. Like Mays had sought out Sandy independent of his teammates and was pouring it out about the pressures he faced from the town, the team, and his father, that being in exponentially ascending order. Like Mays was concerned about his injury and feared that maybe, maybe, his career was in jeopardy.

It would have been helpful in my workup on Mays to know about his leadership in the room, even with older players around. And it would have been useful in my workup to know that he was genuinely wounded by the deaths of the coach and the team doctor—he'd had more to do with Bones than most of his teammates. Yeah, there would have been a whole bunch of things she could have told me that might have been helpful, and even though a glass of wine or two might loosen her tongue a bit, the whole patient privilege thing had to be taken into account. If she violated that, she'd be slapped down by the folks in the province who oversee her profession. So even if she did tell me something that would have been helpful, like those things I mentioned, I couldn't tell you what it was.

"There are just some things that I can't tell you," she said.

There are just Some Things I Came to Know. Let's leave it at that.

17

I picked up the morning paper to check out the coverage of the memorial service. The news story grabbed a few quotes from former Peterborough players and several of the league's general managers who, unlike my own, were able to make it to the event. I hoped to see a story of Peterborough police busting the professional autograph collectors who'd planted themselves on the sidewalk outside the funeral home and beside the most expensive cars in the hotel parking lot. Alas, the ghouls fled the scenes.

One item did pique my interest: a column by Gus Stern, the guy who had bumped Harley Hackenbush. THE MAYSES KEEP RED'S MEMORY ALIVE: that was the headline.

> *We'll never see the likes of Red Hanratty again, and that's a shame. That Red didn't live to see the best days of the greatest player Peterborough has ever had is a lesser tragedy, but a tragedy nonetheless. Barring an unforeseen contract snag with the club that is lucky enough to draft him, Billy Mays Jr. has played his*

last game for Peterborough. He gave Red two great years. Red
returned the favour.

I shook my head to reload. You usually have to swat away flies
from fruit this ripe.

"I had a chance to go another direction and take a scholarship to
a school in the States, but the coach was the reason I came here,"
Billy Mays Jr. said after the memorial service yesterday. "I owe
the coach everything for the opportunity he gave me and all he
taught me as a player and us as a team. I'm going to dedicate the
rest of my career to his memory. I mean that with all my heart."

Impressive. It made me wonder if Ollie Buckhold had put
this through a focus group or something.

Mays is, of course, the second in his family to lug a hockey bag
from Toronto up to these parts. The father of the wunderkind,
William Mays Sr., played one full season season in Peterborough
before enrolling at York University and focusing on his studies.
After graduating from business school with honours he quickly
established himself as a titan of industry.

"Red was a great man and he did right by my boy," Mays Sr.
said. "Doc had a part in my son's success too."

Mays Sr. said that he's planning to set up a scholarship fund
in Hanratty's name that will be directed toward the best students
in Peterborough's bantam and midget leagues. He said he'll do
the same thing in the Markham league where he coached his son.

Doc McGarry isn't going to be overlooked. Mays Sr. also
said that he's looking into creating the Doc McGarry Memorial
Scholarship, which will be available to junior players who plan to
study science or medicine in university. Doc's son, Dr. Theodore

McGarry, Mays Sr.'s former teammate and roommate, would administer the scholarship.

"I've always considered philanthropy to be not an option but a duty," Mays Sr. said. "And I've always been a major contributor to my alma mater, but, unfortunately, I never took an active role in a charity associated with junior hockey. It's only young Billy's accomplishments that drew me back into the fold and back up to Peterborough."

I sniffed. I could smell either the coffee brewing or a major tax deduction coming to a boil.

Of course, if such scholarships were already in place, Billy Mays Jr. would have been a lock as a candidate. Given that he'll have a seven-figure bank account in a few months, there will be no crying need for that help when he decides to start working toward a degree. And Mays Jr. said that day will come sooner rather than later.

"The plan has always been that I'd pick up courses by correspondence when I turned pro and take classes over the summer," said Mays Jr., who has been accepted by the University of Toronto.

Adds the father: "I'm proud of Billy. I went to school because I didn't have an option of going to the pros. Billy's is a very conscious decision and it shows his maturity and our family values."

Red Hanratty didn't live to see these scholarships take care of his best and brightest players.

That a young man will continue his schooling with Red's memory always fresh in his mind is the one bright spot in this tragedy.

Never let it be said that William Mays Sr. didn't do anything, though you could make a case that he didn't do anything quietly. Still, I gave the old man points. He seemed to accept his lot in the game as a young man, made a choice to go back to school and made the most of it. I'm as cynical as the next guy—at the very least—but it was hard to find much fault with that.

18

I took Sandy back to Toronto a couple of days later. She had postponed a bunch of scheduled appointments so that she could help out with the kids in Peterborough. Sandy had established herself with the players and would make the trip to see them weekly, but she felt obliged to be available for the sad and damaged men, women, and children who went to her for support.

I dropped her off at her office downtown and made it only a few blocks before my BlackBerry rang. Caller ID: Sandy.

"You have to get back here. The office has been broken into and trashed."

"Call the police," I told her.

"I'm in the lobby and I'm not going back up there or doing anything until you get here," she said.

I turned the Rusty Beemer around, sped back to the building, and made three loops of the adjacent underground parking lot before I could find a spot. I finally made my way up to the lobby, where she was staring at the smokers out on the sidewalk, perhaps reconsidering her decision to give up nicotine a few years back. The occasion called for it.

Sandy's mood was as black as a puck.

"What, did you stop for something to eat on the way back?"

"I couldn't find a parking spot," I said.

She threw herself into my arms. I couldn't remember her ever doing that. She was proudly a woman who didn't need hugs in tough times. She was always the supporter, not the supported, the strong one, not the vulnerable.

I walked her back up to her office. It was just her room and a waiting room lined with chairs. She didn't have a receptionist. She thought that the presence of anyone else made it a less private experience for her patients. Maybe she didn't need someone to pick up the phone, but she could have used a guard dog to scare off whoever trashed her office. Her file cabinets had been jimmied open and papers dumped on the floor. Broken lives that had been alphabetically ordered were now strewn in a chaos that was a lot closer to real life.

She was shaking.

"I'm calling Fifty-Two Division," I said.

"No, don't."

She grabbed my arm.

"We have to report this."

"We can't. I can't."

She dug her nails into my arm. I didn't want to wait too long for her to explain. I thought she was going to draw blood and ruin my shirt.

"Whoever did this is a troubled person, someone who needs my help, not prosecution. Maybe he or she will come back and I'll be able to help ..."

It had to be a he and not a she. Your average *he* would have had to use all his strength and then some to break open the cabinets.

"... and if the police started to question my patients, well, they just couldn't do that. I can't give the police my patients' names. If they were questioned, they might be scared off ever seeing me again."

The place was trashed but not vandalized in the usual fashion. The only things broken or damaged were the locks on the file cabinets and drawers. The perp could have taken her computer. Instead, he had tried to log in. Unsuccessfully.

"What's gone? Was anything taken?"

"No, it doesn't look like it."

It wasn't a robbery. It was a search. Not a pro. A pro could have tossed the place and left it like only the cleaners had passed through.

Might have been a guy who wanted to intimidate her. It wouldn't have been someone who broke in looking to do her physical harm. He would have come during business hours or stalked her when she left the office. No, the perp made a point of doing this when she was out of the office. When she checked her calls, she saw a bunch of hang-ups from a payphone. That would have been him doing his advance scouting.

Sandy and I started to clean up the mess. We were under the gun. Her patients would start arriving in forty-five minutes. We barely spoke. I wanted to say that I was concerned for her but she wouldn't want to hear that. It would have only given her more reason to worry. I just told her that I'd have my phone on and would stay in the coffee shop around the corner. That I'd be three minutes away.

Her appointments went off as scheduled. I sat in the coffee shop all day.

We never talked about it again.

19

It was the night of April Fool's when I drove out to London. I had seen London only twice all season, and I like to see the teams in the Ontario league at least three times. This was my last chance. London trailed Sarnia in the opening-round playoff series three games to love.

I came in the back door of the arena. I was wearing my team windbreaker, so the security man didn't ask me to pull out my ID from my wallet. Pembleton was standing outside, having a roll-your-own, close enough to the door that his exhaust was wafting into the otherwise smoke-free building. He didn't catch the bylaw exemption afforded his recently deceased nemesis. Maybe someday the league will approve a move to go to all the arenas and name all the designated smoking areas after Pembleton.

Pembleton looked as nervous as the next pig heading up the conveyor belt at the slaughterhouse. It was just another game but he looked like his whole job was hanging on the outcome of the next sixty minutes. This had been such a recurring theme over the course of his career that it had become his default mode.

"Death row inmate and the clock's striking midnight," I spake to the fellah with the list of credentialed guests of this unstoried franchise. In case he missed my meaning, I gave a nod and a glance back at Pembleton.

"Lately he has been more of a bastard than usual, if you can imagine that," he said, looking to the heavens.

"Shit," I sighed. "I was hoping I could talk to him for five minutes before the game to ask him about the Gillen kid so I might be able to beat traffic."

"Good idea," the security guy said with confidence born of shared misery. "What's your day job, wrestling alligators?"

I took a deep breath, in part to gird myself for the challenge, in part to fill my lungs with O_2 before venturing into the nicotine-tinged fog that surrounded the Coach Ever Down to His Last Chance.

"Coach, I'm Brad Shade," I started. I wasn't allowed to finish. "I'm a scou—"

"I know who the fuck you are," he said.

Professional courtesy was now dispensed with.

"I just wanted to ask you about Gil—"

"After the fuckin' game. You do know there's a fuckin' game tonight."

Ugh. Why bother? I'll admit that my patience and expectations for any useful dope on Gillen were instantaneously exhausted.

"Yes, I can see you're keenly taking note of Windsor's line combinations in the warm-up. Smokes out here, but I guess they let you keep your flask in the office."

"You asshole."

"From you that's a merit badge."

He threw his spent butt across my bow and walked through the door. He made a point of brushing me with his shoulder. He might have been on his tiptoes but only managed to hit me in the mid-latitudes of my ribcage. He reeked of tobacco bought from the reserve and Five Star.

I had been told that Pembleton lacked the social graces but had no idea it could be this bad. After all, even a novice coach knows that you have to have friends in this business. A favour granted here will eventually be repaid. Someday he might be coaching a kid we have drafted, who needs our whispers in his ears, assurances that his coach is doing a good job. Or if we have a Euro import he likes—we can deliver those to him like a pizza or, in his case, like a bottle of rye picked up by a cab driver. A junior coach saying "fuck you" to a guy from the league? Dumb, and this guy didn't last a thousand games behind the bench being dumb.

I looked at the credential list and saw the name of Arnie Hunter. Arnie's a junior-hockey lifer, a sixty-something insurance salesman by day, a bird dog for London by night. He told me that this would be one of three regular-season games he'd see his team play this winter.

"Nice way to break up six months of watching minor-midget games," Arnie said.

"At the risk of crossing paths with Mr. Popularity Himself," I replied.

"Ain't that the truth," he said. "I leave the fedora at home when I watch our team play. If we lose I don't want him to be able to pick me out of a crowd. He'll pin it on me, some kid I pushed for. I'll take it. I worked for this franchise for twenty years before him, and God willing I'll be working for it twenty years after he's gone. Which, given his history, could be the end of this season, the end of the week, or 'last minute to play in the third period.'"

Arnie gave me the straight dope on Gillen. The kid was dumb but earnest. He needed someone to show him his stall every time he walked in the dressing room, but he could fight like a Navy SEAL. Not the worst combination. Sort of like a mutt that will never fetch you the newspaper but will bite the leg off a guy doing a B and E. I tapped out a note to that effect on my BlackBerry and filed it in our database: *Not smart but no issues.*

By way of conversation, talk turned to the deaths up in Peterborough.

"Every time I see something like that, well, I'm sorry, but I can't help but think of the insurance implications," Arnie said. His soul-baring was at once warm and creepy. "The benefici- aries would be the widows, but both were widowers. It seems like they both had big families so there's gonna be a significant split between the siblings down the line."

I told Arnie that I played in the old-timers game, that I walked right through the parking lot and by the Ol' Redhead's car just minutes before the blood was spilled on the asphalt. I told him that I had an airtight alibi if the boys in Peterborough ever got around to questioning me. Arnie said he heard the dragnet was in high gear. He read my shrug as a disbelieving one. If their investigation was so thorough, why hadn't they got around to me yet? Arnie felt compelled to spill the beans.

"The cops came in and questioned Pembleton the next day," Arnie said. "He told them that he left right after the game but it can't be true ..."

I asked him how he could know that Pembleton was still there.

"It would be the first time in his life that he ever left right after the game. Rhythms of his life. After every game he's draining a jar and smoking a half pack of cigarettes and vomiting in the can. Whatever. He's the one who keeps the team bus waiting. Players have half an hour to get on board, but they're always waiting there for another half-hour after that."

"Maybe," I said. It was a well-educated guess.

"I'm not just going on habit," Arnie said. "Next day he sent Stark ..."

Stark being the beleaguered London trainer who had so often performed the fireman's carry to deliver Pembleton to his hotel room when he got shit-faced on road trips.

"... to pay a speeding ticket he was hit with. Stark being the inquisitive sort said he was clocked at twenty-five over the limit just outside of Toronto, 4 A.M. If he left right after the game he'd of hit Toronto ..."

"When I did, in time for the 11 o'clock sportscast ..."

"It stuck in my mind—and Stark's—it would have been the first time in Pembleton's life that he'd of been pulled over at 4 A.M. and passed the Breathalyzer. Usually by that time ..."

"He'd be vital signs absent," I said.

He nodded.

I SAT UP in the corner seats, nobody five rows in front of me, nobody five rows behind, all you need to know about the hit a losing team takes on the bottom line. I filed my scouting report on Gillen between the second and third periods: *Awkward skating but tough. Started well but faded when team fell behind 3–zip in the second. Might not have a lot to play with but then his linemates probably say the same thing.*

You can only make wisecracks in your reports if you're dead sure that a kid can't play. You're allowed to be wrong about a kid. So long as you don't diss the kid it's a forgivable error. You carve a kid for laughs and other scouts will needle you forever if he ends up being a player. I wasn't going to get needled about Gillen. Nothing was going to get thrown back at me. He couldn't play, and if you needed a second opinion the kid probably would have backed me up.

I WENT DOWNSTAIRS after the game. I figured I'd take one more shot at Pembleton, even though his team lost and lost bad. My father always told me that life's too short to hold grudges. "You have to recognize who's your enemy and who's just a guy in a bad mood and remember that you've been in a bad mood before," he'd tell me, usually to deaf ears. In a situation like Pembleton's, a guy sometimes is looking for someone to talk to, even if it's just to talk him down from the ledge. I'd extend him a courtesy that he didn't offer his crestfallen players. He didn't even bother saying a word to them after the game. No thanks for coming out.

I was just down the hall from Pembleton's office when I saw a slab of beef draped in a cheap, too-tight suit knock on the door with a buddy, no *GQ* spread himself, riding shotgun and carrying a notebook. A pair of plainclothesmen, though they took the job title too literally. They knocked and entered without waiting for an invitation and didn't bother to look back when they shut the door behind them.

I leaned against the wall outside the door, managing to pass for None-the-Wiser. I played the role of him who's waiting his turn for an audience with this guy barely hanging on to his job and the game. I had three concussions so far as I know in my career, but none of them seemed to have damaged my hearing and I could pick up a fair bit of the conversation. I couldn't tell the detectives apart, if it was one of them talking or both taking turns. No matter really, they were speaking as one. Pembleton's growl was now a rasp.

"Okay, one more time, after the game what did you do?"

"Straight home."

"Straight home?"

"Straight home, didn't talk to nobody."

"Nobody. Nobody saw you."

"Well, I wasn't signing autographs or stopping for a drink ..."

I imagined that this could have been true. He was so well-practised that he probably could knock back doubles in a dead sprint without spilling a drop.

"You just left the arena?"

"Yeah."

"What car were you driving?"

"My old Kia."

"Where did you park?"

"What the hell do you mean, where did I park? There's no spots reserved for me. I dunno. I had to pay five bucks to park in a lot before a game I'm volunteering for."

"If you'd asked somebody they would have reimbursed you. Probably paid your gas ..."

And given you a gift certificate, I wanted to interject but wisely demurred.

" ... but you chose to leave immediately, what, ten minutes, fifteen minutes after the end."

"Yeah."

"Couple of things, coach. One, your speeding ticket."

"Yeah, if you left right after the game and were stopped in Toronto at 4 A.M. you wouldn't have been speeding, you would have been pulled over for driving your tractor on the 401."

"I stopped to eat on the way. My ulcer ..."

An ulcer for a career coach is like a carpenter's callus, I guess.

"You stopped for something to eat. So where did you stop?"

"I stopped at Tim Hortons ..."

"For a doughnut for your ulcer."

"Some diet you got there."

"No, for a soup."

"Did you eat it or make it?"

"Yeah, coach, I guess you could have done both seeing as you took about five hours to make an hour-and-a-half trip."

These guys weren't all-stars, not even first-liners, but they had enough to grind Pembleton on.

"I was sleeping it off. I don't like night driving. Not after having a pinch or two. Need 'em to steady my nerves."

"Right, steady your nerves before a pressure-packed situation like an old-timers game."

"I don't like crowds."

"Or the coach of the other team who turns up dead."

"That's got nothing to do with anything. So you say I didn't like him. If it was such a problem I wouldn't of come out to the game outta my own pocket."

"I suppose. But the problem I have is that you show up on a security video."

"Yeah, coach, there are a bunch of security cameras at the arena and, funny, you show up on the camera right at the exit, the door nearest where Mr. Hanratty's car was parked ..."

"Where Mr. Hanratty and the doctor were lying dead later ..."

"... where we drew chalk lines around them."

They had Pembleton in a head spin.

Voices lowered. Some of what they said fell out of earshot. Not the tone, though. For the plainclothesmen it was interrogation by insinuation. For the coach, it was furious back-pedal. He left and stopped. Or make that, he had a drink and then stopped. Couldn't remember going to his car but, yeah, it musta been parked close to there, except that was the reserved parking and he said that he had paid out of his own pocket. Must have been mistaken.

"We'll be in touch, coach," the one said. A sigh was heaved.

I STEPPED AWAY from the door, lest I be made for eavesdropping. I kept my head down and eyes on the BlackBerry's screen as if I were studying the notes on Gillen I'd dashed off.

"Brad Shade ...," the one plainclothesman said, parked in front of me. Two hundred and seventy pounds, he would have had to parallel park.

"That's me."

"Detective Madison, OPP up in Peterborough. That's my partner, Detective Freel. I recognized you 'cause I coached against your father's teams. He's a good man. Helluva coach. Talked about you, real proud ..."

He made this sound either inexplicable or as a loving leap.

"... How's he doing?"

"Retired but not tired."

"Give 'em my best. Tell him he's not missing much, off the ice anyway."

"You're a long way from your arena, detective."

"Thanks for reminding me about filing for mileage. Fact is, it's the Red Hanratty deal. You mighta put that together. We're questioning practically anybody who was within the city limits the week of ... well, you know how it is. Only case where I got autographs for my kids along the way. I guess technically I shouldn't of asked for them."

I dialed him back to the subject at hand.

"Yeah, I was there that night."

"What were you doing there?"

"Playing in the game, one of the old-timers."

Okay, I don't lack for self-worth clinically or chronically, but somehow my name didn't show up on the list of those to be questioned. As it would turn out, I wasn't listed in the program because I'd been a late addition to the lineup. Didn't know that. And I didn't end up on the score sheet. Which I did know. On a night of a hundred stars, I was the guy working the curtain. Again.

Detective Madison's oversight was more embarrassing to him than my enduring anonymity was to me.

"Brad, I guess we're going to have to question you too. You understand. Not saying you're a suspect or anything."

I asked him if it could wait until I was finished with Pembleton. Told him it was a working night for me too, that I was scouting for L.A. Told him I'd have a brief and hopefully polite conversation with Snidely Tonguelash, the fellow he and his partner had left in a puddle behind his desk in his office. Told him I just wanted to ask about a kid who was a near-prospect.

Detective Madison told me that their questions could wait until sometime down the line and left unsaid that he and his partner had about a four-hour drive back to Peterpatch. I gave him my number. The 416 area code let him know that I was in Toronto, so I didn't bother mentioning it. He gave me his card. I told him I'd be back in Peterborough on work in the next week, and he said that he might have some pictures to look at.

The trip from Peterborough was useful for the two detectives. Pembleton and me, a bird and a half with one stone. The trip to London was potentially useful to me. An audience with the black hat and another with two guys with badges, two birds in a bush. It seemed that I was more likely to trip into some useful dope on Mays and the Peterborough players from Madison and Freel than they were to find out anything from me about the murders at the arena.

Madison and Freel said their goodbyes, and as they walked off I swallowed hard. I knocked on the door. I heard a garbled "Fuck!" A pause and then an exasperated "What?" I didn't bother for a proper invitation. I opened the door.

PEMBLETON SAT behind his desk. He had been at work with an almost spent packet of tobacco and rolling papers when the detectives had walked in and was waiting to return to the business at hand once his hand stopped shaking. He was leaning back in his swivel chair, staring at a filing cabinet on the far wall, not turning to look at me, not bothering to ask who I was or what I wanted. He was lost in a train wreck of thought.

He had been a nice hue of shale before the game but now looked waxy, a bit of ash mixed in. I can only imagine what his blood was like, some toxic sludge run off rye, nicotine, and recrimination, but whatever its composition it had run completely out of the face of this little tough guy. London had lost the game and he was inching closer to another pink slip. The boys from Peterborough had asked him some uncomfortable questions and he was inching toward, well, I didn't know what.

"Coach, I'm Brad Shade. I spoke to you briefly before the game. I'm a scout with L.A. and ..."

"I got all that the first time. You were on my fuckin' team in the fuckin' old-timers game, right?"

I wasn't about to be deterred at this point. I could have made my getaway about forty-five minutes earlier. I didn't want to have to come out to London again. I wanted to finish my report on Gillen and be done with him for the year.

"Yeah, but I thought you didn't know who I was 'cause you called me 'Hey, you' and my name wasn't on my sweater. Look, I just wanted to ask you about Gillen."

"I don't have a bad word to say about him 'cept he can't fuckin' skate, which I'm sure you put in your fuckin' report."

I took a deep breath, suspecting that the next sentence I managed to get out would be the last sentence I got in.

"Look, you know why I'm here and I know you know, so let's cut the shit. I'm not new. Just let me know about the Gillen kid, what I should know for me to do my job like you do your job."

Pembleton wasn't much good at the pushback, like the one the detectives gave him, like the one I was giving him. He sighed.

"I like Gillen as much as any kid on the team," he said. "More than most that come this way. I don't need to tell you he isn't the sharpest skate. I don't need to tell you about his father, 'cause you've already been through that before."

We had looked at Gillen's older, smaller, tamer brother a year before. At that time we found out that dad was a lush who was occasionally violent, those occasions being when his synapses were firing on most cylinders and he could stand without leaning against a wall.

"Has he had trouble?"

"Trouble" being the great miscellaneous that captures curfew, chasing puck bunnies, catching puck bunnies, fathering children by puck bunnies, fights, drinking, fights and drinking, criminal charges, et cetera.

"No trouble like mine. Wouldn't wish it on anybody, not my worst enemy."

Despite his lukewarm co-operation, I was still irked by the little tyrant. I aimed low.

"Here I thought your worst enemy was as dead as Georges Vézina." I put the snarl back in the whimpering little mutt.

"Look, you fucker, I don't have to take shit from you. I'd have you thrown out on your ass if I felt like it."

"If you felt like anyone would listen is more like it."

Okay, it was clear. I had overstepped.

"Just so you fuckin' know, I never had a problem with Hanratty. I wasn't his buddy. Never said I was, never pretended I was. But I had no problem with him. All that other fuckin' stuff gets ink, sells tickets, and lets our bosses know that we're doing our job. Be serious ... I kill the guy after an old-timers game. I'm mad about that how? Why the hell did I drive up to that fuckin' game? Because he asked me. I didn't have to pick up the phone. It didn't matter that he beat us in the playoffs three years running and cost me my job in Brantford. Those dumb cops thinking that I'd want to kill him. What do they know about the game?"

His mind was racing but he had spun out on the second turn. He was about to say something more but it was gone.

"They're just doing their job and questioning everybody," I told him. "They're questioning everybody and just looking for any leads they can sweat out. Shoulda just given them a straight story. You slept one off in the parking lot and got away when you shoulda blown over. But you have no alibi. And not having an alibi, well, that's the slippery slope."

"The ice is slippery when it's flat so long as the Zamboni just rolled over it."

"Point taken," I said.

"So how'd you become such a police expert?"

"My father was a cop. He actually knew the bigger guy of the two that were just questioning you. And as far as what they know about hockey, trust me, you've got guys coaching in this league who don't know the game as well as the one guy. Did you see the scar over his eyebrow and the seam in his lip? Did you think he did that fencing maybe?"

"Didn't notice."

"Didn't think so." He didn't put it together that I basically hung it out there that I'd been listening in on the interview.

"So what do I tell them?"

"Try the truth if you didn't do it."

"I didn't."

"Okay, you didn't. You have no one to back up your story, but at the minimum you're not talking your way into a jam, which is where the hard evidence is taking you. The time on the speeding ticket."

He was rattled. That I knew details of the night he had misspent fazed him.

"Truth is, I had a skinful over the course of the day and night. A bunch of it in Hanratty's office going from about 3 P.M. I went out to my car—and no, I can't remember where it was—and fell asleep in the back seat."

"You decided not to drive."

"Sorta. I couldn't even get my keys in the ignition. Or maybe I did. I don't know, not sure."

"Right. If you give 'em the straight story then maybe something else that you don't know will sort things out. Hell, if you have no alibi at all and you were driving home, they could run your car for bloodstains—there was a ton of blood and it would have to drip in the car. If there's no blood in your car, well, it's not an absolute alibi but it goes a long way."

"Right."

Something was just a bit off. I tried to figure it out. "How long did you know him?"

"Going back to high school. We dated the same cheerleader."

"How'd that work out?"

"He married her. That doctor was his best man."

"Oh."

So the sainted Judy had fired Pembleton before six junior clubs had given him the pink slip. Then she married Hanratty and predeceased him.

"Tell it to them straight and maybe something will back up your story."

I tried to sound more confident in the Everything-Will-Work-Out than I was at that point. Likewise, I tried to sound more credulous about his version of events than I had become.

20

A week later I put in a call to Duke Avildsen, a Hockey Semi-Legend. I talk to him a few times a month. Duke grew up in a small town on the north shore of Lake Superior. His father drove an eighteen-wheeler, and when Duke was fourteen, he rode in the front seat next to his old man, who dropped him off in Timmins to play midget hockey. Duke's only been back to that town once over the years, when he was nineteen and had to bury his father.

Duke blew into the league back in '61 and decided to stick around a half century. Two hundred stitches and a few million air miles later he was still at it. He scouted for five L.A. GMs over the last fifteen years. Duke had filed reports from 250 games a season for the first couple of decades after he hung up his skates. He was one of the first scouts to go behind the Iron Curtain and smuggle out players, risking their lives and his. He had the nerves of a burglar. Now, in something like semi-retirement, he works weekends—a game Friday night a short drive from Toronto and a game Sunday afternoon, where he holds court in the scouts' dining room at Mississauga arena, just down the street from the old house in the new subdivision he calls home. He still looks like he could play. The only thing that jiggles on him is a forty-year-old dental plate. When someone drops the name of an old-timer he scrapped with, his gums must involuntarily flex or something because his set of store-bought teeth lose their grip and start to float about his mouth.

Duke is still a sharp hockey man. He has a good eye, knows the game. He gives us good value and has been behind a few late-round finds that he can dine out on if he's ever so inclined. When Hunts brought me out of exile I did my best to befriend Duke. Our conversations were informative and entertaining.

I phoned Duke at breakfast and told him about crossing paths with Pembleton and the Peterborough detectives the night before. Nothing came as news to him. He called Pembleton "a good hockey man when dry, which is sort of like saying that Vancouver's pretty near the end of a drought." He said Pembleton had been telling it straight when he downplayed his so-called rivalry with Hanratty.

"They had a lot more in common than you'd think. They'd look at players like they had the same set of eyes. The difference was all in the packaging. Pembleton was a pretty decent guy, dry, but he always came off as a mean fucker. Hanratty seemed like your bartender at your corner tavern—y'know, all hey-how-are-you-buddy and singing 'Danny Boy' and that crap—but underneath he steamrolled guys, guys like Harry Bush, dozens, maybe hundred of players whose only problem was that Hanratty just didn't like them. The Father Flanagan stuff was a dangle. Pembleton talked tough and he was never a pussycat or anything, but he was probably even fairer to his players than Hanratty was to the kids in Peterborough ..."

I took "fairer" to be "more even-handed" or "less arbitrary."

And even in my limited time working the Ontario league I'd heard tales, credible enough, that Hanratty's mood could go as dark as a coal mine after midnight.

Duke has always been a good judge of character. I came away with the feeling that he didn't particularly like either Pembleton or Hanratty, even though they were pretty much contemporaries and shared old-school values. I also came away with the impression that he might have trusted Pembleton more than Hanratty.

"... Pembleton and Hanratty weren't really players. Hanratty was a career minor-leaguer. I talked to Floyd Jones, who played a long time in the league but was on Hanratty's line in Syracuse, and he told me to ask Hanratty next time I saw him about how he used to 'deflect' the puck to his wingers. But Pembleton wasn't even that, didn't even get out of juniors, so I never played a shift against them. All I know of them is what I came across in the Ontario league. Hanratty was all blarney and bullshit. The game gives him an audience and attention. Pembleton's a loner. If it weren't for the game he'd be a drifter or a hobo or something. Pretty much is even with it."

Only later did I realize that Duke hadn't called Hanratty "Red" or any variation on his nickname the whole time. Red was the character, Hanratty the actor. And only later did it occur to me that Pembleton had no nickname.

Duke asked me about my list, about games I had worked. The usual shooting of the scouting breeze. I told him about sitting on Mays. Duke said that he saw him a couple of times at the start of the season and that he was the real article. I asked him if Mays reminded him of any player. I figured he'd drop the name of a Hall of Famer or all-star or something. Nope.

"To me, Sorensen has some of the same game, same skating. Who he doesn't remind me of is his father. I only ever saw the old man as an underager. He never did play in his draft year or after that. Not very big, not like the kid. He's a head taller than the old man. And the father wasn't real athletic. This kid is a horse, the power he generates with every stride. He could pick his sport, I bet. They both have the same head for the game, though. Great hockey sense. The father clearly schooled this kid and did everything he could to make sure he developed into a physical package. I suppose the father could've played, but he didn't want it bad enough and ended up going to university. York U. I even kept an eye out for him to see if he'd play some hockey for the school team, but he never did. I guess it worked out okay. He made a helluva lot more money with those money schemes than he ever would've lacing up his skates."

Some scouts I'd take with a grain of salt, but not Duke. He planted a seed that was sprouting without watering: What happens if the game eventually doesn't mean a whole heck of a lot to Billy Mays Jr., just like it did with his father? A kid with holes in his game can still help you. A kid who doesn't want it is of no use to you at all. Did the team shut Billy Jr. down? Did his father? Or did the kid just decide to pull the chute? The last two possibilities were red flags. Our first-round draft pick was riding on the intel. So were our jobs, I figured.

21

I drove up to Peterborough the next day. Some more door knocking. I called Harley Hackenbush at 5 P.M. Start of his shift. I figured I might be the last human voice he'd hear through his eight-hour shift unless the guy who takes his pizza order counts. I asked him about William Mays Sr. as a player.

"He c-c-cc-could play but he didn't get hardly any ice time. Hanratty told me that he thought M-M-MM-Mays played better and harder playing eight minutes a game than eighteen. And then he started to be a healthy scratch. I asked Hanratty about it. He said, 'The k-k-kk-kid helps us more by not playing at all than playing eight minutes.'"

"I guess that's not exactly mutually exclusive," I said.

I tried to puzzle it out, but Hackenbush was holding an important piece.

"If old man Mays couldn't have played, then why the h-h-hh-hell did other teams try to get Hanratty to trade him?" he wondered. "P-PP-Pembleton wanted him too."

"Are you sure of it?"

"Sure as I'm s-ss-sitting here. Probably has a lot to do with me sitting here."

"How's that?"

"I never got along with H-H-HH-the coach. Or at least he never wanted to get along. He'd call me Quackenbush and Hackenschmidt and s-ss-stuff like that to embarrass me in front of his players. He'd r-rr-rip me. He wouldn't talk to me after games. He'd s-ss-swear a blue streak. Just m-mm-messing with me, making my job impossible. And then I wrote a story about WW-W-William Mays Sr. deciding not to come back to the team after his rookie year. That's when he went to our p-pp-publisher and said, 'Look, we save a seat on our b-bb-bus for one of your reporters. If you want a reporter's ass in one of those s-ss-seats, it's not gonna be H-Harley H-Hackenbush's.' H-Hanratty's h-h-had that sort of clout. That's why I h-h-haven't seen the team play in over twenty years. That's why I only draw such p-pp-plum assignments as old-timers games. I'm two years from r-retirement and I'm getting treated like s-some s-sort of intern. If I make any n-noise, next thing I'll be f-fetching coffee and running errands for the n-night n-news desk."

"So you hadn't been to the arena twenty years and ..."

"I'd been to the arena but for b-bantam and m-midget games and stuff."

"Okay, the first time you're back at the arena for a game Hanratty is coaching and he ends up dead in the parking lot."

"Yeah, sh-sh-shame about Bones though. He was still my G-G-G-GP all these years. Saw him just a c-c-couple of weeks before about my gout."

So if Hackenbush's eyes ever got moist when he was talking about the Ol' Redhead's premature demise, it just meant that his big toe was throbbing.

MY FIRST TRIP around the Ontario league, I sat beside Duke Avildsen in the scouts' room in Mississauga and couldn't help but notice that he was reading a newspaper that was spotted with coffee stains, torn and unevenly folded. The pages had been shuffled into a random order. I wanted to check to see if snow was in the forecast for a drive to Sudbury the next day and I couldn't find the weather. It had been ripped out.

"What did it say?" I asked.

"Couldn't tell you, Shadow," Duke said. "I wasn't the one who ripped it out. I picked up the paper at a diner. I've never paid for a paper my whole life. No self-respecting scout ever has."

It's an unusual rite of scouting but not so unexpected I guess. Just as they forage for information, so it is that scouts try to find news in its natural state rather than buy it. Plus, teams don't let scouts put newspapers on expense accounts. I'm not a joiner but I didn't see the harm of falling in with this convention. It might mean waiting, and that day it did. I didn't find a newspaper until I ducked out for dinner after talking to Hackenbush. I sat at the counter of an all-day breakfast joint down the street from the arena. Eggs, bacon, beer.

The lead story on the front section of the Peterborough paper that day:

VIS, CITY IN TALKS FOR ARENA PARTNERSHIP

Peterborough mayor Arthur Smythe and Woodbridge entrepreneur Giuseppe Visicale met yesterday to discuss a private-public partnership for a commercial and residential development with a renovated and upgraded City Arena as its main attraction.

Smythe and Visicale say that they are looking for input from city councillors and the public with regard to the arena improvements.

> "We're proud to say that we are the best hockey town in this
> country, and Mr. Visicale and I would like to set about making
> our arena the best in hockey. Our vision is that the arena would
> be a centrepiece for the downtown core, a magnet for investment
> attracting high-tech businesses and high-end service operations."

Yadda, yadda, yadda. It was the usual pie-in-the-sky stuff for
Smythe and rare public exposure for Visicale. I looked at the
photo of the two just below the newspaper banner: the mayor
whose smile revealed teeth gapped like a picket fence and the
Hockey Don's poker-faced mien. There wasn't much doubt
about who was playing and who was getting played. Midway
down the story:

> As part of the proposed deal, Vis Hockey Enterprises would secure
> a minority share in the Peterborough junior team with options
> to purchase incrementally larger shares in the community-owned
> franchise if the commercial-residential development hits certain
> city tax-revenue targets. Part of the city's contribution to the
> arena development would be realized from a tax on hotel rooms
> and an increase in metered-parking rates in the downtown core.

Yeah, like Vis Enterprises went into anything to be a silent
partner. Those targets would be hit easily. A marksman would
have a harder time firing a couple of rounds inside a tractor tire
at thirty yards.

Further down a quote from Visicale:

> "I'd like to see City Arena be renamed the Red Hanratty Centre
> and to pay some sort of special tribute to our late legendary coach
> and Doc McGarry, the team's long-time doctor, who both lost
> their lives so tragically just days ago."

All this had been in the works for a while. I had heard rumbles about it. Then again, every team in the Ontario league had received a cold call from Giuseppe Visicale.

The counterman cleared his throat and interrupted. He had spotted the L.A. logo on my clipboard and jacket.

"You a scout?"

"Yup." I volunteered nothing more than that off the hop.

"You were at the funeral."

That was a good guess.

"How'd you know?"

"I was there too. I recognized you just now. My son wanted to go up and ask you for an autograph. He said you were a player but I said that I didn't think so."

I didn't bother correcting him.

"You went to the funeral. Did everyone in town go?" I asked.

"I went because Red used to come in here with Doc and the other team guys. The players would come in after a Saturday-morning skate. And teams in the league come in here too. We have a good rep."

"What's gonna happen with this development they're talking about?"

"Might have to sell the lot here, which would be bad 'cause my father started out this business. Red told us he signed his first contract with the team over in that booth. I can tell you he would have fought this deal tooth and nail. Said so when he first got wind of it."

"How's that?"

"Red was his own man and the team was his own team, that's all. Didn't want no interference or nothing. Those guys on the board of directors rubber-stamped whatever Red put in front of them. He wasn't a control freak or anything. He could just do his job better than anyone else could. The directors knew that.

If Red didn't want the team sold or to be in that deal, it wasn't gonna be in that deal. Red was coach for life, the biggest draw really, no matter who played for him. He wouldn't have stayed on if someone in ownership was gonna crowd him. And if the team was sold against his wishes and he quit, there'd be rioting in the streets. No one would go to games in that brand-spanking-new arena if he quit."

Yeah, I thought, if Red weren't dead already, a statue of him being unveiled in front of an arena controlled by Vis Hockey Enterprises would be enough to kill him. Nothing had ever stopped Visicale and crew from running a show that they wanted in on, but then again they'd never worked Peterborough before. Hanratty was a boss of a different sort. Everyone saw Hanratty's demise as untimely, or at least everyone except Pippo Visicale.

A bell rang and the counterman turned back to the kitchen to pick up a BLT for the tow-truck driver in the window seat. I looked down at the last two paragraphs of the story.

> William Mays Sr., a former Peterborough player and father of current star Billy Mays Jr., expressed an interest in investing in the proposed development. "I've always believed in Peterborough, and I've longed to come back and give back," said Mays Sr. "I've been incredibly lucky by being future-directed, not lingering on the past or reliving it. It's all about moving forward and making a better world for future generations. I think this would move Peterborough and the team forward into the new millennium in the right direction."

It struck me as bogus. I would have bet that he wouldn't have been so "future-directed" and intent on "not lingering on the past or reliving it" if he hadn't seen the paperwork. If Vis Enterprises' numbers and performance didn't fit his Metrics for Success, he probably would have been vouching for the virtues of the Old School.

22

April 10, or thereabouts, I found Detective Madison's card and called his number. My father always advised me that it's far better to call them than to wait for them to call you, no matter who the them is. I didn't have anything to hide or anything to fear from hostile questioning, and I thought that it might go more quickly if I was proactive. I also figured that I might be able to squeeze the detective for any juice about the Peterborough team and Mays in particular.

"When can you come in, Brad?"

I was a little disappointed that Pembleton was worth a trip to London but they wouldn't make the drive to Toronto to interview me. I just tossed it atop the heap of slights and indignities that I suppose are more perceived than real.

"I'm yours. My calendar is pretty open. I was thinking of coming up to Peterborough anyway to look after some business."

"Does Friday work?"

We set it up for after lunch.

I then called Ollie Buckhold. I asked him if I could sit down

with Mays that Friday morning. I figured that the visit to police
headquarters might either start later or run longer than I hoped.

"Bradley, anything for you, my friend," Buckhold said. "You're
going to love Billy. He's a wonderful young man. Let me call him
and set things up. Would lunch work?"

"Lunch would work."

"I'll pick up Billy and meet you at—"

"Ollie, if it's all the same to you, I'd like my session with Billy
to be just me and him. There's plenty of time down the line for
us to sit down with you and your client. God knows that we'll be
spending whole workweeks in the same room or on a conference
call if we're trying to do a contract. And really I just wanted to
get a sense of what Billy thinks of our organization. I'd like to
make a good first impression and that's easier if the set-up is
more personal."

"I understand completely, Brad."

I'm pretty sure he did. He understood that I was dissem-
bling. I was emphasizing only the most minor of reasons for the
meeting. I wasn't worried at all about first impressions. That
would have been presuming a lot, too much really. If he's our
player, the top name on our scouts' list when our pick comes up
and we're on the clock, we're taking him and we'll worry about
making an impression when we pose for a picture on the stage
and walk him back to our table on the arena floor. But that was
way down the line. I wanted to get a read on the kid. I suspected
he'd be okay, more than okay. I suspected I could put three big
check marks beside his name in the character ratings. But I
have to see it, know it. To trust my instincts would have been
presuming way too much.

"Let me call you Friday A.M. and we'll set something up."

"Done," I said. I suspected that I'd have to call him rather
than wait for his call, but we'd struck our bargain.

23

I was three bites into a corned-beef sandwich, the lunch special at the Merry Widow, when my cellphone burst into the opening bars of "Tears of a Clown," my ring tone of the day. Unknown number. I answered with a grunt. Had to be one of those 1-800 deals.

"Mr. Brad Shade, please?"

The guy on the other end of the line had a bag-of-gravel voice that made it sound like he didn't say "mister" a whole lot.

"Speaking."

"Mr. Shade, my name is Lou DiNatale. I'm with Viz Enterprises. Our records show that you came out to our charity game in Peterborough a week or two back."

"Yup."

I looked to the peeling paint on the bar ceiling.

"Mr. Visicale appreciated you comin' out, Mr. Shade. May I call you Brad?"

He just did.

"Brad, I run one of Viz Enterprises' summer hockey academies ..."

I only ever went to hockey school. I guess calling them "academies" kicked in at a certain price point.

"... and I wondered if you'd be interested in appearing as a featured-guest instructor at a few sessions in August."

I hemmed and hawed.

"We can make it worth your while for a few days."

"We can discuss it, sure. I'll have to see what summer tournaments I'm working—I know I'm in the Czech Republic the second week of August. Otherwise, though, I should be clear until Labour Day."

"We'll send over one of our representatives with a contract for you. The camp'll be in Peterborough. At the arena. We put you up at the best hotel there, or you can be Mr. Visicale's personal guest at his vacation property on Stoney Lake."

So much for discussion.

I still had a couple of bites left in my sandwich when a shiny black Lincoln Town Car pulled up in front of the Merry Widow. Out of the front seat bounded a monster in a dark suit and shades. He walked into the premises with papers in hand and went directly to my stool without asking my name or anything. He laid out a contract for me. I looked out into the street. I saw the opaque rear window of the Town Car power down a couple of inches.

24 _____

I had to drive to St. Catharines. Game 200 of the season in my log fell on Wednesday. There'd be no candles, no cake. Just a round number when I logged into the team's database. There'd be a couple of dozen more before the junior playoffs were over, and then I'd cross over and look at some minor pro teams. I had targeted 250 games but was probably going to fall short. But when I saw 200 pop up on the screen, it hit home how purely passive my life had become. I was a watcher. I attended. All my life I had been engaged, involved, in action. I never gave a thought to those in the seats when I was playing. I never gave a thought to what it was to be one of them.

Before going out on the drive, I scanned my bookmarks and the league website, just to see if there was any news, injuries, or suspensions I should be up on. I saw an item from Peterborough.

> *Peterborough has renounced the rights to Valery Markov for nonattendance at practice and breaking curfew at his billets. Markov left the team last month, and neither the player nor his*

representation has been in contact with Peterborough's interim
manager, Harry Bush. It is presumed that Markov will return
to Russia immediately and rejoin his club team, Dynamo, next
season. Markov's agent did not return calls yesterday.

The suspension was the barn door and Markov was the horse
gone. They thought he was returning to Russia immediately?
No, they thought he was already back there and just hadn't let
him in on the fact. It seemed like Red Hanratty's last practice
with the team was Markov's too. Not that it mattered much
to Peterborough. The team was going to fall three-and-out to
Ottawa. It might have mattered to Markov, a blow to his draft
stock, which wasn't very high to start with.

St. Catharines was an inglorious waste of time. Number 200
bore no significance whatsoever. The players of interest did
nothing of interest for sixty uninteresting minutes. Good games,
good players, I'd work almost for free. I earned my money that
night staying awake in the stands.

25

I set out for Peterborough at seven Friday morning. A two-hour drive with a stop for coffee. I figured I could get there well ahead of my lunch meeting with Mays and grab breakfast at the Tim Hortons beside the arena. I'd try to catch up on the Late-Breaking Dope, maybe come away with a line or two on my report on Mays.

The boys from the arena were sitting at the table where I had left them a few weeks before.

"How you guys doin'?"

"Good. We had a short day yesterday," the Zamboni driver said.

"Howz that?"

"The cops brought us in for questioning."

"No way."

"Way. But I don't think they had us as suspects or anything."

Which is to say that the police didn't give them undeserved credit for ambition or anything.

The security guard piped up.

"Really, they just wanted to see if we saw anything unusual, anybody who shouldn't have been there, and they wanted us to name guys who showed up on the security videos by the team-only exits."

"And by the offices and the dressing room," the maintenance man said. He was trying to jump in on the intrigue.

"What did you see?"

"Nothin'," the Zamboni driver said.

I thought he'd make a compelling witness for sure.

"Nothin'?" I tried to capture his inflection IQ point for IQ point and stopped at eighty-eight.

"Well, we saw all the usual guys who work there, but they were gone long before Red and Doc packed up. And the old-timers all went out as a group. They had a bus back to their hotel."

"There was nothing going on in the parking lot either," the security guard said. "For a game like this I have to keep an eye on the VIP parking lot, make sure no one sneaks in there to try and steal a hubcap or get an autograph or something."

"We sat there for hours watching those goddamn tapes. We hadda ID everybody who went in and out of the offices, the dressing rooms, and whatever," the Zamboni driver's assistant said. "It was just about the worst night for it 'cause you had the mayor and all the rest in there."

"'Course the detectives know a lot of 'em already. I mean, they're well-known and all," the guy on the security detail said. "I couldn't figure out who all the old-timers were. Y'know, they don't look like their hockey cards at all anymore ..."

This came as no news to me, but they were blissfully unaware.

"... Others, you know, I don't know all their names or anything, but I know who they are, like the Italian guy from Toronto and the thugs who are his wingers."

"So what came out of it?"

"Only a few went out to the VIP lot before or right around when Red and Doc were out. But most went out two or three or four at a time and, y'know, they had alibis or whatever."

"Red was smashed," said the Zamboni driver. "Doc had to be driving him home. He went out to start the car up. It didn't even look like Red was gonna be able to make it to his car on his own."

I took a professional curiosity in the investigation. But more immediately, I just wanted to get an idea of the wringer I'd be rolled through that afternoon. The account they gave me made it sound like I could be sitting in front of the video screen for hours.

I EXCUSED myself from Peterborough's version of the Algonquin Round Table and speed-dialed Ollie Buckhold.

"Brad, my friend, great to hear from you," Buckhold said. "I've put in a call to the young man and left a message about your request. I'm sure that everything is going to be all right. Would noon be good?"

"Noon's good."

I had no reason to suspect it wouldn't be.

I RE-ENTERED the conversation between the arena workers in mid-sentence and motioned to the waitress to refill my cup with that coffee-like fluid that she used to deter all but the iron-stomached customers from overstaying their welcomes.

"... so like I say, there wasn't anyone who we couldn't out and out say shouldn't of been hanging around the exit. No one who shouldn't of been in and out of the dressing rooms or coach's office. And, like, the team is awfully, awfully tight with those VIP passes for parking ..."

"... team makes so much of their money from the parking lot ..."

Including five bucks of mine that night.

"... Yeah, they issue parking passes on a night-to-night basis for everybody 'cept Red and Doc. Even Spike the trainer never gets one. We get a list each night and the detectives took it from that night."

The security guard shook his head and took a deep, nervous breath. He seemed shaky.

"The detectives kept asking me if anybody could of got by me. I told them there was no way. I didn't leave my booth all night. I hit the pisser before I opened the gate and never left until I made my rounds and Red's and Doc's bodies were found.

"I figure it had to be someone in that lot, someone who had a pass. Nobody went into that lot from the arena."

Out of the mouths of the unqualified came a conclusion that concurred with the detectives'.

I looked out at the arena from the window. The way the parking lot was set up, the area around the door into the arena was in a blind spot from the booth at the gate where the security guard checked passes. So Hanratty's parking spot would have been hidden from view. He'd arranged it that way to avoid out-of-town fans egging his old Cadillac.

I believed the security guard, even if the detectives were looking for holes. He didn't have many options in life, I figured. Employment opportunities in Peterborough would have been limited for a guy like him. He would have lost possibly the only job he was qualified for if Red Hanratty had been ambushed in the parking lot for nothing more than an autograph. No matter how much he professed to be a man of the people, the Ol' Redhead was a one-strike-and-you're-out guy. Yeah, nobody got by the security guard.

NOON. STILL NO CALL or email from Ollie Buckhold. I wasn't going to wait any longer. I speed-dialed him.

"Brad, my friend, I'm glad you called. I've tried Billy and the young man must have turned off his phone while he's in class. You know he's an outstanding student and plans to do his degrees by correspondence while he's playing in the league ..."

If I let him go on with the testimonial I'd be late for my appointment with Detectives Madison and Freel.

"Ollie, I'm going to be tied up from two to four. Leave a message for me and ask your client if I can meet him off-site or at his billets or something."

My patience was fast running out. Buckhold had to sense it.

I had Mays the Elder's card. I called through to his voicemail. I emailed him. I asked him to give me a shout. Maybe Superboy was back at home unbeknownst to the agent. If he was still in Peterborough, maybe the father would have better luck getting the son to pick up than the agent had.

I drove over to police headquarters and checked in at the front desk.

"COFFEE, BRAD?" Detective Madison asked.

"No thanks. I've been sitting all morning in Tim's. My date stood me up and I held out hope."

Madison, who'd soon be familiar enough to answer to Maddy, and Freel, who preferred Detective Freel and Sir, sat across from me.

"Brad, we could use your help with the IDs on the old-timers going out to the parking lot, but first we have a few questions. When did you leave the arena?"

That was the first of about twenty consecutive questions without comment on my answers. Who saw you? Where did you go? Then what? And then what? All in Joe Friday's monotone. If I wasn't a suspect, they made it seem I was going in. As they'd tell me later, they decided that for the sake of fairness they'd treat me like everybody else, a cold-blooded killer until my alibi convinced them otherwise. Which it did pretty quickly. Yeah, I went out into the lot before the Ol' Redhead and Bones, which could have given me access, but I hadn't stuck around a minute, didn't even warm up the Rusty Beemer. Nobody saw me leave, but I arrived at the Merry Widow just twenty minutes after the time of deaths. I was certifiably out of the area code when Hanratty and Doc departed this mortal coil.

We spent ninety minutes going over the IDs of the guys lugging their hockey bags and sticks, of others coming and going in the security camera videos. Arena workers had identi-fied most but not all. I tried to fill in the blanks as much as I could. We started with the view outside the coach's office before the game.

"Him?" Maddy said. A lanky guy going into the coach's office before the game and leaving quickly.

"The ref," I said. "Johns. Don't know his first name."

"Him?" A pudgy guy waiting outside the coach's office only to be blown off when the Ol' Redhead made a beeline for a television camera.

"Harley Hackenbush. Disgruntled *Times* employee. If purple prose were a crime, he'd be your man."

Maddy fast-forwarded the video. A blur of a guy going into Hanratty's office, a freeze-frame of him exiting. He was carrying a file folder. He had on the handiwork of an Italian designer.

"Him?"

"William Mays Sr., a not-quite-self-made millionaire whose son will make his first million single-handedly before he buys his first razor."

"Him?" A guy walked through the frame, though not out the exit.

"Double J. Jackie Jameson. Long-time scout based here, known mutt."

Freel tapped his fingers on the tabletop impatiently. It seemed he didn't much care for my running commentary, so I stuck with the straight, unadorned answers thereafter. There were some I didn't know but I was sure that the detectives would be able to fill in the holes. Between those I knew and those I just saw, not a one seemed reasonably inclined to want to rid the world of the winningest coach in the history of junior hockey.

Then we went to the after-game, the camera looking out at the exit to the secure parking lot.

"Him, him, and him?" Freeze-frame. Several hundred dollars' worth of sleeve were draped over the shoulders of a tall blond kid and a shorter, thick-bodied kid who didn't own a comb.

"That's William Mays again, in the middle, Junior on his right, and Markov on his left." The video rolled forward. The old guy let loose the headlocks. He shook Markov's hand and wrapped his left hand around the Russian's wrist as if he were trying to hold him in place.

Markov turned and headed out the door to the parking lot. The Mayses walked toward the main entrance, where fans would have been milling around.

"Okay, that's you," Maddy said.

Obvious to all of us and faintly striking up a memory that I had suppressed. William Mays did the same double-up on the handshake and then, well, a hug. I was uncomfortable but not surprised. I remembered reading an interview with him in an investment magazine. He was touting a new business-management book with the theme of "instant intimacy." He claimed that "first impressions are lost opportunities" for you and me, but not for him. He claimed that "knocking down the walls between us" was the key to his success. He also claimed that "delegating was the anti-empathy" and that the smart executive should get to know the lives of "those whom others would call 'the little people.'"

William Mays was challenged on one news show about this idea, but he backed it up. A dogged newsman walked Mays through his office and down to the street and he aced the ambush test, to the blow-dried baritone's unmistakable disappointment. Mays knew the names as well as the life histories of not only his buxom secretaries, which is to be expected, but also the beaten-down woman who came around to clean his office, the minimum-wage security guards on the ground floor of the business tower, the nose-pierced baristas pouring his coffee at the nearest Starbucks, and the old, internet-obsolete guy flogging newspapers on the sidewalk. And they seemed to like him. To love him, really. I wasn't feeling it. His hands patted my back and mine his. We were like two seals wrestling and I was trying to tap out a submission.

"Awkward," I said.

"Yeah," Freel said. He smirked.

I watched myself head out the door and William Mays turn back inside and walk out of the frame. "He said he had to go to the can before he started the drive back."

Involuntary memory is sometimes almost too vivid.

"Too much information," Freel said. The video advanced. A couple of minutes later Mays did exit the lot. He was followed by a few other old-timers who all vouched for each other. About half an hour later Hanratty and Doc. Fifteen minutes later, the security guard who found the bodies.

Maddy bade me farewell. Freel nodded. I made my exit.

I HAD TURNED my BlackBerry off while in police headquarters. When I powered it up in the visitors' section of the parking lot

I had no new messages. No voicemail from Buckhold or Mays the Elder. No replies to emails out. Once more into the breach.

"Brad, I'm glad you called," Buckhold said. "I haven't been able to reach the young man, but I promise you when I do, he'll be in touch. He might be involved in an after-school event or perhaps one of the charities he works for in Peterborough. He knows that you're out that way, and I'm sure that he's sorry for any inconvenience he's caused you. I know he respects you as a former player. He told me that he has your hockey card. And I know he really respects Hunts and your organization. He's talked about L.A. as one of the teams he hopes to be drafted by."

I tapped the steering wheel once for each lie in a cascade of them. As the volume of bullshit built up, so did my sense of Buckhold's desperation. The one bit of truth: He was having no luck in getting a hold of Billy Mays Jr. For Buckhold, the worry was not that I was going to be stiffed. No, the worry was that the kid's failure to return calls might be an omen of the agent's worst nightmare: a star client who defects before signing his first contract. If an agent gets a client a contract or two before he defects, at least the agent has come away with his piece of the action. But if Mays or some other teenager bolts before signing his first deal in the league, the agent has done a lot of chasing and hand-holding for nothing. It would be a wasted investment of time and resources, a lot of bad coffee cake scarfed down, a lot of undeserved flattery extended, and, in some cases, dough advanced that, off the books and on the honour system, would likely never be repaid.

Charities, respect for me, the hockey card, the hopes of being drafted by L.A.: All of it was fiction. What was real, though, was Buckhold's desperation. Losing a client like Junior would be embarrassing, but he'd be a laughingstock in the trade if his fresh-faced client showed up on the side of a milk carton.

I tried William Mays Sr. again. By phone, I had no luck, straight through into voicemail. By email, I caught a break, a reply in two minutes.

> *In meetings all day. Can't discuss. Billy is in Peterborough. He hasn't been home for a couple of days. Messaged me that he won't be back until the weekend. Try Ollie to get in touch. He has the details.*

I decided that I'd try to cut out the middlemen. The league keeps a database with information on the top draft-eligible players. League-supervised measurements of height and weight so that we get the straight dope on a player rather than the exaggerated numbers you see in the programs or on game broadcasts. The league gets them to fill out questionnaires. It's cursory stuff really: father's and mother's occupations, their school, any family ties to the game or other pro sports. One section lists contact information. This includes addresses, summer being the family homes and winter being the billeting homes. Phone numbers are given for each.

I strained my eyes to read the details on my BlackBerry's tiny screen. I opened the PDF of Mays's form. Some of the questionnaires can serve as indictments of our school system, rife with spelling mistakes and written in a first-grader's scrawl. Thankfully, Mays's was filled out in clean, uniform penmanship worthy of an architect or cartographer.

The billets' address was listed: 23 Rainy Road, Peterborough. Their names and home phone number were alongside: 705-555-9189, Sarah and James Storms. His cellphone was listed further down the page: 647-555-2729.

I decided to go out to the billets' home. I wasn't about to count on someone picking up with call display. And with an answered door knock, I could tell if I was getting the straight goods. I figured that, unlike Ollie Buckhold or Madison and Freel or, for that matter, the late Red Hanratty or me, the folks at 23 Rainy didn't have to lie for a living.

THE STORMS WERE retirees and had been ensconced for a half century in their comfortable four-bedroom home overlooking the river. Their children and the town were grown. When the last of the younger Storms blew out of Peterborough for better things in a bigger city, Sarah and Jim started taking in players. They'd later tell me that Billy Mays Jr. was their favourite one ever and that Markov was the quietest. That would be relayed to me down the line, on about my fourth visit in my background checks. On my first trip they couldn't offer me much.

"Billy should be back in the city, I think," James said. "We haven't seen him for a couple of days."

"Three," Sarah said.

"Usually he's good about letting us know what his schedule is, but since his injury he's really back and forth a lot, seeing specialists about his shoulder, in to see his agent and other people."

Sarah jumped in. "He had to do a television spot the other day down in one of those studios in Toronto."

"We haven't spoken since then," James said. "We figured he just stayed on at his father's place."

"Yes, he wouldn't have been at his mother's. I believe she's in ... where is that place, Jim?"

"Turks and Caicos," he said.

I gave them a very brief outline of my plight. They were sympathetic and tried to be helpful, but said that they really didn't know much more than they'd already told me.

I tried to small talk them for any faint leads.

"How many billeting players have you had this season?"

"We started with two, the Russian boy and Billy, who was with us last year as well," she said. "It's so quiet now with neither of them around."

"How did you find out about the Markov boy going back to Russia?"

"We had no idea. Billy and the Russian boy came home late after that game at the arena the night Coach Hanratty and the doctor were killed, but we didn't stay up. He and Billy had breakfast but we weren't here. We left them here because we had some morning errands to run. Billy went to school. The Russian boy would usually have been at home at lunchtime, but he wasn't. His things were gone."

James jumped in. "He couldn't tell us anything, dear," he said. "His English was very limited. We got by with just a few words here and there. He spent a lot of time on the computer. Sometimes he got in touch with his agent, a guy in New York, who could do some translation for him. Like when he didn't know the words for ketchup or Aspirin."

They said that they had heard nothing more from him or about him since.

"How did Billy take it?"

"Coach Hanratty's death or the Russian boy leaving?"

The latter, I told him.

"He didn't talk about it."

"Didn't like to talk about it," she said.

"I think Billy was bothered," he said. "He did like him and he wanted him to do well. Billy thought they could go to the finals this year if he stayed healthy and the Russian boy could play up to his ability."

"Probably true," I said. It was a reach, but I didn't want to come off mean-spirited.

"Billy told us that he'd be back," she said.

"You mean Billy said he was coming back from Toronto after the television appearance?"

"No," she replied. "He said that the Russian boy was going to be back."

"From Russia?"

"No, Billy said that he hadn't gone to Russia. People just thought that."

The lunch appointment, whiff. The call to Buckhold, whiff. And then Ma and Pa Storms, a third strike.

As I left the Storms I saw their next-door neighbour staggering up the path to his porch steps. Harley Hackenbush looked out of sorts and unkempt. Three days of razor stubble. Shirt stained by his lunch. Blazer and pants wrinkled. One shoe untied. His property looked even less maintained. Grass knee-high, weeds higher. Litter blown into a bereft flower bed. He didn't look like a man something bad happened to. He looked like one who'd never been cut an even break and was now in an undignified and indignant death spiral. I saw Ma Storms looking out the living-room window at Hackenbush. The guy who was lowering the block's property values didn't anger her. She pitied him.

I STILL HAD Wonder Boy's cellphone number. A last resort. I decided to make the call from a payphone and put it on my credit card long distance. Mays's number was a Toronto exchange. The number connected and the phone picked up after one ring.

The words were unintelligible. They weren't even English. They were angry, though. Clearly not Billy Mays Jr. Clearly the voice of someone older. The guy who picked up the phone sounded like he had a shovelful of iron filings down his throat. He sounded like he was spitting out each word through a filter of gold teeth.

To my ear, it was a Russian guy. My ear was semi-educated on that count. I had played a few weeks of my last season of pro hockey for Omsk, a cultural exchange that saw me stiffed for a paycheque. I didn't much appreciate the billionaire oil-baron owner's attempt to restore my amateur status against my wishes, but I was thankful just to find another gig in Helsinki a few days later.

My first guess was that it was Markov on the line, but I shelved that idea. I'd only heard the kid mumble a few words, but he had a boy's voice. The rasp on the other end belonged to a guy who smoked two packs of unfiltered darts a day and gargled with broken glass.

A Russian had Billy Mays Jr.'s cellphone. A Russian guy who sounded like trouble. There seemed to be a pretty good shot that the Russian guy had Billy Mays Jr. or, to tamp down the drama, at least knew where he was. I had no reason to believe the kid was in Peterborough. I wondered if he might be in Russia. I turned out to be right on the first count and close on the second.

I HAD my gym stuff with me. I had planned to lift at 5 P.M. after the drive back to Toronto. It was already 6:30 and I was still in Peterborough, chasing my tail. I'm not as righteous as some guys in the trade about working out. Away from the arena, a few spend every waking hour lifting, running, riding the bike, or whatever. They're probably in better shape in their forties than they were in their early twenties. Others spend their spare time catching up on the vices they had to forgo in order to pull down million-dollar salaries. You wonder if they're going to live to see their pensions kick in. I'm in the middle ground, a little on the side of the health conscious without being fanatical about it. Good genes, too. Sarge never wore more than a thirty-four-inch waist, stretched across six feet two.

I ducked into the gym in Peterborough. In the weight room I found Beef at the squat rack. The Olympic bar was at rest on the rack. He had just finished a set with four plates. His chalky hands were still gripping the bar and his legs were wobbly under it. He looked like Jesus on the crucifix, albeit Jesus with a fifty on the body mass index. His green eyes looked like two basil leaves in a big bowl of tomato soup. I thought he was going to faint dead away, but eventually he staggered up, panting.

"That was pretty good," I told him. When in doubt, flatter.

Recognition wasn't immediate. The fog lifted when his heartbeat lowered into a less life-threatening range.

"You're the accountant."

"I'm not really an accountant," I said.

"I know," he said. "My father was an accountant. When my parents divorced, my mother said that she'd never marry another one."

I let that slide. I saw no sense in making jest of a kid's real-life pain, though I was sorely tested.

"I know you're a hockey scout," he said. "That you used to be a player. That all came out after we cleaned up that mess at O'Murphy's. I got that you used to be married to that actress when I Googled your name."

"Okay, you got me. I'm sorry about telling you that. And about the fight."

"That's nothing, mister. That's what I get paid for."

"We all get paid for something."

"That's the truth. You get paid a ton of money to go watch hockey games, and I get paid minimum wage to bus tables and break up fights between drunks."

I suspected that he didn't resent me so much as his lot in life.

"I was just trying to do a workup on the Mays kid. Understand that my team might be risking millions on him. I've gotta do whatever it takes."

"No problem, mister."

"Have you seen him lately? I was supposed to meet with him today but he stood me up."

"Yeah, I know that feeling. He hasn't been at school for a few days now. I think some of the guys on the team were covering for him, saying that he was in Toronto doing stuff. But I don't know. It seemed like he didn't get assignments in and that's normally stuff that he'd always get done on time, even if he was on the road or something."

Confirmed. MIA. AWOL. Circumstances Out of the Ordinary.

"You heard anything at all? Anything around the team or whatever?"

"Mister, I work for a dollar above minimum wage and a split of tips from my waiters. You woulda had the crap beaten out of you and got arrested, and I helped you out. At the end of my night, my share of the tips was eight bucks."

Beef was all baby fat but no child. I hinted at some sort of compensation off the books. His father wouldn't have to declare it when he did Beef's return.

"Supposedly the Russian guy on the team is, uh, *big*."

"Big?"

"You know, mister, real *big*," Beef said, glancing down at his own loins sheepishly. "*Big*. Bunch of the girls at school. It's all over the league. The guys on the team make jokes about it. Not Mays, not really anyway. But they all say that if the Russian guy doesn't turn pro he can make it in porn movies. And they said he already passed his audition."

Beef left me hanging.

"And?"

"And anyway, they said that someone had a video of him."

"When did all this go down?"

"Right around the time the coach was killed."

"Right before or right after?"

"Well, I figure the video had to be before and, yeah, maybe it was right before that they were talking about it 'cause they took all the guys on the team out of class for a few days after the coach was killed. So yeah, I'd say before."

I went to the locker room and took two double sawbucks out of my wallet. I went back onto the gym floor and gave them to Beef, who thanked me but didn't shake my hand. He stuffed the bills in his sock and threw plates on a bar to do his dead lifts.

TWO HOURS LATER my cellphone rang. Unknown caller.

"Hello."

"Brad?"

"Yeah."

"It's Paul Madison, the fellah you were speaking to down at police headquarters in Peterborough."

"My memory is better than you think."

"I have a personal favour to ask you. Completely unrelated to our ongoing investigation. I don't normally like to tap my day job for this sort of stuff, but I wanted to ask you ... Well, I coach a bantam triple-A team and we're putting on a fundraiser for travel tournaments for next season. I was wondering if I could convince you to come out and talk to the kids and parents."

"No sweat. I'd be glad to."

With all the retired players in Peterborough I wondered why Madison would need to import names for an event like this, but then I realized that no one was going to buy a ticket to meet their kids' friends' fathers. I just put it down to the price

I'd have to pay for my workup on Mays. If I had an in with the Peterborough force, I'd get straight dope about the whole Peterborough team.

I gave him my email and told him to message me the details. He said he'd do it from his personal account. I told him that was a good idea. Otherwise it might go to spam.

26

I thought my glutes were calcifying on the drive back to Toronto. I arrived at the Merry Widow at a not-so-late hour. Nick, as ever, was on the bar. The Irregulars lined it. Games played out on the screens. Nick knew the betting lines, the scores, and the times left in each. He knew the starting goaltenders and those who'd been pulled and replaced. The Irregulars gazed foggily at the game directly in front of them, and some didn't even recognize the teams' sweaters. Nick didn't have a deep bench. The third-liners among the Irregulars were fractured souls, some displaced, and the fourth-liners irreparably broken.

Polo was the Irregular sitting closest to the door. Nick and the Irregulars called him Polo because they'd given up trying to pronounce his surname. Polo was reading a back issue of *Lidové Noviny* that his sister had sent him from Prague. Polo's an owlish, unassuming old-timer who went to the Merry Widow to immerse himself in hockey, the game he loved, and to forget the women who passed through his life, though with less frequency lately. Left to his own, he wouldn't say much more than the name of the beer he was drinking and "I'll have my tab." And mostly he was left to his own. The Irregulars did not know and did not care what his story was. He'd shared his story with me a couple of years back on a night when there was only a late game. He stuck it out to watch it because it featured one of his countrymen.

Back in the '70s Polo had been a guest in Pankrác, a barred hospice for those who couldn't get their politics right. He would have made hard time there look like a membership at the spa. Polo was a hard guy who didn't look like one to those who didn't know him. He didn't like being called a dissident because he thought the term in the West had been watered down like Nick's Red Label scotch. "I was strident but thought no different than everybody else," he said. "They call those who didn't go to prison dissidents too. So I am not a dissident. I must be something else."

I didn't question his logic. I'm sure he arrived at his findings honestly with six years of gruel and meditation.

I wouldn't say that you meet the most interesting people in the Merry Widow. Actually, most you meet are pitiful and predictable. Polo was more interesting than most, but his genius was being wasted at the bar, the genius being a gift for language. He spoke Czech, German, and Russian flawlessly. He spoke English and French well, if heavily accented. He could carry on a decent conversation with Nick in Greek and worked on his Italian when he played poker down the street in a men's club of Juventus supporters.

I didn't go to the Merry Widow to prevail upon Polo. Actually, I hadn't given it any thought at all. But when I saw him there, catching up on events in a country that he'd forsaken long ago, it struck me.

"Can you do me a favour, Polo? Nick, get Polo a beer."

Nick went to the Czechvar stashed on the bottom row of the fridge, Polo's private stock.

"What it is, brudder?"

Actually, Polo's English was better than it looks on the page. He dumbed it down for me and the other members of the Legion of Stupor Heroes.

"I have this number," I told him. "I think it's a Russian guy who answers it. I want to know who it is and where he is and how to find him."

I spilled out the details in point form. A Russian kid gone missing. A Canadian kid gone to look for him. Some black bear answering the Canadian kid's phone.

"Maybe they shouldn't hear the sound of the bar. I'll go in the street. Give me a minute."

Polo exited the bar. I saw him dial his cellphone. His caller ID was hidden, maybe because it would just fill up the screen. He pressed the phone to his ear. He was talking animatedly, his free hand doing something like International Sign Language, something he must have picked up at the poker game.

Ten minutes later he walked back in the front door.

"They are in Little Moscow at Steeles and Yonge. We can go."

I never did find out what he said and how he extracted the dope. I didn't want to know. I trusted it just as he presented it.

POLO AND I PILED into a taxi. Seventy dollars later we got out of the cab. We were at a shabby strip mall at the city limits, the 300 block of Steeles Avenue West, right up the city's main artery, Yonge Street. I felt like I was deplaning at the Moscow airport. The architecture didn't say Russia, but every grill and every overheard conversation sure as hell did. I was made as a foreigner, naturally. Three generations ago Shade was Shaad,

German, but the pedigree was now mixed, and even a pureblood Deutschlander would stand out in a throng of Russians.

Polo, however, managed to pass. Especially as soon as he opened his mouth. He'd later tell me that he even came equipped with a backstory. He had, in fact, lived in Moscow briefly. That seemed to be an unlikely situation for someone holding a belt one degree higher than dissident, sort of like the Grand Wizard taking out a sublet in Harlem. But Polo had picked up the languages as he went from place to place. Whenever I asked him about what he did for work along the way, he changed the subject.

I let Polo do the talking when we went to the Kontinental, a restaurant that catered to Russian émigrés, just like every other perogy joint and grocery store in the mall. A tableful of thugs by the door were in an animated conversation when we walked in, but they went dead silent and burned holes in the back of our heads with their heat vision as we made our way to the counter.

We sat on barstools with our backs to them and without a backwards glance. Polo spoke to the counterman, I presumed to order us coffee. The counterman brought me a double of premium vodka and Polo a large glass of kefir. Polo's reading of the situation was a good one. In this situation he needed to be sober and I needed to be half drunk.

I made out that Polo asked for a guy named Sergei. No surname. Who this Sergei was and what we were doing at the Kontinental I had no idea. Polo hadn't spelled out in advance any details about our meeting. Three minutes into our car ride he had fallen asleep, his head resting against the window.

The counterman pointed us to a door in the darkened back half of the restaurant. I had a notion that the Kontinental's viability rested not on the profits from the single table at the front door, but rather on whatever went on in the back. Polo led the way. He showed no outward signs of nerves, but later he told me that he was a reasonable man and was as scared shitless as I was.

IT WAS LIKE trying to make out figures in a steam room, but instead of vapour the room was clouded with smoke from unfiltered Russian cigarettes. Two huge wooden crates of the smokes were sitting on a skid. They had been stolen out of a cargo hold and were almost certainly stolen once or twice before that. I gave the five found-ins high points for criminality but none for originality.

A poker game was running. After a brief interview and a few words between Polo and the dealer, the only Russian who was talking, my finder sat down at the table and pulled out a wad of cash that had never been in view at the Merry Widow. It was enough for a down payment on a condo and made me wonder why Polo resided in a basement apartment around the corner from our local.

Intermittent conversation ensued, Polo and the dealer being the only participants. "Intermittent" is inadequate, really. It was a couple of mumbled words from the dealer and a couple back from Polo and then a full hand played silently, cash tossed, and hands folded across a green felt table that, like the smokes, had been purloined. Half an hour into the session, Polo spoke up, seizing the initiative finally. About halfway through what passed for a soliloquy, Polo pointed at me and said "Los Angeles" in unaccented English.

"Player?" the dealer asked me.

I shook my head in the negative. At that point I was rattled enough to forget what I once was.

Polo explained that I was working for L.A. and that he was my friend and that we were looking for a Peterborough kid or kids. Markov and Mays.

Nothing more was said through the hand. Or the next. Or the one after that. For an hour.

I was going to start breathing through the sleeve of my shirt. My palate felt like a rat had crawled in my mouth, farted, and died. Polo was unbothered. He was sitting behind stacks and spires of chips that faintly resembled the Kremlin against the Moscow skyline. He went all in. A bear-faced guy who hadn't said a word called the bet. Polo had a flush on the turn. Ungentle Ben had two pair. Polo didn't reach for the pot. I was surprisingly all right with his hesitance. He said a couple of words and the dealer took out his wallet, extracted a Russian wholesaler's business card, and on the back wrote down an address. Polo pulled his cash out of the pot but left the loser's share on the table in case it was needed for bail or bribe.

I didn't ask Polo what happened, not when we walked through the now-darkened Kontinental, out the unlocked front door, and into the parking lot.

"We can walk," he said. I felt like running. Home.

It was a Russian rave, which is to say that the vice of choice was vodka, not Ecstasy, and every leggy blonde looked like a Sharapova sister. Polo and I were a generation and a half older than anyone in attendance, save a bald bouncer who'd likely brought home the Olympic gold in Greco-Roman's super-heavyweight division and shaken Leonid Brezhnev's hand. I felt like turning around and walking out whence we came. Polo walked up to the no-neck and tried to shout over the booming Eminem. The wrestler pointed across the room. There, standing against the wall on the far side of the room was Markov amid a cluster of girls talking animatedly. Slightly to his side, hands in pockets, head down, Billy Mays Jr. He was oblivious to our presence and to a willowy former figure skater undressing him with her Baltic blue eyes.

I could take it from here. Polo walked in my wake.

I opted for the nice-weather-isn't-it approach to conversation.

"Does your father have any idea what your phone bill is going to be?" I shouted at the top of my voice over "Love the Way You Lie."

Mays looked up slowly. It was late. He was tired, not sharp. So at first he showed puzzlement upon hearing someone speaking English. Then shock that someone was speaking to him in a room full of strangers. Then fear, that I shouldn't be there, knowing what I know. Too puzzled, then too shocked, and then too afraid to form a thought.

I coloured inside the lines for him. "I tried calling you," I said. "I think some Russian lifted your phone." My throat was already starting to hurt.

"I left it in the car charging," he shouted back, "yesterday."

"Not anymore. Some Russian broke in there and took it. That's who answered when I called. Smash and grab."

I didn't bother noting that his father was going to have no trouble covering a bill with hour-long charges to Moscow long distance. It wasn't the prospect of getting reamed out that had him out of rhythm. He wanted to go underground, but he was coming to the stark realization that he'd never be able to go unnoticed so long as he was pulling down a seven- or eight-figure cheque from the league.

"Nice little cultural exchange program you have going here," I said.

"It's not what you think."

"I'm not sure anymore what I think."

"I came to get him."

"I want to believe you," I said. I looked over at the blonde who was now smiling at him. "You probably could be having more fun. Here, I mean."

"Markov's in trouble. He knows it."

"I dunno if they can fix it with the team. I think they'd probably have him back. They sure as hell could use him next season."

"It's not the team. He didn't go because he was afraid that he was going to get arrested for killing the coach. He's been hiding out here with his girlfriend."

That seemed a hell of a leap, but then again I'm not seventeen, Russian, and under the thumb of tyrants on two continents.

"This is his girlfriend?"

"Well, I guess she's *a* girlfriend. She took a camera-phone video of him and he came to get her to take it down off the internet so that his girlfriend back in Russia doesn't find it."

I just let the video stuff drop. Too much information. The videographer in the club was a stunner, so I could imagine what the girl back home looked like.

"He didn't come home with me the night Coach and Doc McGarry were killed."

"So you don't know where he was. And he walked out into the parking lot ..."

"Just to pull my car around front of the arena. He told me before the game that he had to go to Toronto. He wanted me to drive him but I told him I had a test first thing in the morning. My father gave me my weekly spending money at the game and I gave it to Valery. A couple hundred bucks, maybe more. I told him I'd cover for him for a day but to get back."

"He wouldn't have wanted to take Hanratty's Caddy, would he? He would have walked right by it."

"I don't think Valery would steal a car, and nobody would take that old car. Everyone would know whose it was."

Good point. It would be like stealing the clown car at the circus. All you need to make a getaway, everyone seeing the car and beeping horns and waving.

Young Mays kept on filling in the blanks.

"I told him the next day that Coach and Dr. McGarry had been killed and how it happened. He freaked out. He said they were going to arrest him. I tried to convince him to come back and just answer questions. He wouldn't do it. He's been hiding out with this girl ever since."

The video. I had to ask.

"Why was he so worried about a girl in Russia seeing him in action on the computer screen?"

"She's coming over. In a couple of weeks. Markov went to these guys ..."

I thought about all "these guys" I had seen in the last couple of hours. I tried to figure out which one had shipped Markov's girlfriend to Canada in a cargo container along with six crates of smokes, a couple of skids of Stoli, and enough AK-47s to outfit a working crew.

"... and they managed to get her a flight and a visa."

"What about her?" I pointed to the girl on Markov's arm.

"She's a student."

Sure, kid. She probably cracks her textbooks between sets in the change room at a strip joint.

"It's not that. She's older than Markov."

I did the five-second visual inspection. She was.

"She was a nurse back in Kazakhstan. She's trying to get certified here. She's doing English classes and working part time. Markov's agent set it up."

Plausible. If Markov's agent had enough clout to get him out of Russia, he had to know enough palms in need of grease to get this girl her letters of transit.

"So what the hell are you thinking?"

"I was going to get him to come back."

"No, I mean what the hell are you thinking? You're standing

here like you're at a funeral and that blonde over there wants to have you over for breakfast. Buddy, if you're going to break curfew you at least have to get laid."

"No, she's just a friend of Markov's girlfriend."

That wouldn't be *the* girlfriend but rather *a* girlfriend.

"So are all those girls," he said. "They all went to school with her and worked with her. Markov told them we're on the same team."

The kid was a Boy Scout. An abundance of talent around him and he lacked the imagination to leave with anything more than a postcard and T-shirt. I envied and pitied him.

There was no use to trying to jump-start the kid. I turned to the girl and kept it businesslike so I didn't look like a dirty old man. I kept the language as basic as possible so it wouldn't get read the wrong way.

"He likes you," I told her, nodding my head in Mays's direction.

"He's a nice boy," she said. "I met him at work."

She nursed a screwdriver as a prop and kept glancing in his direction, never catching his eye. He sighed. It just died there and she didn't get it. This kid who could have dined out on his celebrity was content to be a wallflower.

Polo and I left. I had to pull Polo by the arm. He walked west and leered east.

"If they're looking at you, they want you to pay or roll you or both."

"It would be worth it," he said.

POLO AGAIN fell asleep in the cab ride back to the Merry Widow. His head again was pressed against the window. He was smiling.

I thought about Billy Mays Jr. Maybe rich kids and top prospects have to be more suspicious about girls who can sniff out money the way that French pigs can sniff out truffles. I probably was a little too xenophobic in my thinking. Puck bunnies are puck bunnies no matter what country issued their passports. If these girls had gone to school and were legit and working and studying, then who was I to judge them so hard? And Markov's girl and the one eyeballing Mays were stunning.

I was going soft.

27

The next morning I got out of bed with a head that softly drummed a beat left over from the Russian club. I drank stale coffee out of a stained cup. I called Ollie Buckhold.

"It's not my business, but I'd see about getting your client's cellphone account shut down," I said.

"What's that supposed to mean?"

"My guess is that there are several thousand dollars' worth of long-distance calls to the Russian underworld on Billy Mays's account."

Puzzled silence. No sense keeping him dangling.

"I saw your client last night in a Russian club with the Markov kid. I just wanted to let you know that he's okay and that maybe you shouldn't call him unless you want to aggravate some sort of Alexei Capone type. Somehow your client's phone ended up in a Russian thug's pocket."

"Where's Billy Jr.?"

"Right now, I don't know. I don't know if he slept in his own bed last night, but I suppose he slept alone."

"What's your problem, asshole? What's all this cryptic shit you're hitting me with?"

"You might do a better job of protecting your client's interest if you kept tabs on him. Like knowing where he is."

I was about to hit Buckhold with a line about Hanratty being right about him. But inevitably our team was going to have to do business with the agent and there was no sense piling up hard feelings. It was one of those rare times when reason and discretion got the better of me.

"He's all right? I got a call from the father asking if I'd talked to him. Billy had an appointment that he missed."

"Yeah, he's all right. He's been trying to talk the Markov kid into going back to Peterborough. Markov thinks the cops like him for the Hanratty murder."

"You're kidding."

"You've forgotten what it's like to be seventeen, the son of a small-town factory worker, and eight time zones from home where you don't speak the language. A lot of North American kids have a problem with authority figures—they don't respect them. Markov's like a lot of the Russian kids—they're scared shitless of them. A cop wants to question Markov and he thinks he's in the express line to the gulag."

"Why are you calling me?"

"It's a courtesy call. I want to talk to your client and to his father and to you and anybody else I think I need to do my workup. Quid pro quo. I'll help you protect your client, and you help me protect my job."

We came to an understanding: I was going to get my meeting as soon as the kid was back in the pocket. I spat grounds into the sink.

DETECTIVE MADISON sent me a message from his personal email account. He laid out the details of the fundraiser: a dinner at an Italian family restaurant. May Day. Vito's. I tried to figure out which of my two suits wouldn't clash with red velvet curtains.

I MADE MY CALLS to the guys on our scouting staff just to find out the latest rumours: Who was on thin ice besides us? If Hunts and I and others were going to get whizzed with the arrival of Tomlin and Anderson, I'd need a plan for a job search and another team with staff turnover would present an opportunity. None of the guys said that they'd heard anything out there. Then again, they might have but were just looking to cut me out.

I trusted Duke Avildsen for the clearest read of the situation, mine and ours. "Shadow, jobs on the line is things as they always have been, things as they always will be," Duke said, like he was channelling a cross-legged guru on a mountaintop and David Byrne.

"Yeah, the old it goeth and it cometh, but I was holding out hope for stayeth," I said.

"It's like our whole business," he said, ignoring me. "All thinking ends up as over-thinking. Do what you have to, trust your instincts, and, if necessary, have a short memory."

Yeah, on those terms life is a lot like the game. All thinking is just over-thinking half-defined.

I told Duke to give me a call any time for his words of wisdom. He could have provided the required daily minimum of spiritual reinforcement. I felt minutely better when I hung up the phone.

Seconds later a ring.

"Mr. Shade, this is Billy Mays Jr."

"You're up early, son, or did that blonde keep you awake?"

"No, nothing like that. I think I convinced Markov to go back to Peterborough with me."

"Your Russian must be really good if you could get that message across."

"The girls helped me. He finally agreed when I told him that my father would get him the best lawyer if he needed it. Not that he will or anything."

Yeah, I could see that. The kid's fear of authority was trumped by the new Russian system of belief: that there's nothing money can't buy your way into or out of.

"So when are we going to meet?"

"Well, I'm driving up to Peterborough this afternoon."

I had to do a little relationship maintenance that day and night. Sandy was feeling ignored and with cause. I wanted to avoid three-plus hours in transit, and the Rusty Beemer was in need of a much-delayed oil change.

"Why don't we sit down and have lunch and I'll ask you a few questions. You don't want to sit at a table with Markov and his girl anyway."

"Okay, let's meet at the Hermitage on Steeles just west of Yonge. I can be there at eleven. Markov's girl works around the corner. There's a Russian restaurant they like right there."

I imagined another backroom poker game with the young lovers staring into each other's eyes. Or maybe she dealt cards there. No matter. Our meeting was set. We'd talk about a million-dollar investment and his future over blini.

BILLY MAYS WAS ten minutes early. I was fifteen. He might have been at the appointed coffee shop earlier and left when he didn't see me. A double check mark beside punctuality. He was freshly pressed and had spent some time getting his blond hair neatly messy, the latest in bed-head fashion. A check mark for not wearing a baseball cap turned backwards and flip-flops. Another: bottle of water rather than coffee or some sort of iced drink. Kid knew to stay hydrated.

Markov was in tow. Mays explained to Markov that he was going to lunch at 12:15. He told Markov to sit at another table while we talked. The Russian kid sat down with a large cup of black coffee, downed it in one chug, and didn't look up from his BlackBerry for more than an hour. He managed to hoover back two bagels in approximately two bites apiece.

Mays had a clear idea of who he was, what was lying out there for him, and what the stakes were for the team that called his name on the draft floor. He had a clear idea of the time it was going to take to sort out his game and the help he was going to need to get through life in L.A. with millions in his pocket at age eighteen.

"There'd probably be less to worry about out there if I were in Ottawa or Minnesota," he said.

"Anywhere you play in the league you can find trouble if you go looking for it," I said.

He was a smart, impressive kid, but he was still a kid, not naive but just innocent enough. Only in a small way did he seem like one of the programmed-for-success kids, talents constantly pushed forward by meddling parents, prospects that are high risks for burnout.

"You've been through a lot this year."

"It's like my father says, 'What doesn't kill you makes you stronger.'"

Yup, I read that in one of the magazine profiles of William Mays Sr. I didn't have the heart to tell Junior that Nietzsche beat his old man to the punch. The customs officer in Frankfurt could have recited it line and verse in the original German.

"I've played for coaches who've been fired, lots actually, but I never had a coach die on me," I said. I tried to keep the facts cold and hard, to keep the melodrama to a minimum.

"A lot of people have been there for me from the start of the season. My father. My agent. My teammates, Valery especially, in his own way. The fans. The media. People in hockey like you."

Obviously, Ollie Buckhold had sent the kid the bullet points and he had full command of them. I had to get off them. I had to ask him stuff that he hadn't been prepped for. I didn't go to all this trouble to get scripted answers.

"Tell me about you and your coach ..."

He looked puzzled.

"... How it all started. From the start."

Wonder Boy dialed in.

"It's a funny thing, but I had never met Coach Hanratty before I was drafted by Peterborough. I had met a bunch of coaches and general managers from other teams. They wanted to know my plans before the draft, whether I was planning to go to school in the States on scholarship or play major junior. I had tried to keep my options open 'cause at thirteen or fourteen you just can't know whether you'll be a player or not. But I was pretty determined at fifteen that I was going to play junior. My father felt the same way ..."

I got the idea that this was a chicken-and-egg proposition, with the egg claiming he came first and the chicken came around to it later.

"... Flint had the first pick in the draft, but we told their general manager that if I was going to Michigan it would be to play college hockey. I had no interest in playing for a U.S. team in the Ontario league. So Flint wasn't going to draft me. And I let some other teams know that we couldn't guarantee that I'd play for them. I wasn't going to North Bay. We told teams near Toronto that we were likely to sign on, and teams where there are good universities—Ottawa, Kingston, and the rest—that we'd be interested if I could continue my education.

"Because we hadn't talked to Peterborough and Coach Hanratty, we thought they didn't have an interest in me. My father didn't even consider it. When I met with Coach Pembleton in London he told me straight up that he couldn't see Peterborough drafting me. My father agreed. So we were definitely surprised when we got the news that Peterborough had taken me in the draft."

Yeah, ninety-nine times out of one hundred Hanratty would have steered clear of a potential "father" issue and any kid who had a notion of going to college and not reporting. The kid was a mile-a-minute chatterbox. I forgave him for being overtaken by his enthusiasm. Some might have thought that this recap was spiced with conceit, but I didn't. I find false modesty harder to take anyway, and that's usually in this script.

I asked him to back up. Why did Pembleton tell him that he thought Peterborough wasn't going to take him?

"I honestly don't know. I hadn't given it a lot of thought going in, really. But as soon as he said it, my father agreed with him, which sort of surprised me."

The Ol' Redhead had always been a pretty astute judge of talent. He would have had to recognize that Billy Mays Jr. was a player. He couldn't have got that wrong.

I asked Mays to walk and talk. I wanted to make our meet feel less like an interview or quiz show. He was cool with it. He went over to the table where Markov sat and gave his sleeve a tug. Markov didn't look up right away. Probably composing love sonnets to his already pining girlfriend. But at Mays's urging, he came along in tow, walking a few steps behind us, like one of a potentate's wives.

I wanted to get a sense of the arc of Mays's development

and a read on how he'd changed over the couple of years in Peterborough. I asked him about the first conversation he had with Hanratty.

"He told me that he was going to be fair and that everyone started with a blank slate," he said. "I didn't think anything different, really. That's the way it has been everywhere else and how I've always been treated. I didn't want anything special, just a chance to play and make a positive impact."

"What about your father's experience?"

"My father has never talked about his time in Peterborough much. I think it was hard for him, though. I imagine that it's hard to see your career wind down in junior."

I didn't bother to break to the kid that, if it winds down in junior hockey, you really haven't had a career.

"What about your last conversation with your coach?"

"Yeah, I remember it really well. It was strange and I think about it every day. It was almost like he knew something was coming. Maybe that was just because he'd had a couple of beers. But he told me, 'You'll go on to great things, hockey or not.' And he told me, 'You're part of this team even when you're not on the ice. You get this Russian kid goin', will you. You're the only one who can reach him.'"

I looked behind us. Markov was still tailing us, head down, messaging frantically.

"I figured he was always at him. Calling him Ivan the Terrible and stuff like that. But I think he was frustrated. He could see all this talent but couldn't coach him. And Busher always said the coach's biggest problem was when he couldn't coach a kid ... 'When he can't coach 'em, he forgets about 'em or ignores 'em.' But Spike also said Coach had changed over the years and that he was okay with things changing."

THE TAKEAWAY: Hanratty's last words to Captain Fantastic were a succinct scouting report on the kid's character and leadership.

I made notes of it in my workup on Mays in our database. What really stuck with me, though, was his thinking that Hanratty knew something bad was going to happen. Or already had happened. I would have put it down to a kid's imagination in ninety-nine other cases out of a hundred, but not with Mays, not completely anyway. He was a pretty clear-eyed kid. And he thought that Hanratty was saying goodbye to him. I'd be thinking about something like that every day too.

28

After seeing the kid off, I called William Mays Sr.'s number. Straight to voicemail. I hung up. I'd be way down his list of priorities.

I messaged him. *Mr. Mays, is there any way I can come in and talk to you about your son and our team? Let me know what will work for you.* Automatic out-of-office reply that said he would be in meetings the next two days.

I was about to throw in the towel, but within a minute I had a reply. *I'm available any time today. I will be at the Scarborough Hunt Club for a late tee time today. If you'd like to meet for lunch or even get in a round, let me know.*

Lunch I was good for. I let him know. Declining to play eighteen at an exclusive course wasn't going to impress him. The oak panels in the clubhouse and expensive stogies weren't going to impress me either.

MAYBE MY MESSAGE wasn't clear enough. I was coming up to interview him. I was coming up as part of a get-to-know-you. He must have read my message as a sign-up for one of his business seminars. Rather than talking about his son and the game, he spent the entire hour giving me a summary of his *Seven Keys of Turning Maybes into Wills*™. I felt like the first stop on his book tour. When I tried to budge him off this line, he found a way to segue. When I tried to talk about our team, he said that his lesson plan could put us on a championship course. When I tried to talk about his son, he said that Billy Jr. was but one happy by-product of a life dedicated to the *Seven Keys*™. I felt like I had been put in a cage and restraints and forced to watch late-night info-mercials. I expected him to tell me that telephone lines were open and to call in the next thirty minutes.

The creepiest thing, though, was Mays calling the kid "my creation." A lot of parents get a vicarious thrill from their sons' games but this one crossed every line.

29

A friend of a friend of a friend knew the brother of one of the Peterborough players' fathers and reported back to me that the former Mrs. Mays was a well-preserved former finalist for the title of Miss Canada. By this same very reliable fourth-hand report, Mrs. Mays would have had a better chance at the crown if she had been given the opportunity to show her true gift in the talent competition. Other beauties might have been able to warble or play a fiddle, but she had an almost unmatched aptitude for separating rich men from their sometimes hard-earned millions. She had a way of making wealthy but otherwise normal men feel like Mr. Canada.

Mrs. Mays had one practice marriage before meeting Mr. Mays, and she must have taken the view that their union had to be demonstrably consummated because Billy Jr. was the only foal in her storied career. The three subsequent attempts at something approaching holy matrimony only further padded her assets. As much as Billy Jr. ever stood to make playing hockey, it's likely he would have to be a first all-star five times before his net worth caught up to the trust funds of his mother's lawyer's children. And they were only in grade school.

By all accounts, Mrs. Mays was only an occasional presence at Peterborough games. She spent most of the winter in the Caribbean and other time in Saint-Tropez. She had taken no role in her son's development as a hockey player—though she was a shoe salesman's daughter and grew up in a humble bungalow a block away from Ted Reeve Arena on Toronto's east side, she considered hockey rinks intolerably proletarian. When Mays was taking little Billy to the rink, the then Mrs. Mays absented the abode for the racquet club, where the tennis pro served up what her husband couldn't, not that the detectives he eventually hired could prove it.

I guess I could have minded my own business, but if I were so inclined I'd be better in another line of work. The background noise of a messy family life can fog the minds of thirty-year-olds, never mind a kid barely out of high school who is about to be handed millions of bucks. I had to root around this other branch of Billy Jr.'s family tree.

The former Mrs. Mays's current husband, an only partially disgraced scion to a meat-packing empire, had to return to Toronto for a board meeting, an emergency session prompted by an outbreak of listeria. Presumably the production line was spoiled by a batch of swine with herpes or syphilis. I presumed, rightly, that the former Mrs. Mays would put in an appearance at the tennis club just to jangle her jewellery and catch up with the ponytailed Spaniard who gave her lessons. In some other more bawdy sense, she returned the favour.

I knew one member of the Toronto Lawn Tennis Club: M.T. Smith, a former Los Angeles teammate. M.T. was a different cat. He was the only guy in the league who went by initials rather than a Christian name, and he was the only player in L.A. who took up surfing. He ended up with small bits in Hollywood films, the by-product of friendships he struck up at tennis clubs in SoCal. In fact, he even landed a role in a movie of the pro tennis tour. He played a Swedish middle-rank player with a booming serve. M.T. played the guitar and tennis. He always had something going on, bucks in a golf course here, a housing development there, a new line of equipment with his name. He made millions in the league and millions more in real estate back in the city of his birth.

We'd been in a couple of jams off the ice and somehow talked our way out of them. I had managed to get him inside a couple of Hollywood parties with a simple "He's with me" back when "me" counted for something in movie circles. I didn't have to call in a favour to get him to bring me along as a guest to the club. He even went as far as to find out when the former Mrs. Mays had booked a lesson.

"That's her there," M.T. said.

"Jesus," I said. "How does she get two hands on her racquet?"

"Yeah, I know, it looks like she's wearing two deployed airbags. Her first husband was a plastic surgeon and she was his invention. Doris. We all say that's 'Double D Doris.'"

"No wonder the kid turned out to be Superboy. The breast-milk he scarfed down was poured through a silicone filter."

M.T. and I hit a few balls on a neighbouring court. I never picked up a serious interest in the game, even when my ex had a supporting role in a romantic comedy that was set at a tony tennis club. I don't have tennis whites or even a racquet of my own and I had to blow the cobwebs off my Adidas Stan Smiths, but still I could pass for an occasional player. Between points I managed to give her a "good shot" and a smile. She didn't get five husbands plus à la carte items by ignoring flattery. She had a neediness that neither the Miss Canada title nor even Miss Universe could temporarily sate.

She knew my buddy—he had been the realtor of record in several transactions spilling out of her divorce judgments. It wasn't the hugest surprise that she made her way barside in the lounge after her lesson. Introductions were made. Things started to run their inevitable course. She was an equal opportunity flirt. She looked at M.T. and me and undressed us both, like she was wearing X-Ray Specs.

"You were married to that actress, weren't you?" she asked.

"I was. I have a Cup ring too. Nobody asks about the ring."

I spied the rock on her third finger. Bigger than anything I saw in Hollywood.

"I've actually watched your son play a lot of hockey this season. Our team has an interest in him. I've spoken to him several times. He's a solid young man."

"Billy's wonderful. I wish I could see him more than I do, but the game keeps him away so much. And in the summer, he feels he needs to be around an arena with a gaggle of like-minded kids. He told me that he couldn't get a good game in Cape Cod in July."

The former Mrs. Mays had the wherewithal to make a good game happen in Cape Cod in July. She had the wherewithal to make an all-star game happen in the Netherlands Antilles on Christmas Day. She was happy that Billy was doing well at what he loved. She was otherwise happy that he did not encumber her.

M.T. excused himself when his BlackBerry vibrated. "Better get this," he said. "Feels like money." Mrs. Mays air-kissed him and gave him a hug with a long stroke of his back.

She invited me over for a drink. I told her I'd follow her car. She said it was okay to ride with her. Her driver was discreet. She hired him six months before her first implants.

DIVORCIN' DDORIS DIDN'T HAVE a life story, just serial resent-
ments that she acted upon in her boudoir and elsewhere whenever
she could. I originally presumed that DDoris was exploiting rich
old men when she sicced her lawyer on them. Four hours after
we left the tennis club I realized that she was effectively saving
their lives when she pursued cancellation of their legal bond.
I was pumping her for information about her son and she was
plying me with martinis in her *pied-à-terre*, a fourth-floor walk-up
downtown that she probably maintained through a Swiss bank
account, a numbered company, or something or other that kept
her husband of the moment utterly in the dark.

She was under the impression that somehow I was a kept man
out in Hollywood, and I did nothing to dissuade her—I figured
if she saw me as a kindred spirit she'd be more willing to open
up to me. "Open up" doesn't start to cover it. After a couple
of drinks Pour Us DDoris became Porous DDoris. Our tryst
stretched into triple overtime, and she was at once ecstatic and
unrelenting. She sat up in the saddle and rode me as if I were a
mechanical bull. She was thoroughly uninhibited.

Off in the distance I could hear a construction crew breaking
up an outdated sidewalk. I figured the boys had knocked off for
the day by hour four, the point at which DDoris had worked
up a full head of steam and her sighs and moans had gone from
porno quality to something like the MGM lion. Her pneumatic
riding had lasted a good twenty minutes and the bounce of the
epically constructed breasts was practically hypnotic. Pictures
rattled on the walls. Unnoticed in the din was the fact that
her violent thrashing was shifting the bed from one side of her
bedroom to the other, a distance of fifteen or twenty feet, until
it brought the headboard to an open window. For the life of
me I thought the mattress was going to disassemble and I'd be
skewered with a loosened spring. Thank God she didn't knock

over one of the hundred candles she lit as scene-setting for the event or the entire place would have been engulfed in flames, not that she would have noticed. At the end of her performance, her fourth orgasm in fifteen minutes, she fell onto my chest. She buoyantly rested there, her face eighteen inches above mine. At that point I heard applause from the street and then the start of jackhammers once more.

Don't get me wrong: I love Sandy, or something close to that. This, however, was something along the lines of taking one for the team, doing whatever it takes in the line of duty.

"Maybe we could come to an understanding if your team takes on my son," she said.

I told her that would be great, something to look forward to. She probably knew the name of a good chiropractor too.

She wanted to know about Hollywood. Everything. I suppose she wanted to add a mogul to her collection of former husbands. Getting on TMZ and in the tabs would be like her hanging out a shingle. It would open a whole new field of rich men who would covet her and young men who could change her oil.

I opted for candour. I figured I'd give something up to get something back.

"No matter how full it looks, it's an empty place and people change on you," I said. "Those you think you know best sometimes change the most. That's what happened with me. Met a girl who was a military brat, then a small-town girl, then the teenage sweetheart on an after-school show, then a struggling movie actress. She gets one breakthrough role and files for divorce the day after getting an Oscar nomination."

"Looks full for her," she said.

"Does now, but wait. You walk into any respectable dinner theatre in SoCal and you can find an actress with an Oscar nomination on her credits and crow's feet. Too much like hockey,

I guess. You hang on until you forget what you're hanging on for, something you'd never figure on when you're in the clover."

"I want to be young forever," she said, up to her earlobes in clover. "I work at it."

"Clearly, though it doesn't seem like you go at it like it's work."

I tried to push our discussion toward her second husband, father of her son. She didn't conceal her distaste.

"An angry little man," she called him. This might have struck some as strange, given that the guy stands almost six feet tall. DDoris didn't measure in inches, height-wise anyway. She measured in millions. William Mays counted his by tens, her most recent two husbands by hundreds. I supposed DDoris left a trail of angry men, big and small, as well as an exit line of satisfied boy toys who indulged her surreptitiously, at least to whatever degree you can keep her Sensurround earth-moving and banshee-wailing on the down low.

"It was doomed, of course it was," she said. "He had no special place for me, at least not until our son came along. After that, he spent all his time with him and that silly game. He always said that he wished to be the father that he never had. His father died of a heart attack when he was twelve. Dead away in a second. But he clung on to things, memories, in the worst way. He had these awful tin and plastic trophies left over from his own youth that he insisted on putting on the mantel beside Billy's, like they were brothers. It was all so tasteless. Even when Billy was six or seven I thought the relationship, if that's the word, was unhealthy. He didn't do it for Billy. Billy wouldn't fight him. He'd go to the rink, but at age three or four or five he was hardly in a position to put up any resistance ..."

I imagined a little more maternal involvement might have established a more balanced childhood, but I also imagined that she was astraddle a clay-court specialist from Madrid, a pro from the golf club who won the long-driving competition, or a busboy from the Granite Club.

We could have talked and frolicked all day but at 3 P.M. my BlackBerry pinged with a reminder. I had the promised date at Vito's that night. I had to go.

SHE LIT A SMOKE, my cue to bid farewell. My loins felt sandpapered but I was otherwise refreshed. As I was slipping my shoes on, I saw a tortoiseshell-framed photograph on the mantel: left to right, DDoris, Junior, and Ollie Buckhold. I didn't think it remarkable at a glance. Buckhold was going to play a large role in her somewhat beloved son's life. I remarked, "Ollie's a good man."

"He's a wonderful man," DDoris said, lingering over the first syllable of "wonderful." This was no standard character reference or testimonial.

I shot her a sideways glance.

"You like Ollie," I said, "as an agent."

"I love him in every way imaginable," she said.

I was having trouble picturing him at the top of the list with regard to DDoris's intimate feelings toward the opposite gender. She left no doubt with the way her eyes glazed over. She sighed.

"I wish I had met him long ago. So much could be so different ..."

I held off saying that his innate sexuality might have been one of those never-to-be-changed items. I let her continue with her delusions, but they were better founded than I expected.

"I recommended to my son that he sign with Oliver after we met privately," she told me. "We have struck up a bond. Ollie is a regular visitor. As I hope you will be too."

I wasn't about to explain the differences between Ollie and me, though anyone in hockey could have told you what Item Number One was.

"He's such a gentle man," she said, deliberately breaking the word into two. "So fine and cultured and educated. Not to mention physically ravishing."

The mental picture I was drawing featured Ollie in the supine position with eyes closed, head turned, teeth gritted, and face contorted as if he were bench-pressing 325 pounds. Which is to say, labouring. And yet I didn't doubt that she felt something for him that she didn't for me, despite her screams. He was her *objet d'art* even if she wasn't the ideal of his affections by just about the longest shot possible. Erecting him would be the ultimate exercise of her power. I always thought figuratively that there was nothing Ollie wouldn't do to secure a client, but my eyes were opened. His desire to secure fresh meat wasn't bound by his own biological imperatives.

Funny how it goes. It happens for us when we leave the game. It happens for the wives and girlfriends at just about the same time. Life and life's problems change and we change with them. After lives of action and aggression, players become passive, feminine really, more like those who wait on us as trainers or scribble words into notepads like boy Fridays. And the women at that stage throw their pants on, empowered by our retreat. So it was with DDoris. Her attraction wasn't to a man of a conventional sort but to a gentle one who had to be won.

For Ollie, the situation was more complex, to say the least. After serial stealthy relationships with attractive young men on his various cruises, he had gone to this sexual tigress. She was a mother figure of sorts, but in some ways more masculine than others who had buried their faces in his pillows. Okay, I'm reaching. That's the best I could do. I'll admit, if he hadn't been an agent I wouldn't have thought the love match was possible.

"You and Ollie see each other regularly?"

"Nightly," she said. "I send my driver for him. Ollie is very discreet."

I'm not sure whether "discreet" meant holding the truth from her son, from the hockey world that believed Ollie swung only from the other side of the plate, or from Ollie's many buff boyfriends past.

"Wherever Ollie goes for his work, my driver fetches him," she said. "The many times he goes to Peterborough to look after my son. Game nights. Other nights."

I boiled it down. She talked about the worst nights of the winter. Friday nights. Saturday afternoon. Whenever. Ollie was chauffeured to the arena and back to jungle gym.

"In March?" I asked.

"Every night in March," she said. "My husband was in meetings in San Diego. An hour or so in a boardroom every day and then six hours on a golf course. Such a bore."

I reduced it down to paste.

"St. Patrick's Day?"

"My maiden name is O'Reilly. Of course, the national holiday. I insisted on no alcohol. It dulls the senses. I made sure that he rushed back. He said that he was in negotiations with the coach about another young player, a player nearly as talented as Billy. I told Oliver that any talks with that coach were going to have to wait and they did. Oliver said he had all the cards and the coach had to get along with him for his own good. Oliver liked that coach to lick his boots."

Ollie, who probably wouldn't have minded sucking a cowboy's toes, was alibied up. At the time a cinder block was creasing the crania of Red and Bones, he was in the back seat of a limo on the 401, trying to summon up a stiffening in his loins in defiance of nature, like Dust Bowlers looking to the heavens for the Great Flood. Somehow that night and all the others he managed to feed Her Insatiableness, though the refrigerator was bare and his stove wasn't plugged in. Ollie was elsewhere that night but in the last place and the last position you'd think of, unless you thought he was trying to return to the womb.

30

I felt like I'd been through two seven-game series when I left DDoris's, but I wasn't going to have a chance to recuperate. I had another calendar reminder flash on my BlackBerry: Vito's 7 P.M. Yeah, I had to keep that promised appointment with Detective Madison, the fundraiser at the Italian restaurant in Peterborough. Bad timing. I needed to carbo-load before my session with DDoris, not after. Still, duty called and I set out once again for Peterborough. I had an hour and a half to think of how I'd be able to claim the mileage on this trip on my expense account.

When I got to the restaurant, the place was filled to capacity, maybe not quite a hundred, with a makeshift head table. Madison came up to me and offered a handshake and a word of thanks. When we sat down, we could look out past our plates to those locals who'd paid seventy dollars for their veal and signed up for various items in the silent auction. Kids came up to me for autographs and pictures. I didn't allow myself to get fooled. Most had no idea who I was. They just knew that I had to be somebody to get in without paying.

I made small talk with Madison as our waitress, Vito's mother, dropped Caprese salads in front of us.

"How goes the investigation?"

"I was hoping that you wouldn't bring it up. I was hoping that everyone else wouldn't too."

I could take a hint to let it drop, but he felt he had to talk over the clatter of knives and forks and glasses chin-chining.

"We're getting hammered in the press," he said. "Forensics hasn't turned up anything, and I've lost count of how many I've interviewed and re-interviewed. We have persons of interest, but that's for the paper and television stations. It's not a cold case, y'know, but it's sort of fallen below room temperature."

Madison knew that he had said as much as he could and maybe more than he should, even with a person of so little interest as me and even in a setting so informal as a family joint with "That's Amore" playing in the background. He switched conversation over to hockey. I feigned enthusiasm and I've forgotten what we talked about.

Speeches were made by the organizers. Madison knew not to ask me to prepare a speech. That would have been a sure way to scare me off. Instead, he ambushed me, asking me to stand up to take a few questions from the floor.

The first one was about shutting down the Great One in the finals back in '93. "Jacques told me to stay close enough to him so that I could tell him what brand of gum Gretz was chewing," I said. "After game three I told him, 'Juicy Fruit.'" It got a laugh, as always. I didn't say anything like that and neither did he. It was just a line I cribbed from *Hoosiers*, an in-flight movie I sat through three times one season. I visualized Jacques being played by Gene Hackman.

Next came a question from a kid who wanted to know what I thought of Billy Mays Jr. Before I could form an answer, the kid's father stood up and asked if L.A. was going to draft him. "He's a player of interest for us, that's for sure," I said, shooting a glance at Maddy. "When the late coach here said Billy was the best to ever play for him, I'm sure he meant it."

And on it went. It didn't take long. I guess I couldn't sustain their interest for more than a half-dozen questions. The kids didn't want to have to wait for their gelato, and parents looked at their watches. When I sat down, I leaned back in my chair and glanced back at the wall behind the head table. It was covered in autographed photos of former players, celebrities who'd passed through, and community leaders. I picked out a photo of Vito and Hanratty, Vito and players from the old-timers game, Vito and the mayor. Prominently displayed and larger than others was a photo of Vito and Giuseppe Visicale.

I said nothing to Madison about it. He was preoccupied with organizers' duties, counting the take, paying the bills, and sorting out disputes with the silent auction. Vito himself came up to thank me when the tables were being bussed.

"I hope you come back," he said. "I'll make something special for you, you see."

"I see that Mr. Visicale comes here," I said. "Is he a regular?"

"I make a special *cuscusu* for him. He says it's like his mother's. He comes in after the games when he's in town. I keep the place open for him. Put up the closed sign but he comes to the back door and we sit and talk about the old country."

Vito talked about Don Visicale's favourite meals. I asked Vito if this special customer was in on St. Patrick's Day. Affirmative.

"I remember because he came with other people, including the mayor. He called me from the arena to let me know to expect a big sitting. He apologized that he didn't tell me before but he was very generous after."

The CEO of Vis Hockey Enterprises was in the company of

the mayor that night. If you are a person of interest, the mayor wouldn't be a bad one to vouch for your whereabouts.

"It was so sad," Vito continued unprompted. "The coach was supposed to come that night too."

"I can't see that. I thought that Hanratty didn't want Visicale buying into the arena and the team."

"They came here together many times after games, the three of them. Pippo came with the coach and the doctor"—Vito crossed himself—"and he told me that he was going to buy the team. 'Don't worry what the newspaper says, the coach will help me,' he told me. The way he said it, the coach wanted the money to come into the team but didn't want it to seem that way, not at the start. It was better for the coach if he said he didn't want the deal because many people here don't. Then when he said he'd changed his mind, he could tell other people to change theirs. No, Pippo really appreciated what the coach was going to do. Now with the coach gone, I'm worried that his deal won't happen. People here don't like Pippo and me."

Visicale couldn't have had blood on his hands or else Vito would have remembered seeing it on the white tablecloths. Bloodstains are harder to get out than his tomato sauce. That wouldn't have meant that he couldn't have had the job done, but whoever did it wasn't a professional. What's more, Hanratty was worth more to Visicale alive than dead. Fact is, the guy who had taken out the Ol' Redhead and Bones had to fear Visicale as much as the law. Visicale was likely a guy who didn't oppose capital punishment.

On my way out the door at night's end Woody McMullin cornered me. He had emceed the event and with his work done had dived into his jars. He might have been knocking back one of the better vintages of Vito's mom's stock of dandelion wine. I tried to gently bring up the idea of Hanratty being in bed with

Visicale even though the townspeople thought there'd be hard feelings between them. "With money on the line, Red developed a taste for pasta," he said and then stifled a belch. "Different guys for sure, but Red thought that the team needed more of a budget for scouting and an arena upgrade to compete. Visicale could give him all that."

The next belch he unsuccessfully stifled and I beat a retreat. He said goodbye with a flourish, like he was throwing to a commercial.

31

It was the second week of May and Hunts was making a trip he dreaded: Toronto. He suffers through these trips twice a year. The first is the annual road game that L.A. plays here. On the team's last trip in, Hunts didn't fly out after the game with the team. We had two days of meetings at the Royal York with the scouting staff and coaches from our minor-league affiliate. We also brought in a couple of people for interviews: a personal trainer who was looking for a job in player development and a nutritionist who claimed he could raise our team's performance with some sort of organic rocket fuel.

Hunts only made it as far as the Royal York lobby over the course of the meetings. I practically had to drag him out of the hotel on the night before his flight. I wanted to take him to an Irish bar around the corner. It wasn't even a five-minute walk. I thought it would do him good to relax a bit. Instead, he looked like he was marching to the gallows.

"I never have liked this city," he said. "I never played any good here. Got pulled every other game it seems like, and against teams that couldn't score if they picked up the puck and tried to carry it in. And there's never any getting away from the game here. It's maybe the only time I get recognized—people come up to me and tell me something they suppose that I don't know about hockey. Doesn't happen in L.A., never. Hardly ever happens anywhere else."

Hunts isn't a particularly social animal, and that's a liability in his position. It's right there in his job description: The GM is the face of the franchise. He takes no pleasure in the PR part of the job, whether it's making small talk with fans or signing an autograph, or a professional consideration like taking questions from reporters. I suppose he's still a lot like the sixteen-year-old from Morden who used to rush back to the farm in Manitoba at the end of the season. Cities are an inconvenience to him and Toronto isn't just a big city but, worse, the biggest hockey city.

Hunts's second dreaded annual trip to the city is for the league's scouting combine that convenes in Toronto every May. Hunts and I do the breakfast buffet at the Sheraton out by Pearson International Airport when he blows into town for the physical testing and team interviews with the top one hundred draft-eligible prospects. The hotel is as close as Hunts would ever want to get to downtown: forty-five minutes away if there's no traffic, and only five minutes from first-class check-in for the flight back to L.A. The prospect of a quick and easy escape brightens his mood. He always gets a room at the hotel where the league does its testing and his suite serves as our team's headquarters, where we conduct our scouting war-room sessions and player interviews.

Hunts's BlackBerry was pinging with messages from the league HQ with combine updates, players who'd be attending and those bowing out, the interview schedule, and some such. He glanced at the screen but didn't put down his knife and fork as he laid into his cheese omelette. With his attention divided between news and his plate, I thought it was the perfect opportunity to squeeze in a request that could be problematic if he had follow-up questions.

"Hunts, I was wondering if I could have ten minutes alone with Mays when we bring him in for our interview."

"That's half our time with him. Don't you think the rest of the guys would be interested in hearing what he has to say? Maybe they'd have questions they'd want answered."

"I just want to ask him some sensitive stuff, stuff about his family, his mother's problems ..."

I opted not to throw in even a faint suggestion that the problems were avarice and nymphomania.

"... and I figure he'd be a little more forthcoming with me alone, seeing as I've talked to him some and I'm more familiar with him than anyone on the staff."

Hunts kept his head down and kept chewing. He took a bite of his toast. I figured I shouldn't let the silence hang out there.

"I'll write it up in notes and send it off to the guys."

He chewed. Chewing wasn't an answer.

"Look, I know it's our pick and by 'our' I mean you and me. It doesn't matter what the other guys think so much. You and I own this pick. We're gonna wear it for better or worse. It's the team but it's also our jobs. I need you to trust me on this one. Ten minutes."

Hunts was just about to take another bite. At that moment, however, a waitress came by the table to freshen our coffees and take away empty plates. She lingered. She seized the silence.

"Hey Chad, whaddaya figure you're gonna do with Harris this season? He's got one year left on his contract, right?"

Hunts looked at his plate, his head as motionless and his eyes as focused downwards as Tiger Woods at the top of his backswing. He rolled his eyes upwards.

"He's got a year left to prove that he's worth another contract. If I didn't think he could prove it he wouldn't be in L.A."

"He's my neighbour's cousin," she said.

"Everybody's got a neighbour and every neighbour's got a cousin."

"Yeah, but not every neighbour's cousin makes four-point-five and is a year away from being an unrestricted free agent."

He raised his head and looked to his left, not Tiger Woods any longer, more like a guy who couldn't break a hundred, like me.

"That's one helluva point you got there. I think I'm gonna get that engraved on the back of my watch."

The waitress walked away with two of our empty side plates and her coffee pot.

"Hunts, the ten minutes at the end of Mays's interview ..."

"Yeah, yeah, not a problem. I gotta tell you, I can't get out of this city soon enough. It's not like everybody's a fan here or an expert. They all talk like agents."

THE PHYSICAL TESTING is always ugly. Any kid putting in half an effort on the stationary bikes for the aerobic testing is on his knees barfing afterward. I've never paid too much attention to the results. You can always make these kids physically bigger, better, stronger, fitter, whatever. I just like to get an idea of their physical maturity—some are men and have little room for growth, others are boys and have a chance to improve a lot.

All the GMs and scouts stand around watching the kids go through their assorted ordeals. When you see one of us smiling as a kid faints dead away, you're looking at a sadist. And when you scan the floor at the combine, you'll see a lot of smiles. I don't smile. It's too much like team hazing and I dropped a guy on a minor-midget team because he gave me a hard time about not wanting to get involved. The rest of the team backed off on his recommendation. They didn't stop hazing other guys but they kept clear of me. I wish someday a kid would see a GM or scout smiling at the combine and then get up off his knees and sucker the creep. I'd draft that kid.

The league physicals are more important to me than a kid's VO_2 capacity or his vertical jump. I want to know if a kid has had concussions, if he has had or is going to need surgery, if he has physical issues that make the investment of a pick too risky. We see all kinds of things show up on those medicals. A kid who gets a completely clean bill of health is like a car that gets a mechanic's certification. And just like the mechanic's sign-off doesn't mean you're going to be able to drive the car forever, a clean bill of health is no guarantee. A kid can shred his ACL on his first shift after signing his contract or his first concussion can end his career.

THE LEAGUE SENT US the schedule for interviews. Some players had only three or four interviews. Some had twenty-five or more. Some meetings were scheduled before their physical testing, some after. With a hundred players involved, the making of the interview schedule was probably as complex as making the league's schedule of regular-season games. Mays was going to be our second-last interview. L.A. would be the last team he'd talk to.

The combine interviews remind me of my film studies class at B.C. The funniest film we did in a course-load of doom and gloom was Mel Brooks's *The Producers*. In that flick Bialystock and Bloom, played by Zero Mostel and Gene Wilder, are auditioning actors for the role of the Führer in *Springtime for Hitler*. I remember watching the movie in class and splitting a gut. Determined to produce a Broadway bust, Bialystock and

Bloom have a cattle call and bring in the world's worst actors for auditions to play Adolph Hitler. They settle on Dick Shawn, a stoned hippie, for the lead role, but it's the others that stuck with me. After watching it I thought that Sarge must have gone through the same sort of thing when he was questioning witnesses and suspects. Life's rich parade passes by.

Back at B.C. I never imagined that I'd sit across from eighteen-year-old kids and feel like Bialystock or Bloom, but that's exactly how I felt now. There was a sneering Russian goaltender who looked like Eminem, with gold chains as thick as a construction worker's index finger and a ball cap turned backwards. There was a big, rough winger from Thief River Falls who was stumped when I asked him what he planned to major in when he enrolled at State in Mankato in the fall. There was a skilled centre from Port-Cartier who spoke not a word of English and hadn't been out of Quebec until his seventeenth birthday, when he played a road game in Moncton. There was Sorensen, a Swedish kid who was at number five on my list but whom I liked a little less in the interview because he reminded me of the other guy in Wham!

Farm kids. Rich kids. Goofy talkers. Damaged silent types. There were kids who seemed awfully impressed with themselves and thought that they were locks to be stars in the league, though most weren't even close. There were kids who seemed a little shaky, even though everyone in the room figured they'd be in the league in a couple of years.

Duke Avildsen did a slow burn through the whole ordeal. He piped up every once in a while with a question that always hit home, usually something no one else had thought to ask, usually producing a Useful Bit of Dope. He had contempt for the process, though. "We're tipping our hand," he said. "Teams know who we're interested in or at least who we're not interested in when they look at our list of interviews or ask kids about their chat with us."

All these prospects passed through the interview room before the one that mattered, the one that I had sat on for weeks by then: Billy Mays Jr.

"TAKE A SEAT, Billy," Hunts said.

Our room was set up so that the tables formed a U and Hunts sat directly across from the kids who were brought in. Hunts caught him straight ahead. I sat hard by kids on their right side, seeing them all in profile. That's how we were set up for Billy Mays. He went around the room, shook hands, made eye contact, and tried to remember names, just as Ollie Buckhold had instructed all his young clients. Mays remembered more than most kids. A lot didn't remember anything at all.

Mays had already done more interviews than he could recall and would have done more, but a few teams didn't bother because they thought they'd have no shot at drafting him. It was a weird deal. He had to believe that he was going to have to answer the same questions that came up in all the other interviews and that he wasn't going to hear anything new. That was true for the first half of the session.

"What are your strengths and weaknesses?"

"Mr. Hunt, I'd say that skating is my strongest asset. I think at the next level I'll be more of a playmaker than a scorer, but that's what you'd expect from a centre. I eventually want to develop into a player who can contribute on the power play and penalty kill. I know my defensive game is going to need work, but I think that my skating and strength will help me with that ..."

He was right on every count. How much was sincere and self-aware, and how much was Ollie Buckhold's pre-combine coaching? I thought it was more of the former.

"Who have been the most important people in your development?"

"Mr. Hunt, obviously my father. He's a former player and he had me on skates at two or three. He enrolled me in the best programs here in the city and in hockey schools. My coaches in peewee and bantam were very important as well. My bantam coach, Russ Crawford, played for Dallas for a few seasons, and I learned a lot about seeing the ice and awareness of situations from him. And of course there was Coach Hanratty, who taught me about the commitment it takes to be a professional. He used to say that he wasn't just looking for a season's commitment ... he wanted to see it on every shift no matter which game it was or what the score."

"You didn't do the physical testing here because of your mono and your shoulder injury. When do you expect to resume training?"

"My doctor says that I won't be ready for summer prospects' camp if the league team brings in players in July. I think I'm probably closer than he thinks. I'm hoping to start skating in August. We're going to see what the doctors say and how I feel. Personally, I think I might be closer than they say. I really want to get back out there, but then again I don't want to do anything that might risk my career in the long run. My father says, 'You have to be tough to come back and play after something like this, but it's even tougher to be patient and smart.'"

That's how it went for the first ten minutes. Hunts asked most of the questions but others jumped in. Our guy in Michigan asked Mays why he decided to play junior after being recruited by the top schools in the States. Mays said that he and his father had given the move serious thought but ultimately decided that he'd get the chance to play more in Peterborough. Besides, his father said he had a good time there. Duke Avildsen asked the kid how much he followed the league. Mays told him he knew that Duke had played for three Cup winners and scored about 300 goals in his career. It was actually 292. I suspect the kid knew to fudge up. Sven asked him what he thought of the game he'd played against Sweden at the summer 18s, because it was one of two games that Sven had ever seen him play and because Sven could never get enough of talk about Sweden. Mays gave him a pretty comprehensive scouting report of the players on the Swedish team, a somewhat generous one, enough so that Sven was beaming until the last player's name came up: Sorensen. I was sort of heartened that Mays was high on Sorensen like I was. Sven didn't take that as well.

"I couldn't shake him," Mays said. "I was busting it trying to keep up with him and he wasn't even breathing hard."

I looked at my watch. We had Mays booked until 2:40 and it was half past. Hunts looked over at me and I nodded.

"Gentlemen, if I could meet with you outside the room. Let Shadow here handle the rest of the interview. Billy, don't get fooled. He's smarter than he looks. Thanks for your time and best of luck."

The rest of the staff looked puzzled at this turn of events but followed Hunts out the door.

I PULLED MY SEAT around the side of the table and parked it about arm's length away from Mays. I wanted to win his trust. I started by telling him about cards I wasn't going to show my boss, not now anyway.

"The Markov thing didn't happen," I said. "Nobody in this room knows anything about it. I gotta believe that no one you've talked to in the last couple of days knows anything either. I haven't told a soul. I think you were wrong but for all the right reasons. Sometimes life's like that. You were in a tough spot."

"Thanks," he said. He looked down at the floor between his Cole Haans. Embarrassment and relief. I don't know if Markov's end of it would stay dead and buried or if it might follow the Russian kid down the line. Videos are like that. That Mays tried to help him wasn't likely to surface.

I moved directly to some business-as-usual stuff to snuff the uncomfortable moment.

"Any teams here give you the third degree? Try to sweat you?"

"A couple were in my face, trying to push my buttons. You can't let it bother you."

"Well, I'm not here to bother you. Tell me about your father."

"I wouldn't be here without him. I appreciate all that he's done for me."

"How much does he push you and how much do you do on your own?"

"I pride myself as a self-starter. It's one of the messages my father has driven home again and again, my whole life. 'You've got to do it for yourself because you can't wait for someone to do it for you.' He says that all the time. Another one is: 'When you do it on your own, you own it.'"

"Good messages," I said. I suspect that the kid took them to heart, but I thought that the maxims were a bit rich coming from William Mays Sr. Mr. Self-Reliance grew up Old Money, skating out of Rosedale and into the best schools, Upper Canada College and all, before heading off to Peterborough for a single season in junior.

I paused and looked down at some notes I'd scribbled.

"What's tough about being the son of a famous father?"

"I honestly don't think anything is tough. I know I've had opportunities that others didn't. My father's in business but he knows all about hockey. I think that's been the most important thing—his support. Yeah, I've been able to get the best coaching and off-ice work from private instructors, but my father knew what it was going to take from his own experience as a player. He always says he wished that he'd had the same sort of encouragement. My grandfather sailed and rode horses. He didn't care about hockey at all and only came to see my father play a few times, never even went to Peterborough to see him. He died young. I guess my father knew some of the things that can be tough about being the son of a famous father and made sure that I didn't have to worry about them."

Since I first crossed paths with William Mays Sr. I never imagined that I'd pity him, but at that moment I did.

I tried to segue as softly as I could. A little interview shell game.

"Your father make it out here today? I didn't see any Jaguar or Lamborghini in the parking lot."

"Yeah, he's here. He never brings one of his good cars to stuff like this, a hockey thing, anyway. He thinks some people might see it as showing off. He gets a rental. It's what he's done since I started playing. Didn't want other parents to dislike us."

"So he has those great rides and takes rentals?"

"Yeah."

I could see that being a write-off in his business expenses. I could also see Senior doing it so that a hockey bag didn't turn his Lamborghini into a Toxic Bacterial Incubator.

"Disappointed that you couldn't do the testing?"

"Yeah, really disappointed. I was aiming to get back in time to do some of it. I wouldn't be able to do the bench because of my shoulder rehab, but I did think I'd have a chance to do the stationary bike stuff, the VO_2, and the rest. That's what I'd been working on when Doc McGarry shut me down because of the relapse with the mono."

Now we were getting to the Juice Not from Concentrate. I wanted to know what he knew about his health issues, what other teams had asked, what he had told them. And I wanted to ask him all this before he had a chance to talk to his father and Ollie Buckhold.

"Yeah, help me out with that, Billy. What was the timeline on that? I'm not really sure from talking to people. It would have been something that I woulda wanted to ask Doc McGarry myself. How and when were you shut down?"

"Doc gave me the go-ahead to start skating again in early November. I had been diagnosed by my GP with mono back in the summer, 'round Labour Day. I'll admit that I felt pretty tired the first week back from the summer 18s, but I pushed through it. I was completely revved when I got into games ..."

"You were playing really well. I saw a bunch of those games."

"Thanks. When I hurt my shoulder in early February, I missed a few days of off-ice stuff. I was really limited and had to improvise a bit. Because of the shoulder I was practically off lifting completely—no squats, no cleans, no bench. But I used a deep-sea diver's weight belt to do lunges and other stuff with resistance, and a Swiss ball for my core strength. And I used the bike. I figured there was nothing wrong with getting cardio and it would help me come back for the playoffs, which was the timeline we were looking at."

"And so what happened that changed all that?"

"I felt a little short of breath the one workout. I had the resistance on the stationary bike set at seventeen out of twenty, which was my normal number. I could do seventy rpms for forty-five minutes pretty easily, maybe more if I felt like pushing it. But this time I felt a little sluggish and dizzy. I thought it was the flu or something so I went to Doc. Coach Hanratty had me on a sked for workouts and I could miss a day only if I had medical clearance, so I went to Doc to get him to sign for me. He gave me a checkup and sent me for tests."

It sounded like Beef's story was the straight goods.

"I've felt crappy like that in workouts," I said, just to give him the Old I Understand. "Just out of the blue. A cold. Flu. Something you ate didn't agree with you."

"My meals the night before and that day were the same as usual, the stuff that my nutritionist set me up with. My billet family is great about all that. No, Doc brought me in and did the usual stuff ..."

"Like?"

"Temperature, blood pressure, checking my throat, my ears, checking my pulse, getting blood, and having me give a urine sample. He told me to stay out of the gym until he said it was okay to go back. Then he sent me for more tests at his son's clinic."

"And what did they do there?"

"They monitored me walking on a treadmill. They did some imaging."

"And what did Doc tell you was wrong?"

"Well, it was Doc's son who told me about the relapse and told me that I had to shut it down for the season. Doc got the results when we were on the road. He wanted me to see my father before telling me that I had to stop. Y'know, in case there were any questions. But then Doc and coach got killed. And it ended up that my father met with Doc's son. My father said Doc was a guy who would tape me up and send me out to play in the playoffs. He said his son had all the tech stuff and he'd look after me best."

Evidently Senior didn't let his son in on the fact that he had met with the Ol' Redhead and Bones before the old-timers game. Noted.

"Did Theo put you on any meds?"

"Just a few pills a day to take."

"What were they?"

"Vitamin supplements. He said that I might be anemic."

"You know the names of those vitamins? B_{12} maybe?"

"I don't know. I didn't have to get a prescription filled or buy them over the counter. He gave me samples that he had from a drug company. He put them in brown plastic containers and said he'd look after the refill. I took three a day of the one bunch for a week and felt pretty lousy. Must have been some sort of reaction. Then it was down to one each and I started feeling better. A little tired but better."

So the pills weren't drugs, by Bones II's account anyway. They were vitamins. But a drug company was handing them out as samples to doctors. And they gave them to Bones II, who gave them to Wonder Boy. They made him feel worse before they made him feel better.

"How did your father take the news when you told him?"

"He'd already met with Doc's son the day before. I go up to his clinic every week, just waiting to get the green light to be ready to go. But Dr. McGarry says that won't happen until after the draft."

"He didn't want to send you to a specialist in Toronto?"

I wasn't quite sure which type of specialist that would be if we were talking about mono, but I imagined there had to be one. And if there wasn't, if it was basic garden-variety doctoring, why not send the kid to a good GP rather than steal time from Peterborough's only home-based cardiologist?

"My father said that he only wanted the best and he trusted Doc's son. They were roommates when they were on the team."

"Yeah, I knew that. Tell me, when you've talked to other teams, how much have they asked you about your mono and your visits to the doctor and all that?"

"Almost none at all. Some ask how I've been feeling or about my shoulder. That's about it."

"Nothing about meds or anything or seeing Doc's son?"

"Nothing."

"Billy, I hope you don't mind, but I'd like to be able to visit with you and your father off-site. Twenty minutes isn't a heckuva lot of time, especially when we're talking about investing millions and the future of the franchise. There are still things I'd like to talk to you about. Will you be around the city the next few weeks? You're not going out of town, are you?"

He said that he'd be around Monday morning to Thursday afternoon the next couple of weeks. His father decamped with son to a spread in Bala on weekends. In the old man's income bracket, weekends start at lunch on Thursday. Mays said his father was competing in the masters division of the Muskoka triathlon. I suggested meeting at his home. He said that would be fine. I told him I had his father's card and would be in touch.

MAYS AND I EXITED the room together. Hunts was standing there. He shook the kid's hand and gave me a dirty look. He understood kicking everyone else out of the room. He didn't like being shut out himself. He was going to simmer on that all day and the next. Then he'd probably simmer on that on his flight back to L.A.

It wouldn't be the last thing I'd do independent of him.

32

I called our team doctor in L.A. He had served in his role for the last decade and worked with four general managers. He joked that his work was evenly divided between the GMs' ulcer maintenance and the players' STDs. There was a kernel of truth in that.

I told him I had a bunch of questions that would take a few minutes, maybe half an hour. I asked him if there was a good time to talk. He told me to call him back at 6 P.M., West Coast time. He was on the back nine at Torrey Pines and should be home in time for dinner.

I called at the appointed hour. He picked up on the first ring. I filled him in on what I knew of Mays's medical history. The sequence of the mono, the shoulder injury, and relapse. I told him that I didn't have Mays's charts but I'd ask Ollie Buckhold for copies of them, routine stuff with top draftees. He was probably making copies already anyway.

"A relapse from mono isn't the usual thing we see. Lingering effects of it, sure. The likelihood is that he played with it for a while before he was diagnosed and he came back too early, which exacerbated the effects. Shutting him down for more than a couple of months seems a little extreme, but I guess they might want to err on the side of caution the second time out. And with the shoulder injury, again, I could see them saying that even minimal risks of reinjury in the short term weren't worth it."

I told him the facts as Mays had laid them out. He gave me the thumbnail read of them.

The vitamins? "No vitamin treatment for mono other than taking the usual multivitamin."

Samples? "Lots of companies give out samples to specialists, but vitamins to a cardiologist, I can't see it. He'd be given something a lot closer to his practice, if anything at all."

Three times a day with one pill and then one pill a day for the duration? "Loading of a drug is standard treatment with a lot of meds. It's common enough with antibiotics, though not for a week and indefinitely thereafter. It's the protocol with other drugs, too. I've never heard of it with vitamins, but there's a lot of quackery out there and unfortunately many in the medical profession aren't immune."

Feeling lousy after loading them but better later on? "Never heard of it with vitamins, but as I said, I don't subscribe to alternative-health holistic journals, such as they are. If he was taking eye of newt or St. John's wort or something, maybe he did have a reaction."

Treadmill test? "Reasonable measure to take as a precaution if he was reporting shortness of breath."

Imaging? "Well, that's a little more extreme but again, as a precaution, if the technology is available and you're not worried about incurring cost, sure."

Seeing a cardiologist in Peterborough rather than a GP in Toronto? "A GP should be able to handle a case of mono. That's the sort of thing a GP is for. I can't diagnose motives but I would guess that his family might have been unhappy with their GP ... maybe he missed the mono symptoms in the first place."

Our team physician's bedside manner is a beatific calm, something that a golf pro walks with through life off the course. He comes by it honestly. He's a four handicap.

33

A chill blew over my relationship with Hunts. He didn't call for a few days after the combine. My calls went straight to voicemail. I messaged him about setting up a meeting with the Mayses. No reply. I went into our database and posted my impressions of the interview with Mays but left out the medical stuff we'd discussed. Normally Hunts would be on the phone to me five minutes after he read it. Nothing.

I hadn't read the papers for days. I went to my bookmarks of the columnists and beat writers at the L.A. papers and the silent treatment started to make sense: The drumbeat had started for a new GM in L.A. Everyone in the media was taking it up. Everyone was speculating about candidates and, yeah, Grant Tomlin's name was always in the mix, placed there, no doubt, by Grant Tomlin.

If it was just stress, Hunts would be on the phone to me. It wasn't just stress. No, to his mind it was betrayal. He thought I was out there talking to other teams, trying to line up another job in case he got axed. He might have thought that I already

208

had a handshake deal in place with another team. That sort of thing is done all the time all around the league. I had thought about looking around, but anyone in my position would. Hunts wasn't thinking that I had considered it. He thought I had already booked my ticket out of Dodge.

Maybe he heard a bad rumour or someone was yanking his chain. Maybe he thought that the private interview with Mays at the combine was so out of the ordinary that it meant something was up. It wasn't something that we were ever going to discuss. We were going to get over it by not talking about it.

34 _____

A week after the combine there was a knock at the door. I presumed it was Sandy. She was the only one who would know my ritual comings and goings. It wasn't. It was a large Italian gentleman dressed like he was going to a wedding or a funeral.

"Brad, Mr. Visicale has sent me to pick you up for a meeting."

"I'm supposed to …"

"It's very important to Mr. Visicale that you see him today."

Mr. Visicale was going to get his way. I suppose he always does. I went along peacefully.

CASA VISICALE WAS a spread that was once owned by Jack Kent Cooke. It looked like it had been decorated by a guy from Little Italy who'd worked in construction. That was exactly what Mr. Visicale used to do before he enjoyed his business success and others suffered from it. The major differences between his childhood home and his million-dollar crib were: (a) Those were originals, not copies, on the wall; and (b) The plastic was off the sofa and people were allowed to sit in the living room.

It was the only house on Old Post Road where families used a basement kitchen and ate there on a Formica table. The large gentleman who had knocked on my door took me downstairs, where we found Mr. Visicale sitting at that table with a cold espresso and a copy of *Corriere Canadese*.

"Take a seat, Brad," Mr. Visicale said, putting his tiny cup back on its saucer.

I had been given no more details on the ride up. The driver volunteered only what he'd told me at my door: His employer wanted to see me.

"Brad, I'm gonna be upfront," Visicale said. "I'm gonna buy this Peterborough team. Not a matter of if I can. It's gonna get done."

I wasn't about to express any opposition. I didn't want to say that I didn't give a shit what he did. And I didn't want to ask why he cared to let me in on this. He probably figured these out, though.

"I'll be direct," he said. "It's my nature. I'm a businessman and I've done well because I get good people and treat them honourably ..."

He looked over at the 250 pounds of prosciutto standing to his right and nodded.

"... and I want you to come work for me."

"As what" came to mind but not to my tongue.

"I had my son here pick you up on the recommendation of Nick Gucciarde."

Two things again came to mind: (a) His son had put on a lot of weight since he played for Windsor a few years back and was almost unrecognizable behind the sunglasses he wore, even in the basement. (b) Gooch owed me no favours from that season we spent together in Hershey near the end and hadn't done me any by putting in a good word with the continually investigated, often charged, but never convicted Visicale, who lists his occupation as plumber. Gooch had gone on from a career as Hershey's stone-handed winger to coach in the juniors and minor pro leagues. Only at this point was I putting it together that at every stop along the way Gooch happened to coach one of the Visicale boys. I was getting an idea that this wasn't exactly a coincidence but the by-product of a few guys getting their doors knocked.

"Brad, I'd like to bring you in as coach in Peterborough when I take control of the team. Nick will be general manager and he said that you were someone he could work with. I'm not interested in someone who has coached a team in the O. I think they have a way of doing business and I have mine. There's usually no getting people to change and that's even more true of junior coaches. Nick understands how I like to do things, and he thinks you would be great for a team that I want to be the best junior franchise in Canada. It will be the best."

Anything less than certainty didn't last any longer than a breath for Don Visicale.

"I'm under contract to L.A., Mr. Visicale."

True as far as it went. I was under contract to scout for the team until July 1. That's when scouts' deals expire. Some get two-year deals, some even longer. I wasn't lucky on that count. Hunts could give me only a year. It came down from upstairs.

"I'm sure the team will understand," he said.

"I don't know that they'd stand in my way. And, of course, I might get fired. Happens."

"Yes, shit does happen, Brad. I heard all about the situation in L.A. And you might be looking for work. I come to you with something that you should take into consideration. I think you could do better with our company than you would in L.A., unless you have aspirations to coach or be a general manager with one of the big clubs. And I wouldn't rule out the possibility that one day we will buy one of those franchises. In that event you and Nick would, of course, be strongly considered for top roles."

"Mr. Visicale, I promise you that I will think about it. I'm a loyal type of guy, a team guy, and my boss is not just my boss but an old teammate and maybe my closest friend. I can't walk out on him right now with the draft coming like Christmas."

"I respect that. I think we could become friends. Good friends."

The son nodded. I took that as a cue that I should nod too.

"Anyone going into the Peterborough job has a tough act to follow. What were you planning to do if Coach Hanratty were still around?"

"He's not."

"He didn't want the team sold. He had a pretty good gig there."

"He was a fool, to tell you the truth. It's one thing to remember the past and another thing to live in it."

"How did he feel about the franchise being sold?"

I played dumb. It was easy. I knew he had said the sale would be made over his dead body, a tragically and almost comically prophetic statement.

"He told me that he thought his coaching days were about over," he said. "He told me he was interested in staying on in some sort of smaller capacity, something suitable for his age. In a word, Brad, I bought him. He was not in my way."

I wasn't for sale, at least not yet. On the drive home I kept trying to come up with a way to extricate myself from this jam. The son finally piped up.

"I think you'd be good in that old coach's place," he said.

He was probably talking about the place behind the Peterborough bench. Of course, the place might be the spot in the parking lot if things ever went sideways in any friendship with Don Visicale.

35

I messaged William Mays Sr. and asked to come out to their spread. Wednesday. Tuesday Junior had an appointment up in Peterborough. Senior would send a car for me. I was going to insist on driving myself but reconsidered. I couldn't imagine pulling up in the Mays driveway and parking the Rusty Beemer next to the Lamborghini or vintage Porsche or one of the other collectors' rides. There's only so much humbling I can stand and I don't actively seek it out.

The driver walked me to the door. He punched in the security code. Before going inside, I took a quick look around the grounds. A security camera above the front door. Cameras high up in the corners of the courtyard. There were more cameras and angles of the action than you'd find in the arena for game seven of the Cup finals. I'm sure the coach house was converted into some sort of production studio. The driver walked me into the foyer. While we waited for my host, I looked for more discreetly positioned cameras. When I saw one near the top of the spiral staircase I gave a little wave. Should have brought my Hi Mom! sign.

"Great to see you, Brad," Senior said. He handed me a copy of *The Seven Keys of Turning Maybes into Wills*™. He'd inscribed it: "To Brad, Let Key #8 for L.A. be Billy." Cute. Junior wore number eight for Peterborough. William Sr. had scrawled his name at the bottom of the title page and all I could make out was a stretched-out *M*.

"Come on with me," he said. He struck me as a guy who liked to walk people through his house with a commentary like a museum guide. He talked up his collection of artwork. I feigned interest. He talked about buying the paintings at auctions and dropped dollar signs in there. This meant nothing to me but explained the presence of the security cameras.

I followed him out to his backyard. He stretched back on a chaise lounge. I sat up at the foot of mine, feeling like I could have used something with a hard back. My ass was too low, my knees were at a tight angle, and Arthur said hello.

"I think your son is a great player," I said. "Don't get me wrong. I can see him being a major player in the league for a long time ..."

"Cigar?"

"No thanks. But the thing is, I don't like seeing kids in the league at eighteen. It's too young for anyone except the ones who are really physically mature. If we draft Billy, I can see him coming to our training camp but going back to Peterborough for one more season before coming up to the big club. We're looking at signing Billy in June or July after next season."

"I think Billy will play for you next year."

Too typical. After thousands of drives to the arenas with their kids' hockey bags in the trunk, after thousands of hours standing in arenas where their coffees go bone cold in ten minutes, parents start thinking in millions when their kids are a step or two away from the league.

"If he didn't miss as many games as he did this year, I might agree with you. But I think he needs to be thicker through the shoulders and lower body. The contact he's going to see in the league, it's different from what he's ever experienced. We don't want to put him in a position where he's in danger of getting really injured."

"Brad, I appreciate your concern, I really do. But I'm going to manage ..."

The Oh No Moment in Bad Hockey Parenting was upon us.

"... Billy's career using the same principles that I've put into play with my own enterprises. Start with a Vision, one of the Seven Keys. Everything starts with a vision, and a vision starts with knowledge and imagination ..."

My vision was escape as soon as possible, safe in the knowledge that the Franchise Prospect had the ultimate Father Who Tests a General Manager's Soul.

"... What we have to look at is who Billy will be, not who he was this season or is today, but who he will be. I know Billy, in some ways better than I know myself. That's the knowledge that I possess and I alone. The imagination is to see things as they may be. That's the theme in *Seven Keys*™. Maybes to Will Bes. And you must act upon things as they *may be* to make them come to fruition. The team that drafts Billy is not drafting Billy for what he has done but who he will be. That's a big difference. After we sign ..."

My aching head, he was in the dreaded First-Person Plural.

"... with the team that drafts Billy, he'll go to training camp and he *will* make the roster and he will be a contender for the Rookie of the Year."

His son hadn't played a game in the league and already this guy was trying to find a place to hang his son's plaque at the Hall of Fame. I tried to jump in. I shouldn't have bothered.

"I think a team would have to see Billy perform in training camp before they would have a vision with a contract in it. Unless he makes the team coming out of training camp, a team would probably hold off doing a contract at least until next winter."

Fire, meet gasoline.

"Brad, I don't mean to sound didactic, but the fact is Billy will be offered a contract this summer, he will go to training camp, he will play on the top two lines of the team that drafts him and signs him. That's our vision. And part of the *Seven Keys*™ is Eliminating Obstacles. We'll eliminate any team that does not intend or in fact commit to negotiating a contract in good faith with Billy this summer. I want to make that clear to you. And another of the *Seven Keys*™ is Achieving Opportunity and Minimizing Risk ..."

I was going to ask if those should be two Keys but bit my lip.

"Training camp with a contract is an opportunity. Training camp without a contract is a significant risk. We're not intending Billy to go to a training camp without a contract in his hands. I want you and your team to understand that we are unequivocal in our position. We think it would be best for all involved that we're dealing with a team that shares our vision and commits to eliminating obstacles and minimizing risk."

Senior went through five more chapters of the *Seven Keys*™ as they were going to apply to Junior's career. I drifted off. I looked over at a cast-iron statue by the pool. Something along the lines of Rodin. It captured a young man holding a scroll. I tried to have a vision of Junior holding a contract drawn up by L.A. lawyers. I figured there was a better chance of the kid in the statue autographing the scroll than there was of Billy Mays signing a contract with us this summer.

36

I got a call from Harley Hackenbush. He had my number from the call I made about old man Mays's days in P'boro.

Hackenbush said he was on the junior beat again. Temporarily, I guess. The kid who was covering the team was having back surgery and would be stretched out for at least a couple of months. Hackenbush had to write up a story on the likelihood of Mays going in the top five of the draft and the possibility that he'd play in the league at age eighteen rather than heading back for another year of junior.

"The l-ll-league's gain would be our l-ll-loss," Hackenbush said.

Never-say-die Hackenbush. The Ol' Redhead had opened the trap door beneath Harley's feet and he still talked about the franchise as if he were in the team photo.

I spelled it out for him.

"Everybody thinks that these kids should be back in junior for at least another year and almost nobody is ready to play pro at age eighteen," I said. "Physically they're not up for it. Almost all of them get banged up. But then again, everybody thinks that about everybody else's draft pick. Every general manager thinks his player is the exception."

Hackenbush got his money quote. Small talk ensued. He wanted to know about other kids on the Peterborough team who were draft eligible. I told him I had a limited interest in Markov, and that was true. I didn't tell him that I thought L.A. was about the worst place for a player who was willing and eager to take pictures of his Johnson on his iPhone. He'd have his own spot on TMZ. And I told Hackenbush that I had a limited interest in the others, "limited" in its application here being none whatsoever.

I nudged our conversation over to the subject of Bones II. Hackenbush was a fan.

"If it weren't for h-h-him, I-I-I wouldn't be alive," he said.

"Howz that?"

"Stress. I got taken off the beat because the stress was killing me. My ticker was out of whack."

I imagined that the cause and effect might be reversed. I imagined that it was the stress of being sentenced to the night desk that got to him. And I imagined that there was an intermediate causation as well. He was demoted, he hit the bottle, and every double made his heart skip a beat.

"I was coming to my six-month regular appointment with him and called his office, but they said he won't be back in until next week. He's been off for two weeks or so."

I bade him farewell. It seemed screwy that Mays had an appointment with a doctor on holiday and Hackenbush could have been at death's door and had to wait. I couldn't wholly trust Hackenbush's version of events. He could have muffed the timeline and the details the same way he'd mangled my quotes at the old-timers game. The same way he was going to mangle my quote about kids not being ready to play in the league at age eighteen. Then again, if there was something he wasn't going to muff it would be a visit to his cardiologist that would sustain his life, such that it was.

37

I put in a call to Spike. I wanted to ask him about Markov. I looked at Duke Avildsen's reports on him from mid-winter and Duke gave him pretty positive reviews. Spike confirmed that Markov had been nothing but a good citizen. "Better as the year went on," Spike said.

We made small talk. Of course, our discussion went back to the murders. It had been the first topic of conversation in Peterborough for weeks. I told him that I'd seen a couple of detectives grilling Norm Pembleton.

"They're barking up the wrong tree," Spike said.

"How's that?"

"They're friends ... they *were* friends. A couple of times when Pembleton was heading for a bad fall, in a bad, bad way, it was Red who stepped in and got him to dry out. It was Red who helped Norm get a couple of his jobs. All that other stuff was an act."

"Could have fooled me."

"It fooled everyone. Like Red used to say, 'There's no cowboys if there's no Indians.' Red was the good guy, Pembleton the black hat. And when their teams played, people came out just to see the guys behind the bench. Doesn't happen often. But they did get together, real low profile. They didn't want their players or reporters to know. It woulda ruined a good thing for them. Fact is, they were an awful lot alike."

"What about the cheerleader they dated? Mrs. Red. Pembleton had to have a gripe about that ..."

"Hah, Judy was a cheerleader, all upright and uptight. She'd been crazy about Pembleton but he liked his stuff fast and loose."

I could see that. I could see him later regretting it. He couldn't have held it against Hanratty that he had something that he'd passed up, someone he didn't want to hurt.

38

I rolled around the bed. There was no sleeping. I was glad that Sandy wasn't there. She wouldn't have been able to sleep with me turning the light on and off, starting a book and putting it down, turning on the television in the bedroom. *Chinatown* was on. I needed someone to come up to me and say, "Forget about it, Shade, it's hockey." But there'd be no forgetting about it. My job was on the line. *Our* jobs were on the line. If we ended up making the wrong decision about our pick, the owner was going to kick all of us out to the curb. It looked like our pick would be Mays, but there were big holes in our background check on the kid, holes six feet deep where they'd lowered the Ol' Redhead and Bones.

"Detective Madison, please."

A pause.

"Madison."

We exchanged niceties by rote.

I stuttered out a thought that was instinctive rather than well founded. "Something has been bothering me about ... well, 'bothering' isn't the right word, but something occurred to me after talking to you and watching the security video."

"What is it?"

"Just something about the people coming and going. It could be nothing. I don't know. Could I maybe drop in and watch the video with you when I'm up in Peterborough this week?"

39

June was not quite upon us. It didn't feel like hockey season. It might have if the Merry Widow's air conditioning worked. I sat at barside in front of Nick's most recently serviced flat screen. It was game night, game seven of the Eastern Conference final, and, as such occasions demand, Nick had the music off and the sound of the broadcast turned up high.

My father sat beside me. I'd like to think that he stood out from and above the mangy clientele, but, fact is, he'd made a career of blending in and getting along, just as the Irregulars had scratched out their bare existence by rising to the minimum standards of human decency or thereabouts.

Sarge had lost the coin flip with my mother. She wanted to watch some godawful show where celebrities dance ballroom style, utterly lacking talent for the task. Actually, Sarge threw the coin flip—she'd called heads and it landed tails when he tossed it. He put his act over. He wanted to get out. He wanted a chance to catch up with me now that my season on the road was over but for the draft. It wasn't just my company he wanted, though.

The game was one thing to watch at home, another to share communally. Sarge wanted to be in the company of men, of fans who could name all those dancing their own dance on the ice, who could appreciate excellence. Larry, his German shepherd, retired from the canine division, was tied up out on the curb, looking through the window, not at his master but at the game.

In the panel talk during intermission, the main topic of conversation was a hit on Broadhurst, the Boston captain. Hoskins, New York's knuckle-dragger, had given him the flying elbow and rightly got five and a game. The Irregulars winced when they saw it happen. My father shook his head. Larry strained at his collar. Broadhurst was knocked out of his senses and out of the game and, from the looks of it, from the rest of the playoffs if Boston was going to survive this night.

I've been there on both ends of that elbow. It really doesn't merit analysis. It is what it is. Broadhurst was doing what he does, playing his game, getting a little too comfortable or reckless or both with the stakes so high. Hoskins was doing what he does, playing his game, right up to the line marking acceptable behaviour and occasionally, if need be, just on the dark side of that line.

It was done. There wasn't anything more you could say about the play. That didn't stop Grant Tomlin from weighing in with a dissertation that might have gone all night if it weren't for commercials and the puck drop for the third period.

"What you just saw there was a breach of The Code," Tomlin shouted at a host sitting only an arm's length away and whose glasses doubled as a spittle shield. "Given the level of these players' ability and size, each of them could take out an opponent on every shift if they were so inclined. But they play by The Code. They know that when they step on the ice, they're in against guys just like them who understand what this game is about and respect their teammates and the guys on the other side just as much. When you don't demonstrate that respect, when you don't play the game the way it's supposed to be played, you've violated The Code."

He went on and with every next word took a step farther from the truth of the matter.

The Code is a nice notion, one that gets thrown around by reporters and talking heads. It sells a narrative of honour and nobility. Those guys in the seats and in front of the screens buy it. They lap it up. These are their knights, in shoulder pads and shin pads, not shining armour; with sticks, not lances; all in the service of coaches, not kings.

The Code is a notion as bogus as any campaign ever cooked up by an advertising agency and twice as effective for drumming up business. Nobody takes an oath, one hand over his heart, other hand raised, vowing to uphold the game's values and traditions. Every player on the ice signs a contract to play the game and there's not a line in it about respect.

The game is no different from life outside the boards. What players do on the ice is regulated only by conscience, and conscience is the sum of experience in large part, necessity in some part, and intelligence when any is in stock. Most will do their best. A few will do whatever it takes. Broadhurst was doing his best. Hoskins was doing whatever it was going to take, at least to the best of his limited judgment.

There's nothing understood between those on one side of the ice and those on the other. There's the knowledge that Broadhurst is going to do what he's going to do seventeen out of twenty shifts in a game. There's the possibility that in six minutes of Hoskins's ice time he might slash a player across the arm hard enough to break it or, as he did with Broadhurst, leave a star on his back at centre ice, eyes open but the arena as dark as an unlit closet in Carlsbad Caverns. Broadhurst has his own Code, Hoskins a very different one.

"What a steaming pile of crap," Sarge said at the end of Tomlin's soliloquy.

Sarge got it. As it is in hockey, so it is in life. Sarge had his Code. He mostly coloured by the numbers and inside the lines. Others on the force stretched and bent and ignored the rules, worse than Hoskins ever did.

I'm not like Sarge. Somewhere in an old file in our team's office you can find proof of it. Back when I was in my first season in L.A., management brought in a sports psychologist to do testing. Another steaming pile of crap, but no matter. One of the tests involved a big sheet of numbers, running up to 200. They were jumbled, out of order, and in different typefaces and colours. Some were sideways. I got dizzy just looking at them. The psychologist gave us a few minutes and told us to circle numbers in order, going up from 1, and said that a good score was in the high 40s or so. He told us that we couldn't skip a number or he'd have to void tests and register them as failures. I got to 23 but was stuck on 24. I spent about five seconds and then said to hell with it. I could see 25 and so I circled it and just kept going. I thought that if I had trouble finding 24, the guy marking the tests might too and he'd probably just want to see the highest number I got to. I ended up getting to 47. At the bottom of the page I wrote my name and wrote down "Total: 47!" just to make his job easy.

There was no 24. I had thought the test was set up to rate the ability to process information, to check the wiring of the synapses. No, it was set up to sort out those who would take instruction, follow it to a T, and stop at 23 even if that meant failure. Those were one type of player. Those were Keepers of

The Code. I was the other type, the one who'd try to get away with something to get the desired result, the one who went from 23 to 25 with a sideways glance to see if the coast was clear.

The test was a waste of time. I could have told them that I'd do that in life and on the ice.

I'm my father's son in a lot of ways but not on this count. I was like Hoskins in many ways, but smarter, sneakier. I never once did something impulsive on the ice. I picked my spots. And I had no loyalties, no friendships. I would do to an ex-teammate and a friend exactly what I'd do to a total stranger—in fact, I might have even gone at it harder with guys I had run and drunk with, just because I feared that I might go soft and sentimental. Players and general managers and coaches used to say that I was "greasy," which I took as the highest compliment. If you look at the names engraved on the cup, you'll find a lot of greasy guys. Greasy guys are great to play with but brutal to play against. "Greasy" is whatever it takes with a lot of liberties and lubrication. I still think of myself that way. I couldn't be greasier if I jumped in a deep fryer and started doing the backstroke.

40

It was just after midnight and I was waiting for Sandy down in the parking lot. She had asked me for a ride home that I knew would turn out to be a drink first and breakfast the next morning. Her car was on a hoist at the garage.

Sandy's office is downtown in a building that dates back to the turn of the last century and serves as a time capsule of old Toronto, as severe as the columns at the front door, as colourful as the light grey limestone walls. City Hall designated this four-storey cottage a historic landmark and protected it from development or renovation. It's like a pebble in the shoe of the skyscrapers that surround it, but the old building is fully updated, owing to the fact that it's home to one of Toronto's most prominent law firms.

At any time of day you need a digital passkey to get around anywhere. In a larger building you could go to the front desk and count on a security guard checking your credentials, giving you a long look, and then calling upstairs to have someone come down to buzz you through the various doors. No such luck after hours with this building. Trying to get in would be like knocking on the door of a well-maintained crypt. There's video surveillance but it's off-site. There's no old-timer doing crosswords at a front desk.

There was no waiting outside the building either. Construction crews had gutted the main arteries to repair the street-car tracks. Four lanes were down to two. No Parking and No Stopping signs lined every street in every direction for seven blocks in the downtown. I pulled up in a lot that was $4.50 for a half-hour all day and all night. It was an automated lot and you had to buy time at a machine with your credit card. I was staying in the Rusty Beemer, so I wasn't worried about any of the parking lot crew ticketing my car or having it towed. I didn't even mind waiting. With my job I had a lot to make up for. Small courtesies were a way to inch up to a break-even. I had called Sandy just as I pulled up into the lot down the street. The call went to voicemail. Messaged her. She replied quickly. *On the last page down in a minute.* She had a patient on the phone at this late hour. Someone in some sort of crisis.

If she could have told me, she would have told me that it was a player. If she could have told me, she would have told me that it was Mays. But she couldn't, of course. Matter of privilege and confidentiality. She could ask me and, a couple of days before, she did ask me what it was like to be a player and how I responded to stress. Stress on the ice and off. How others did too. I told her that some were dumb enough not to recognize a pressure situation and were probably better for it. I told her that others were smart enough to put themselves in the best possible position to succeed. And still others had all kinds of talent but melted like butter in a pan the first time the heat was turned up higher than room temperature. Some were nonchalant. Others conscientious. Me, I was in the middle of the pack, I guess.

She asked me if I knew any who were anxious. I told her there were lots of them. I played with two goaltenders who threw up before every game. I played with a tough guy in L.A. for about fifteen games, his entire career in the league, and on game day, as the hours leading up to the puck drop passed, he'd talk faster and faster, until in the ten minutes before we went out there, he was practically speaking in tongues. One guy I played with in Montreal, a centre with the security of a five-year deal, broke down like a little lost child when someone ripped off his shipment of sticks and he had to borrow mine. I saw the same thing at a lot of other stops with guys who were confidence distilled until something or someone disrupted their precious routines.

If she could have told me, she would have told me that she was asking all this because Billy Mays had sought her out after the grief counselling. He thought he was having anxiety attacks when his injury knocked him out of the lineup. Shortness of breath. Panic. Elevated heart rate. He even blacked out one time, out of the blue, and came to in a cold sweat. If she could have, she would have told me that Mays's dad told him that all of this would pass, just a phase, the mono thing, and saying anything about this to teams that were interviewing him would be the kiss of death. Said to not even tell his agent. But she couldn't tell me any of this. Matter of privilege and confidentiality.

I turned off the ignition of the Rusty Beemer and the rumble ceased. I put my head back on the rest and closed my eyes. If I had flown, I'd say it was jet lag, but his was fatigue from all the highway miles to Peterborough and back. I could see the front door of the building through one not-quite-closed eye. I heard nothing but my deep breath. Head tipping forward and then snapping straight up. I grabbed the wheel. Small bit of panic for me. I thought I had fallen asleep at the wheel on some sort of road trip.

Just at that moment I saw Sandy at the front door of her building. I looked down at my cell. Three missed calls. All hers. All in the last fifteen minutes. Somehow I had managed to turn the sound off. Some Explaining to Do. I opened my car door, but before I could set a foot on the pavement I saw a guy wearing a black track suit jump Sandy on the empty street. Someone who wasn't a cop's son would ask where the boys in blue are when you really need them. I broke out into a dead sprint, the car door swinging behind me. He wrestled her to the ground. I screamed a profanity and the guy looked up. I was close enough to see that he had a ski mask on. He took off. That made me relatively confident that he wasn't armed or any real physical threat in a mano-a-mano. Split-second intuitive call: I gave chase rather than attend to Sandy, who by my quick reckoning seemed roughed up but not life-threatened.

I have always hated running. Not that I wasn't good enough at it in short bursts. Just that I never worked at it, could never see it as exercise I wanted to do in workouts. My quads and glutes were designed for travel on the ice, not the sidewalk. And Arthur was an issue that made me completely disinclined to run. I made an exception here. I figured I had to catch him within a block or concede the race to this perp. Thankfully, if he had been a member of the high school track team he must have thrown a javelin. He ran down what had been a lane between two buildings a block away from Yonge Street. Bad move. Construction had turned it into a cul-de-sac.

I tackled him. A knife fell out of his hand when he went to break his fall. I aimed for the bull's eye, the point north of the mouth hole and south of the eye holes. Left hand. Blood gushed. I ripped off the ski mask.

Mays the Elder. He'd left his finishing kick at the Muskoka Triathlon.

I snapped his head again with a left hand. I must have been gassed by the sprint. I didn't quite knock him out. And he had one of those no-cartilage noses that just spreads rather than breaks, a design flaw his surgeon didn't consider. Even though he was thus physiologically equipped to have the shit kicked out of him, fear still registered. His grill was swelling up fast enough that his attempt to plea for mercy was a thick-tongued mumble. I held him up off the pavement with a handful of hair.

I considered my options. I was breathing hard.

I looked behind me. No one had seen the last leg of the chase. I dragged him into a doorway where we couldn't be seen from the street.

I had reached for my cell but realized it was on the passenger seat of the Rusty Beemer. There was no calling 911 even if I wanted to.

And then I realized that I didn't want to.

The first epiphany took two deep breaths.

There was always a whiff of something wrong about the Mayses. To my mind, anyway. Nice kid, problem father. Q: Was he going to kill Sandy because she knows his kid has some sort of problem emotionally, some sort of anxiety deal? No. That's the sort of thing that a team and an agent and a player would work through, especially with a kid as talented as Billy Mays Jr. It wouldn't have been motive enough. I wasn't sure what the motive was just yet, but I knew it had to be bigger stakes than that. That he was going to try to put the chill on Sandy was all the evidence I needed that he was the guy who broke into Sandy's office and trashed it. You wouldn't have been able to get a conviction on that one in any court, but my standards don't rise as high as reasonable doubt.

Two more deep breaths and another light bulb flashed.

Nobody knew that Mays had taken this run at Sandy. Not

even Sandy. I knew something that no one else did. The cops didn't know. Junior didn't know. And, more importantly for me, the other teams in the league didn't know.

Then there was Mr. Seven Keys himself. He knew only that I'd caught him in attempted assault, a sexual assault or something along those lines. But connecting him with the Peterborough murders was something that I could play dumb to. It wasn't hard. That was, after all, just a theory at this point. I could act as if I didn't know.

I improvised.

"Look, you bastard, I'd call the cops if I thought this would stick, but I know with all your money you'd beat any beef, even attempted murder. You're just a sick fuck who made the mistake of stalking my girlfriend. I don't want to drag her through this. And, yeah, I've had my trouble over the years. Some people might not think that I'm a credible witness. You could probably turn this around on me and I'd get hit with assault or something. You're going to make out a nice fat cheque to me and this will go away. No, make it cash. One-time payment. Six figures. After the draft. Our team likes your son—we don't have to like you, and if we're able, we're going to draft him. But you have nothing to do with him. Nothing from here on. One briefcase, a hundred grand, delivered. Clean. I could squeeze you for a regular payday but I don't want to fuck up our dealing with your son. So after that I don't want to see you in the arena or on the street. Do you hear me?"

He twitched and stiffened. For a split second I thought I had killed him. He was just trying to nod.

"This is how we're going to do it. After the draft, a week or so, I'm going to email you and ask you to buy me lunch. We go to lunch. You give me the suitcase. We're going to say that it's an advance on personal training that I'm doing with your son."

He was a little more lucid. His nod was a little stronger. I suspected this was a piece of business a lot like his regular working day. Maybe not even as dirty.

I let go of his hair and he slumped up against the back door of a Chinese restaurant. I dusted myself off, looked out to the street. No one passing. I walked back to where I'd left Sandy.

"BRAD," SANDY YELLED. "What happened? Are you all right?"

"You're asking me?"

Sandy was surrounded by cruisers and unmarked cars. Their flashing lights bathed the staid columns of the building behind her with a disco-worthy strobe.

"You're Brad Shade," a young officer with my father's brush-cut said.

He said it like it was an accusation that he could make stick. I gave him a simple "Yup." I wasn't going to start volunteering anything.

"Sandy, are you okay? You could have been killed."

"I tried calling you."

Oh boy, guilty without a good explanation.

"I fell asleep in the car."

"Your knees are out of your jeans," Brushcut said.

"I fell," I said. "I tried to tackle him but he got away."

"Did you get a look at him?"

"He had a ski mask on. Dark ski mask, black Nike outfit, and expensive running shoes. Reflective ones."

I turned to Sandy.

"You think it was one of your patients?" I asked. "I don't like the idea of you working with dangerous guys ..."

She had at least a couple of kids with violent, physical histories, not including me.

"I can't imagine that it's one of them," she said.

They took us to headquarters and walked us through the events. I took them on the route of the chase. I stuck with it as far as the lane, but at that point I had him going straight and getting as far as Yonge Street, which was packed with crowds coming out of the theatres and Gordon Lightfoot's show at Massey Hall.

"... And that's where I lost him," I said for the fourth time.

And no, no one had reason to go after Sandy because of me. I didn't owe anyone money. Of course the detectives doing the questioning knew about my financial troubles over the years.

Sandy was still trembling a full three hours after Mays had tried to snuff out her life and her knowledge of his son's calls to her.

They had our statements. Sandy told them everything she knew and was going to talk to them over the next few days. I told them everything I knew with one large, wholly intentional omission. They closed their notebooks and thanked us. It was the wee small hours. A rookie and an old bull gave us a ride around to the Rusty Beemer, which had a sixty-dollar ticket for illegal parking but thankfully hadn't been towed. They bade us farewell and good night. We could have used a stiff drink but everything was closed.

On the drive back to her place Sandy stared straight ahead. She was pissed.

"Is it because I went after him rather than staying with you? I thought I could catch him."

"No. It's just that I thought I was going to die and the last word I wanted to hear was my name, said softly. Lovingly. No one wants to go down and hear 'Let her go, motherfucker.'"

41

I now liked Mays the Elder for the murder of the Ol' Redhead and Bones. He had established a willingness and a readiness to kill. Still, there was the problem of motive. It wasn't an elephant in the room. It was a bedbug in the room. You could feel the bite but you had no idea where it was.

Of course, William Mays's mind had to be racing too. He'd tell Junior and the folks at the office that he had to go out of town on business and he'd hole up somewhere while the swelling of his face went down. Or maybe he'd call the cops and claim to have been jumped, robbed, and beaten up. That way he wouldn't have to go out of sight. That way he could get some medical attention and I suspected he needed it, even if just for the pain.

I was lucky on one count: I've always been easy to under-estimate. I was that way as a player. How was Gretz to know that I'd be able to find him just about every shift in the final? I was an annoying bastard on the ice but no coach behind the other bench factored me into his game plans in a big way. And that would be how Mays would look at me. He didn't know I was going to try to piece together his assault on Sandy and the Peterborough murders. And if it occurred to him that I might try, he was thinking that I wouldn't be smart enough to pull it off.

Mays figured he was the smartest guy in any room he walked into. Anyone in any room he walked into could learn from him. He had enough conceit to publish his line of self-help books and enough hubris to give Donald Trump a pep talk. We studied personality types in Crim 200. I didn't have to take my textbook out of the box in the closet to remember the stuff about personality and crime. There were two lines of antisocial behaviour: extroversion-introversion and stability-instability. William Mays was a classic case of the extreme extrovert, a guy who lapses without the ability or even the inclination to process his motives and actions. He was willing and able to take the *Seven Keys*™ to the absolute, to complete moral blindness.

There was no defensible reason to kill two people who were trying to save your son's life. It was just psychopathic behaviour. He had only suspicions that Junior had told Sandy something that was going to undo the Mayses' hockey dream. Or maybe that Junior had given up some dark family secret. To break into her office to try to find it, to assault her or even murder her, again, was psychopathic.

I was going to handle him with kid gloves from this point on. I'd do nothing to alarm him. I'd play to his conceit, his dream of his son being a player. I'd quote from *Seven Keys* and his other books. *Yes, Mr. Mays, we're going to draft Billy. Yes, we're going to sign him. Max deal. Best bonuses. Yup, in our lineup next year. You want it, you got it. That thing with Sandy? Grease my palm and bygones are bygones. After all, it's the game that matters.*

The Ol' Redhead, Bones, and Sandy had been in the unfortunate position of being potential obstacles in the way of William

Mays's dream, at least from where he stood. I had to be someone who was going to help his dream come true. I was going to tell him that Sandy and I had talked about Junior's sessions with her and Junior had spoken of him only in worshipful terms. That would take Sandy off his enemies list. That would make her an asset, and me too. And he was even going to talk about bringing in Sandy to help out with a spin-off line of *Seven Keys*™ books for kids. *Sure, Maysie, yeah after the draft, this summer let's talk about it. I'm sure she'd be game.* I was going to talk to him, on the phone, personal visits. I swear there were times that I thought he didn't even remember assaulting Sandy.

I was unsurprised that he was a hugely successful businessman. What made him a killer in investments and the corporate culture made him a killer in a literal sense.

I stared up at the ceiling while Sandy was lights out with the aid of a prescription. I played it out over and over again. No one could put William Mays right at the scene. He seemed to have no motive to go after the coach and the team doctor who had treated his son like gold. I tried to nod off. I couldn't. It was going to be a three-cups-of-coffee drive out to Peterborough the next day.

42

One hour. Two. Three. Madison sighed as he fast-forwarded through the sequences where no bodies passed through the frame, those many minutes during the game when we were putting on a show on the ice and most of the asses in the arena were planted on seats. He was a man of boundless good nature but finite patience.

We arrived at the post-game. As expected, the sequence opened with the crowd milling around as the fans made their way to the exits. They all bore a look of blissful contentedness, happy with their contribution to good works, utterly oblivious to the evil that lurked.

The crowd cleared and Hanratty and Bones walked through the frame to the office, closing the door behind them. There was no sound but I could almost hear the beers opening. I expected a cloud of cigar smoke to blow through the frame. It hadn't occurred to me that these were the last brews and stogies for the two men. Or at least I hadn't thought about their last manly pleasures. If they had been offered last requests, I suspect they might have opted for Scotch and a better cigar than the discount ones in Hanratty's humidor.

The video rolled, more of it in real time now. One by one the old-timers filed by. They dropped their bags and sticks in the hallway and ducked their heads in the doorway to say their goodbyes. Again, it would have been just as the Ol' Redhead and his sidekick would have wanted it.

Fast-forward. Pembleton went by. It wasn't a walk so much as a controlled stagger. He looked dishevelled but probably had at birth. Pembleton carried his suit in a garment bag over his shoulder and wore a ratty sweatshirt. He paused at the door a beat but then kept walking. Out the back door he went, where a bottle and a pack of smokes awaited. So too did a driver's seat that he'd fully reclined in a few minutes, a mile down the road.

Fast-forward. Harley Hackenbush, shooed away. No quotes from the Ol' Redhead in his story, but he'd expected as much. He shut his notepad, stuffed it in the back pocket of his overstuffed Dockers, and tilted his fedora back as he went out the back door.

"We don't see Harley as a likely candidate," Madison said.

"I don't think he'd have the strength to hit *himself* over the head with the cinder block that killed Red and the doctor," I said.

Fast-forward. Billy Mays and Valery Markov walking into view, Mays entering the office, Markov standing in the hallway looking down at his shoes. Not even a minute, a remarkably short time for the conversation as Junior remembered it, but there was no doubting him. Then again, how much time does it take to offer the assurance that everything would be just fine for the best player he had ever coached? Probably not much, nothing that you'd dress up with fudged anecdotes and old jokes. When Junior emerged, his dad and Markov were waiting for him. William Mays put the headlocks on the boys, Instantly

Reheating the Intimacy, seemingly to Markov's discomfort. The Mayses headed toward the front door and Markov exited the door to the parking lot.

I played dumb. "What did the Russian tell you? He didn't have a car. What would he have been doing out there?"

"His alibi's tight," Madison said. "When he finally came in, he told us that Billy Mays sent him around to get the car and pull it around front. Billy Mays vouched for him. The kid was signing autographs and posing for pictures out front of the arena when Markov pulled up. Markov wanted to take a bus to Toronto to catch up with a girl, some Russian. Billy dropped him at the bus station."

"There wouldn't be any buses that time of night."

"No, but there would be cabs. Markov took one. He had a big wad of cash and a driver from Ace Taxi told us the Russian kid was his best fare of the year. It all checks out."

"So at the estimated time of the coach's and doctor's departures the Russian was ..."

"Either in park, violating the town's idling bylaw, or watching a meter click on its way to triple digits but that's about it."

Fast-forward. Don Visicale and his two Goombas entered without knocking, not quite kicking the door down.

"Visicale's alibi is tight too," Madison said. "Italian restaurant."

"Had the veal," I said.

Madison wasn't going to let me one-up him. "And cannoli," he said. "At least that's what we were told by the Mountie who was tailing him."

When Visicale and his crew were making their exit, the Don reached back inside for handshakes with Hanratty and Bones. It seemed like good faith was in play, if not quite peace, love, and understanding. *Fast-forward.* William Mays Sr. He didn't knock. Instead he had his head down and pecked at his iPhone, holding it in his left hand and tapping it with his right index finger. He didn't look up when he pushed the release bar on the door to the lot with his right hand. It was the move of an oblivious nerd and graceful athlete. It was a stark contrast to the guy who'd clumsily spilled coffee on me when he went to shake my hand in the dressing room earlier that evening.

I asked Madison to stop the video when William Sr. reached the door. "The kid's sire," Madison said, presuming that I wasn't able to make him out. If only the detective knew that I'd beaten the shit out of him and extracted a promise of a six-figure payoff for my troubles and silence.

Madison didn't know what I was looking for. He couldn't have, really. He was focusing on those who went in and out of the coach's office. He was taking attendance. Likewise, he was counting heads and taking names of those who walked out the back door into the reserved and guarded parking lot. Again, he had been over all this. There was a scribbled list of names in some drawer of his desk.

I looked at Mays's hands. Other than his iPhone, they were empty. They hadn't been earlier in the evening.

Madison ran the video with a done-that-seen-this sense of boredom. *Fast-forward.* Arena workers, the broom crew, who at high speed looked like a bunch out of a Keystone Kops movie.

Several more innocuous passersby, none of them going out into the parking lot before the Ol' Redhead and Bones, none following them out soon after. The coach and the team doctor hadn't quite shut the lights out behind them but were the last out the door before meeting their maker. Fifty-two minutes in real time after they had gone out to the parking lot, the Broom Pusher looked both ways out the door and, safe in the knowledge that no one was looking, ducked out for a smoke. Madison hit the freeze-frame.

"We checked out this guy's story and we didn't like him as a suspect," Madison said. "There was a lot of blood all over the place. Whoever did the deed would have had a significant amount of blood on him."

"If it matters it splatters, as my father says," I rambled.

Madison let the video run on. Muzz the Broom Pusher was outside a scant twenty-something seconds, not time enough to commit the crime. He stumbled inside the door and looked both ways, this time in desperation. Soundlessly, on the screen, he shouted. One worker, then another, then another arrived, and one by one they ducked their heads outside. When they shut the door, they shared Muzz's stricken look and paralysis.

"A sorry commentary on the arena staff's preparedness, I guess," the detective said. "None of them tried to administer CPR or took any emergency measures."

"From the sounds of it, there wasn't much chance of resuscitating a guy with his grey matter spread out on the asphalt like so many toppings on a pizza."

"Like my father says, it couldn't have hurt," Madison said and coughed. "Sorry, punchline to an old joke."

I shrugged. Yeah, my father told that one too, the one about the guy who jumps ten storeys off a building and onto a street and one bystander tells another Samaritan to go get a glass of water ... oh well, no sense going there. It's not even funny at last call.

Madison stopped the video.

"That's it, really, what you saw before. I don't think there's anything you didn't see before, right?"

"Yeah, I guess," I said. "Do you have any other angles of that hallway?"

The detective took a deep breath. His video-side manner shifted. He was a little less patient this time.

"There are cameras all over the arena. We took the video from the ones outside the dressing rooms. We didn't see anything out of the ordinary. No confrontations, physical or otherwise. We saw Pembleton and the coach exchange dirty looks and that old reporter get brushed off, but really nothing suspicious at all."

"Is there video from another angle outside the visitors' dressing room?"

"There is, but like I say, we went through it frame by frame and didn't see anything suspicious. We checked out everyone who came out of the dressing rooms after the game."

"Can I see the video of the visitors' dressing room before the game?"

Deep breath and a roll of the eyes. If Madison didn't have someplace he had to go, he could have thought of one if given another ten seconds.

"The last thing, I promise," I said emptily. "Just the visitors' and just before the game."

Madison sorted through the other files and with a couple of clicks it was up on the monitor. The dignitaries. "We don't like the mayor for this," Madison said. He then went into a straight play-by-play without any enhancing detail. "The Mays kid and the Russian. Autograph seeker. Harry Bush. Trainer. The Mays kid's father ..."

Madison kept going but I didn't listen. I watched William Mays. He had his hands full: the coffee that he was soon going to splash over me, his iPhone, and the file he emerged from Hanratty's office with. People moved in and out of the frame at the door, and Madison kept reeling off names when he had them, saying just "a fan" or "a kid" or "a worker" when he didn't.

I watched the screen, waiting for the elder Mays to exit. When he did, he walked over to a row of trash cans. They had openings on all sides but were covered, probably so that people in the arena wouldn't overfill them and build a range of small mountains of refuse. Mays tossed in his coffee. He looked around. He tossed in the file. He straightened himself. Looking for coffee that had dripped on him, that was probably what he was doing. I could have assured him it was on me. And then he walked off.

43

I left headquarters. I got into the Rusty Beemer and drove over to O'Murphy's. It would be an hour before the waiters and bartenders checked in for the night shift. That made it just about the time that Beef would have been reporting for his staff dinner. Beef was a growing boy. He was the one I wanted to talk to.

When I walked in the door, the clock was ticking down to happy hour. Beef was sitting at the bar, the only single surface that could fully accommodate his cluster of orders. O'Murphy's had no tables for eight. Beef was gnawing at ribs and licking his fingers or perhaps counting them in case he'd accidentally bitten one off. He was crouched over his plate. I coughed loud enough for him to have heard but he didn't look up. A goaltender facing a penalty shot in overtime of game seven wouldn't have been more focused on the task at hand than Beef was on the spread before him.

"Gonna save me some?" I asked.

"Get your own, mister," he said and then he looked back over his shoulder. "You gonna get into trouble tonight?"

"Nah, I'm Mr. Brotherly Love."

"We're not that kinda place, mister."

"No, I mean, I'm here in peace, as a friend."

"When I need a friend I'll call a friend. When I need an accountant, well, I won't call you."

When his mouth wasn't full and he wasn't wearing out a knife and fork, Beef seemed distracted, as if the food were calling him. I tried to get him to focus.

"There's something I wanted to ask you about, something you mentioned to me at the gym the other day."

"What's that?"

"You talked about how hard Billy Mays trained. That the other guys weren't serious but he was."

"Yeah, that's right."

"I want you to tell me everything you know about that kid working out."

"Aw, mister, geez, I dunno, like what's to say?"

"I'll throw in twenty for a tip."

Beef's recall pro bono was meagre. Sufficiently compensated, though, he was like those guys who commit phone books to memory. Every last detail. The only difference was that Beef was skipping page to page. He'd forgotten nothing but had failed to organize anything. His recollections came out unsorted. Mays was wearing a team T-shirt. He had on two-hundred-dollar New Balances. He had Markov in tow. A couple of his teammates were fooling around on the bench. He heard a couple of guys talking about using creatine. The manager of the gym bawling out Beef for dropping his weights on the floor.

"He expects you to lay them down," Beef said. I told him that I'd check reviews of the gym online to see if this was a common complaint and tried as subtly as possible to get back to the matters at hand.

Beef restarted. Mays saying a couple of things in Russian but mostly showing Markov what they were going to do next in their routine. Mays shouting, "C'mon, c'mon, go, go." Couple of girls sitting at the front desk checking out Mays and Markov, winking at them and miming some sexually explicit stuff. Beef looked uncomfortable recounting this and didn't go into great detail, but I could use my imagination. Markov spotting Mays on the bench, the incline, and other stations. That seemed a normal safeguard given the shoulder injury Junior had suffered, one slip possibly threatening weeks and even months of rehab. Even with the light weights he was working with, one slip could set him back to square one or worse. Markov shouting at Junior in Russian. That was nothing out of the ordinary, I said to Beef.

"It was when he went to get the gym manager," Beef said.

"Why did he want him?"

"He was afraid for Mays."

"Why would he have been afraid for him?"

"He didn't look good."

"It's a workout. You're supposed to look worse the more you go on."

"Nah, it was way more serious than that. After going at it real hard on the leg press, he lost the weight, dropped it. Not that the manager gave him shit for that. I drop an eighty-pound dumbbell six inches and it's the end of the world, and he drops a stack of plates five feet and it's like thunder and the manager doesn't say anything to him."

I tried to massage Beef over to useful dope and away from his grievances with management.

"No big deal," I said. "He dropped a weight."

"Yeah, he was down on his knees, though. He really didn't look good."

"Go in any gym and you see a guy who maxes out and he's a puddle after."

"Mister, I been in gyms and I blacked out or went so hard my nose started to bleed. I seen it. I know what it looks like. This wasn't like that. Usually a couple of minutes and you catch your breath and your head clears up. You're back at it. Y'know, it feels good to be out there at the limit. This wasn't that. He didn't really come out of it. He was in a serious sweat, like he'd been out in the rain."

"Nothing unusual," I said.

"No, the thing is he only had a little sweat on him before he went down. It was like he broke out in that sweat when he was lying on the floor. It was real strange."

"So he got up ..."

"No, he didn't get up really. The Russian guy got the manager to come over and Mays was breathin' real hard, couldn't catch his breath. The manager wanted to call an ambulance. That doesn't happen at the gym every day. Mays started to barf but it was like dry heaves or something, nothing came out. The Russian kid wanted to get Mays's stuff out of his locker—Mays couldn't even tell him which one it was or what his combination was. I mean, he was out of it. And the manager wouldn't let the Russian kid get into the locker. Didn't trust him."

I wasn't too concerned about the recovery of Junior's wallet. Again, I tried to steer Beef on to useful stuff.

"So how did he get out of there?"

"One of the older guys took him. The manager said it was okay if Mays left his car in the lot. He gives anyone else shit if they don't move their cars out of there five minutes after they work out, but just 'cause he's a player ..."

"One of the older guys took him where?"

"Manager told him to take him to the hospital or at least get him to a doctor the next day. I think he was just covering his ass in case he was gonna get sued. If he was on the hook and Mays's career ended there, he could been on the hook for millions.

"Anyway, that was the last time I saw Mays at the gym and he wasn't at school for a couple of days."

"Maybe it was the flu. Fever breaking."

"Nah, he was fine five minutes before. He was pushing real weight. Fine in class that day. He didn't come down with the flu in the middle of a set of eight or anything."

"You hear anything more?"

"I heard him talking to other guys saying he was real, real tired. Pushed it so hard that he wasn't right all the next day. He said that the guy at emergency told him he should go for tests after something like that."

44

I knocked on the front door of the billets. Ma Storms answered. Pa was over her shoulder in a beat. He advised me that Superboy wasn't home. Billy was in and out during his high school exams. She invited me in anyway.

I sat on the couch. He sat in the easy chair. She hovered over us. Coffee. Coffee cake. She looked for ways to busy herself. He wanted to talk hockey and, yeah, about S. Everything about Junior was a celebration, everything about the ex an offering of condolences. I never imagined a Waitress-Slash-Actress and a Flashy Pro Jock ending up in a small town living a peaceful and seemingly uneventful life, but these two seemed thoroughly content. I guess my one and only shot at something like theirs had gone by the boards.

I asked them about their neighbourhood. They told me it was so safe that they never locked their doors. The Canadian Pastoral. I asked them about their house. He told me it was the home he had grown up in. In his family 130 years now. She said that she had grown up just a block over and that her sister still lived in the house. She added that so much about Peterborough had changed. They were Exhibits No. 1 and 1A to the contrary.

I almost felt guilty playing them, but a job is a job.

I asked about Junior. Strictly stuff I already knew. Well-trodden ground. They recounted stories of the son they never had.

"Four daughters, no sons, so each of the boys who comes in here is like a son to us. Billy more than any of the others," she said. Her smile was all the good times, her sigh the realization that at the end of the school year he was leaving home.

They talked about him to shoot down any questions about his character, questions that at this point didn't exist. I kept fishing.

"I guess you never have to worry about him coming in late," I said.

"Well, it is part of their life, when you get down to it, same as all the boys," she said. "When they have road games, trips out of town where they don't stay over, sometimes the boys don't get in until two, three in the morning. We're used to that. Normally we don't get up."

"I'm usually up watching a late movie or have fallen asleep on the couch," he said.

"They come in the side door. Their apartment is in the basement, so it's manageable. They try not to be noisy. Most are pretty considerate. Billy especially. Never had a problem."

"Never? I played—you could never say never about anybody."

"The only time was the other day, but it was hardly Billy's fault," she said. "Coach Hanratty picked him up at the hospital. I guess with a boy under eighteen, the hospital wasn't going to release him unless it was to a parent or guardian and, well, we're not that, so Billy called the coach, God rest his soul. They kept Billy a long time in the hospital that night."

"The coach said that he had a fainting spell," he said.

"So you talked to Red?"

"We did," she said. "He came back with Billy and our young Russian boy, who was at the hospital with Billy the whole time, waiting for the coach to get there."

He jumped back in. "Red told us to keep an eye on him overnight. Which we did, of course. Then the next day I drove him to get his tests. They said they didn't want him driving right away."

"The fainting," she said. "He would have been fine, but they just wanted to be extra safe for the next few days."

"The boy has been right as rain since his father picked up his prescription a few days after the whole thing."

My first thought: maybe not. I pieced together the timeline. Junior works out and crashes. He goes to the hospital. He ends up there for hours, though that might been because of delays or waiting to get blood work back. Still, the doctors in emergency don't release him except to Hanratty. He could have been right as rain and they wouldn't have let him go on his own because it's their policy with minors. But that doesn't square with the rest, Hanratty wanting them to eyeball the kid, Pa taking Junior for tests, Senior picking up a prescription. That and the fact that Bones II gave pills to take before the prescription was filled. That and what Beef told me he'd overheard at school. That and the fact that Hanratty and Bones had shut down Junior for training across the board. Not just weights but the bike, too.

"It's so strange, people blacking out and all," Pa said. "Our neighbour has had his issues."

"Harley Hackenbush?" I asked.

"Yeah, poor Harley. He had to give up covering the team because of his fainting spells. Originally they thought it was low blood sugar. Turned out to be mini-strokes."

"And one maxi-stroke," Ma piped up. "That's when he picked up his stutter."

"Yeah, one full-blown stroke on the team bus. Lucky that Doc McGarry was there. Saved his life and Coach Red did too. Red risked forfeiting a game to take the bus right to the hospital. Harley's really lost use of his right hand for all intents and purposes. He can't even sign his signature to cheques anymore, his hand is so shaky. And we end up shovelling his walk and cutting his grass even though we're so much older. They keep a defibrillator beside his desk at the office. It must be awful for him."

It was just awful enough to eliminate him as a murder suspect. If he couldn't sign his name, he couldn't have picked up a cinder block.

Hackenbush was off the list, though I'd never liked him for the crimes anyway. I made small talk. They said that they had to go to the Legion for a euchre tournament. I thanked them for their time. They got up to show me to the door. I made a point of leaving my clipboard behind. I was going to come back from that, probably at the point when Pa had both black bowers and the ace of spades.

I PARKED down the street. I pretended to be on my cellphone. I looked at the old folks' house in the rearview mirror. It was twenty minutes before they were out the door and into their car. I hoped they were off to the Legion, but it didn't much matter. Even if they were just going to the supermarket, they moved slowly enough that I'd have plenty of time to do a decent search. If someone asked, I was coming back for my clipboard. And I expected someone to ask because this was a Neighbourhood Watch block, even if it wasn't advertised as such. Something out of bounds had a better chance of escaping the notice of the security cameras at the arena than on the street where Ma and Pa Storms lived. Every other house had some cat lady or another species of biddy acting as living-room sentry.

I knocked on the front door to keep up appearances and then walked in. I didn't bother looking side to side. I knew I had to have been seen. I'd have to do a quick toss of the place, starting in the upstairs bathroom. The medicine cabinet was nothing but a dreary glimpse at what the future holds for us all. Pills bought over the counter for back pain, prescription anti-arthritics, drugs for an aching prostate just like Sarge had to take. One surprise: a jar of male-enhancement pills. Maybe old age had hidden pleasures, or could be just longings.

I took a run at the kitchen next. I thought Ma Storms might be charged with keeping tabs on Junior's prescriptions. Nothing on the counters and shelves. Nothing in the glass bowl on the kitchen table or the ceramic one on top of the refrigerator. It was an orderly kitchen, everything in its place. There was no way that a pillbox would have fallen behind a bag of flour or a can of soup. Not even five minutes had passed. I knew I was now on the clock. There was every chance that one of the neighbours had called local law enforcement to alert them to the fact that a stranger was on Rainy Road. I went down to the basement apartment.

It was as I expected, an incomplete mess. One bed made, one not. Clothes, the less expensive ones, were strewn on one side of the room but not the other. Shiny sweats in garish colours with indecipherable words emblazoned were scattered like phosphorescent throw rugs.

I checked the bedside tables. Markov's had a couple of Russian magazines on top, young celebs from Muscovite high society glaring out from their covers. Markov must have hoped that hockey would someday deliver him to that space or, better, deliver him one of the cover girls. I looked over to the table beside Mays's bed. Copies of *The Hockey News*, *Time*, *Newsweek*, and *Bloomberg Businessweek*. *Hockey News* I could get. Even *Businessweek*

I could get. There was probably some mention of Senior's company or an article hyping his motivational courses. But *Time* and *Newsweek* I couldn't figure out. Junior had to be the only self-respecting teenager who reads news weeklies. Maybe he started them in a doctor's office and brought them home to finish.

I checked the drawers of Junior's night table. Bingo. Three little brown plastic pill containers and one larger one, all with white caps. There was a snag, though. None of the containers were labelled. That was too curious to be kosher. Peterborough might be a throwback on every other count but the pharmacy had to be computerized. Even the local druggist would have labelled the scrips. There was a plain white paper bag, no scrip stapled to it. The drugs would have been from a chain store. One by one I opened up the plastic vials and put a pill from each in a Kleenex I pulled from a box on the night table.

I had what I wanted. I beat a retreat. I went back upstairs, grabbed my clipboard, and walked out the front door. I stopped on the sidewalk, leaned against the Rusty Beemer and speed-dialed Hunts. I didn't tell him what I was up to, just that I was in Peterborough doing a little background on Junior. I could have made the call on the road, but I did it on the sidewalk to keep up appearances. I didn't want to be seen making a quick getaway. I looked over my shoulder and saw a set of Venetian blinds snap shut.

45

I went to the L.A. database and looked up our team's physician. I phoned him. No answer. I messaged him.

> *Can you ID pills if I send them along? Analysis or something like that ...*

I didn't get a response for four hours. He must have just set out on the back nine. Finally I got a message back.

> *Why?*

I dialed his cell at that point and he picked up.

"Humour me," I said. "There are these four pills that this kid is taking and I want to know what they are."

"Are you thinking they're steroids or amphetamines?"

"I have an open mind about almost anything at this point except that I don't think they're for acne. The kid's complexion is like a bar of Ivory soap."

"What do they look like?"

"One little pink tablet, one little brown one, a bigger pink one, and a blue gel pill, sort of clearish."

"You don't have anything else to go on?"

"The kid passed out during a workout and they took him to the hospital."

"That's not a lot to go on."

"I did say, 'Humour me.'"

I heard him shout over his shoulder, "I'll be right there." I figured it had to be his designated driver.

"You can send them, but the little pink pill, wet your index finger and press on it a little and then press it against your tongue."

I did as instructed. It tasted like canary shit. I told him that and said I didn't think it was the right time to be playing practical jokes.

"No, no joke there, Bradley. It's strychnine."

"You're trying to poison me."

"No, it's a blood thinner. The player is taking a blood thinner."

I uttered a profanity and repeated it. I can't remember which one.

"The player has some sort of cardiac issue. Send me the pills if you want and I can probably piece it together for you."

"I might do that. I'm gonna see if my father knows someone from the force who does this sort of stuff. If I can't come up with anything, I'll let you know."

"You don't know how delighted I am to be your second choice," he said and then shouted, "Okay, okay, okay!" to his impatient ride. He hung up without a goodbye.

46

I didn't want to ask Sarge. I didn't want to compromise him in any way. I wanted to keep him out of it, but I needed him. I talked around it with him when we went out for a beer at the Merry Widow on a Monday afternoon. The junior season was over, but I had been making the rounds, catching our farm club in the playoffs go all the way to the finals and seeing if there were any minor-league journeymen who might be decent adds for next season. It was largely a time-wasting exercise. I didn't have a game to work that night and my reports for the draft were 99 percent complete. The one remaining percent was what I was working on at that moment. I tried to make it seem like I wasn't working. I offered up hypotheticals.

"If a guy was looking to figure out what a pill or two was, where could he go to get them analyzed?"

"University lab, I guess," he said, biting down on a chicken wing with suicide sauce.

He munched away. I looked at playoff highlights on a flat screen. I thought for a second I must be getting a load on, but then realized that another of Nick's TVs was in need of repair. I waited too long for a follow-up.

"Are you gonna ask me or not?" Sarge said.

"Ask what?"

"I don't know what it is, but you haven't invited me out for a beer on a Monday afternoon in your life and then you ask me about pills out of the thin blue sky. I don't know about the quality of the people you work with and work for, but, Jesus, you mustn't have to worry about being too obvious."

My distance from him, my line of work, and my intelligence. Sarge got off a three-punch combination. I didn't flinch.

"I'll explain it to you later."

"You can explain it to me now and pick up the tab."

I did both. I gave him the story with as many details as I had at the time. I told him I had concerns about Junior. I told him that there had been an incident. I told him that my job and Hunts's were riding on us not screwing up a first-round draft pick, a fourth overall pick to boot. I left out the bit about my inviting myself into Ma and Pa Storms's chateau and putting the wood to DDoris. That would have invited another heaping helping of shame.

"I'll just take it to my pharmacist."

"That's it?" I said.

"That's it. He'll do a favour for me. If you're straight with people they'll do you a favour. One. Just one. I don't suspect that I'll ever have to ask for another one from him. You don't have a pharmacist who'd do you a favour?"

"Sadly, no."

"You should be a little more sociable."

Sarge wasn't much on lectures but was willing to make an exception here. I drained my pint of Guinness and didn't savour it.

I WENT WITH Sarge to the small neighbourhood family pharmacy where he's done his business since he enrolled in the academy. The short-back-and-sides old guy in the white jacket and nicely knotted tie greeted Sarge. It was a good thing that the old guy was on and not one of his kids or younger assistants. It would have been much tougher to finesse a favour out of a less familiar figure. The limits of Sarge's sociability weren't going to be tested here.

"It's a little unofficial investigation," Sarge said. "We're wondering if you could ID these pills."

The pharmacist peered at them through his thick bifocals. "What do you know about the fellah who's taking them or who prescribed them?"

"Blank page," Sarge said.

"We think that one's a blood thinner."

The pharmacist did the same taste test. Same bird flew into his mouth and defecated. "Coumadin, blood thinner," he said. "So much for my coffee."

He walked into the back washroom, poured his takeout cup down the sink, and then rinsed his mouth out.

"I owe you a coffee," Sarge said.

"The guy who took these collapsed," I said.

Sarge gave me a dirty look. He thought I had quickened the pace too much to be sociable. It didn't matter, though. The old pharmacist went behind the back counter and moved around. Unseen drawers and containers were opened and shut. This was going to be less work than Sarge and I had anticipated. I'd envisioned that the samples would have to be sent away.

"This one is amiodarone," the pharmacist said. He pushed the big pill across the table.

"He had a lot more of those than the others," I told him.

"That would make sense," he said. "The fellah was probably on a higher dosage. This is a 200 mil, and at the start of treatment you'd take 400 or 600 mils daily. After that you'd drop down to one pill a day. I see a lot of scrips for this. The cardio clinic is next door."

"What's it for?" I asked.

"He'll get around to it," Sarge said.

"It regulates heart rhythm," the pharmacist said. "This one is a beta blocker, something that slows the heart rate down. The other lowers blood pressure, gives the left ventricle less resistance, as it were, just makes it easier to pump out blood. This is basically what you'd see for someone who has an arrhythmia—an irregular heartbeat. Co-morbidities might be heart enlargement or things along those lines. The blood thinner prevents clots if the blood flow isn't what it should be."

I didn't need just the standard product advisory. I needed to know how this was going to play out, what it would mean down the line for Junior, for the team that was looking to take him.

"So if you started out on these ..."

"You could feel very nauseated with the amiodarone, that's for sure."

"Even an athlete?"

"Even an athlete."

"What could you do if you started out on this stuff?"

"Bed rest would be best, but you'd have to take it easy until you were finished with the loading. Sometimes the heart kicks back into rhythm and it's a one-off. Could there be more to it than that? Sure, but I'm in no position to say."

"If he's an athlete, it might be a risky condition," I said.

"It might be anything," he said. He was tired of speculating. Sarge gave me a look. I had to ask, though.

"So it might be a problem for his athletic career going forward," I said. I offered it up. The old pharmacist hit it like a piñata.

"It might be a problem for his life going forward. It's a heart issue."

It was the best I could do without a doctor, probably a specialist, and the lab work. I could get a specialist. Our team doctor could refer me to one. The lab work was another issue. At that moment I knew that I had seen it from a distance. It had to be the file that William Mays Sr. carried out of Hanratty's office, that caused him to spill his coffee, that he dumped in the trash. What it contained was a question. One guy who knew the answer was the one who gave it to Senior that night and drew his last breath a few hours later. It had to be something less than a clean bill of health.

It sure as hell explained Hanratty's last words to Junior: *You'll go on to great things, hockey or not. You're part of this team even when you're not on the ice.* The kid thought Hanratty was saying farewell, like he had some sort of fatalistic foreknowledge. Nix. The Ol' Redhead was just trying to soften Junior's landing with the imminent end of his career. Bones and Hanratty probably didn't want to tell the kid on his own because Junior didn't turn eighteen until July. He was still a minor, and with something as major as a serious cardiac issue, a doctor and even a crusty old coach wouldn't have wanted to break the news to him without a parent present. And probably they'd have wanted to tell the father first so that he could figure out how to tell his son that it was game over and the first day of the rest of his life.

The file: Senior takes the file saying that he wants to break the news to Junior away from the arena. Or maybe he says that he wants to take the test results to a specialist for a second opinion. I'm leaning toward Door Number One. I liked the idea of

Senior telling the two old guys that he wanted to have a heart-to-heart with Junior about his heart.

Was Senior capable of a show of bogus compassion? Probably the only kind of compassion he was capable of.

47

"What more can you tell us?"

I winced. I had gone through the story of Mays's meds with our team doctor and a heart specialist who was a member at the same golf club and had never been to a hockey game in his life. They were on speakerphone. I had given them all the details, as much as I knew them. I had given them the files but I had blacked out Mays's name. That didn't matter to them, and it mattered to me to keep the circle as small as possible. The drugs as identified by the pharmacist. The sequence of events: Junior's collapse, his hospitalization, the ordering of tests, the shutdown from training, his complaints about nausea and fatigue.

"Everything but a smoking gun," the specialist said.

"Or a blood-stained cinder block," I said.

"What?" the specialist said.

I didn't explain. The whole deal seemed like too much of a coincidence for me. It smelled, no reeked, of cover-up for motive. But all we had was the kid being on these meds. Not a diagnosis.

"It could well be a single irregular episode," the specialist said. "The treatment seems aggressive, but maybe it's been effective."

Our team doctor chimed in. "Brad, I have the reports from the combine and I've shown them to Stan. It says the kid's heartbeat is regular. The blackout episode isn't noted. Not an arrhythmia. No mention of it. As for the drugs, no mention of them."

Yeah, I supposed that mention was in the file folder and in the trash.

"Brad, is there anything more you can tell us?"

"Let me think," I said. I felt like I was on the clock on *Jeopardy!* and had gone into brain lock. I thought back to my last medical. Back to the questions that I've been asked. They've all been pretty mundane. Drinking yeah, smoking no, drugs no. Going back, going through some unfortunate by-products of the magnetic force generated by sports celebrity, a pocketful of cash, and reasonable looks, I was asked about sexual activity. The problem was a treatable infectious condition. The truth was less than the interviewing doctor expected. He wanted a little vicarious entertainment, but the source was hardly hot- and cold-running women. It was something that I'd picked up from the mother of my child after she'd been on location with the junkie actor who took my place.

My mind raced but I was on a treadmill. I was getting nowhere. I thought again about that condition. I felt a little twist in my boxers. I thought that stress might have been causing the long-dormant condition to break out again. Maybe it was a late gift from DDoris. And I felt the existential dread that maybe, maybe, it was a condition I had regifted to Sandy. Thankfully, no, my boxers were just bunched up. As Sarge would say, my knickers were twisted.

DDoris. She talked about the way William Mays smothered

little Billy when she thought she deserved her husband's undivided attention. She talked about how William thought he should have had a career in hockey and that Peterborough had been an awful experience. It was DDoris who wanted and needed the smothering. I was off the treadmill.

"The kid's mom told me that his grandfather on the father's side died young," I said. "Bad heart."

The specialist waited a second to process this information. "Bad heart? Exactly what?"

"I don't know," I said.

"Well, that's interesting," the specialist said. I imagined him doing the physician's chin stroke on the other end. He sounded detached and bemused, as if he had been contemplating a crossword, One Across, five letters with the clue being *The stakes in l'affaire Billy Mays Jr.* and he had been given the first letter of *m*. If he cheated and looked it up he would have found the solution: *my job*. If One Down were six letters with the clue being *What an adverse diagnosis might explain in Peterborough,* he'd have been left puzzling over a couple of words until more letters came in. As it stood, the word could have been either *motive* or *murder*.

"I'm not worried about a hard and fast diagnosis, Doc," I said. "I just need to know what we're looking at on the scale, y'know, from the possible to the probable to the very likely."

The specialist took a deep breath, feeling the safety of not being held accountable or liable. I guess he needed that out of the way. In his day-to-day job he could take a wild stab when it came to putting the paddles to a guy's chest or doing an angioplasty or worse.

"Well, it has to be something, obviously, just taking the medication into consideration," the specialist said. "They're very strong drugs with significant side effects. They aren't prescribed loosely. Certainly with amiodarone, you don't want to keep anyone on it for any length of time as it can cause liver damage. So it's something. Was it a one-time cardiac incident? I'd put that in the possible category. With family history, though, it would take follow-up ..."

I tried to speed him along. "Let's say that there was a follow-up and the kid has been shut down, taken off all exercise," I said.

"That would be standard protocol even it were just a one-off," he said. "If you're asking me to spin the Wheel of Fortune, I'd say that given that this is a young athlete ..."

"A teenager," I said.

"Yes, a teenager, I'd be tempted to investigate hypertrophic cardiomyopathy," he said. He decided not to wait for me to ask to put it into layman's terms. "That's a thickening of the heart that would put him at significant risk of sudden death."

"Later in life?"

"At a young age actually," he said. "I've diagnosed several athletes here, a couple of basketball players in high school just in the last year, and I had to advise them to discontinue playing. I had to put them on beta blockers, and in the case of the one, an anti-arrhythmic med. And I've been approached by a couple of college football players, probably at an agent's request, to prescribe medication, these same beta blockers and anti-arrhythmics, so that they might clear testing. There are millions at stake."

"Same here, Doc," I said.

"Well, I really haven't treated any hockey players, but if those are the stakes, I'm sure that the specialists in your neck of the woods would get the same sort of requests from young athletes. I prescribed the medication to the young men who came to me, but I told them that they should not under any circumstances look at anything above and beyond light recreational exercise, no pushing the envelope. Did they take my advice? I'm not sure. My guess is one or both might not have. Just an athlete's stubbornness and a young man's sense of his immortality."

He was a heart specialist with not even a passing knowledge of hockey, but what he said about a player's headspace was a top-shelf one-timer.

"Is it correctible? Is there an operation?"

"There's treatment but there's no 'fix' per se," he said. "He might be looking at a pacemaker or an implantable cardioverter-defibrillator if he were considered at high risk."

I had the juice that I was looking for. The specialist offered up his Perfunctory Don't-Hold-Me-To-Its, saying in so many words that his opinion was based on incomplete information. I half-expected him to say that it would be accurate within 3 percent nineteen times out of twenty.

I offered my thanks and goodbyes. I suspected our team doctor would bill us and he'd be on the hook for lunch at the golf club.

I DIDN'T TELL the pharmacist, the team doctor, and the specialist that the meds I pulled out of Junior's basement apartment were in unmarked containers. I made sense of that off the hop. Junior didn't take his prescription to the pharmacy in Peterborough. His father did. And Senior brought it back. He could have bought or been given the containers there. He could have told them at the counter that his son was commuting back and forth between Peterborough and Toronto and wanted a stash at each stop.

It even occurred to me that Senior could have taken in the prescription and said it was his own. Same name, no one would have been the wiser. That would have headed off any small-town chatter. Peterborough is small enough that a pharmacist might have recognized Junior and wagged a tongue about his prescription. Or maybe it would have been someone standing in line behind him, eavesdropping when the pharmacist walked the kid through the particulars of his prescriptions.

If it had been anyone else, I could have put everything down to a father guarding his son's privacy. But that would have been the only time that Senior had taken the high road. He didn't strike me as the noble type. To protect Junior, he just had to pick up the drugs. To put them in unwrapped plastic wrappers wasn't protection but concealment. Senior didn't want his son to know anything more than he wanted him to. And if he didn't want his son to know, he sure as hell didn't want teams in the league to know. I suspected that if the son had known exactly what he was taking and why he was taking it, he wouldn't have kept it a secret, not from friends, not from teams in the league. I suspected that the father suspected the same thing. As much as I knew of the son, he made a point of taking the high road. He was too noble for what Senior saw as their own good.

48

The draft was a couple of weeks off. I made an appointment to meet up with Ollie Buckhold over coffee around his offices near the airport.

"I always thought life would be a helluva lot easier if my offices were *in* the airport and I just stayed at one of the hotels out here," he said. "I feel like I live nine months of the year out of my suitcase."

Ollie drank a double espresso. He had been up all night thinking about a defenceman for one of the Sunbelt teams. Ollie didn't say the name. He was mostly a model of discretion, especially when fear of a tampering charge might be involved. It didn't matter. I could read between the lines. He told me that he'd been up going over the notes for an arbitration case that was more than a month off. "It's coming like Christmas," he said. "We're at total impasse. I just don't see any way we can avoid it. It could be a landmark case."

Agents will never settle for fact when hype will do, but in this case Ollie wasn't blowing it up. An all-star defenceman with unrestricted free agency a season away and a one-year arbitration contract for what would likely be a league record number if his boy won. If the kid lost in arb, though, he'd make himself Ollie's ex-client. There'd be rival agents in the kid's ear the same day. Ollie wished a long-term deal would make it all go away.

"Cheer up, Ollie," I said. "You've got Mays coming in. The lord giveth what an arbitrator might take away."

Ollie's mood cheered. "Billy's a wonderful young man," he said.

"His father was a piece of work," I said. I wasn't going to dive deep on that, but I figured it would be disingenuous not to wade in up to my ankles.

"Mr. Mays is a genius in the business that he's in and he believes that his expertise can translate into the business of the league."

"Yeah, which makes your life so much easier."

Ollie smiled and let it drop.

"Look, I'm not telling you anything that you don't know when I say that we're very interested in Mays if he's there when our pick is up," I said.

"He might well be there."

"He might well be, but if things fall the way that we think he *will* be."

Ollie anticipated a question. It was a question that I had to ask, though not the most important one I was going to put to him.

"Brad, Billy would be delighted if he went number four to Los Angeles or higher if you're able to trade up," he said.

"My only concern, I mean, our only concern is his health."

"We'll send you his files. You have looked at the combine physical. He's on the road to complete recovery. It was a shame about the combine. He wished he could have done the testing.

He would have shown you that he's an absolute specimen, a very physically gifted young man."

"I've seen the results from the combine physical, but I'd like to bring Billy out to see our team doctor and to sit down with Hunts so we can get an idea of his comfort level with our franchise."

"Well, Brad, that's a bit of a problem. Billy's not visiting any teams. It's the family's request ..."

Which, of course, meant that it was Senior's demand. I can't imagine that a teenager would blow up an all-expenses-paid trip to L.A. for wining, dining, and the hope of chasing down a starlet. It would be like a ten-year-old turning down a day pass to Disneyland.

"... It's a blanket policy of theirs, Brad. No offence to L.A., but Mr. Mays wants Billy to focus on his studies. The family is willing to talk with GMs in meetings in Toronto if that would suit you. If you'd rather do it than have your boss come in, well, I'm sure that can be arranged."

Ollie wouldn't have been so sure if he'd been aware that I knew Senior had at least attempted to murder Sandy and probably succeeded with the Ol' Redhead and Bones. Ollie wouldn't have been so sure if he'd been aware that Senior was working on the presumption that he was buying my silence for a hundred grand.

"Yeah, I don't really see that happening," I said. "I mean, I liked Billy in our interview ..."

"The young man said that he really enjoyed that meeting."

"... but the stakes are big."

"I recognize that." What Ollie recognized was the fact that Hunts and everyone in our crew might be only a couple of paycheques and a filing of expenses away from job hunting. Ollie also recognized that there was no way that Hunts and anyone in our organization could force the issue. The no-visit policy might have been a ruse. The Mayses might have wanted to go to New York or had an understanding or even a handshake deal with Anderson and Co. Not visiting L.A. or other teams might have been a passive-aggressive hint to shop elsewhere.

Ollie said that he would forward a copy of Junior's personal medical file to our team doctor. All things equal, Ollie would have signed off on the kid making a trip to L.A., but Senior was a genius in the business he was in, and in this case his expertise did translate perfectly to the business of the league. Senior recognized that our club and others were in the position to ask politely for small considerations and that he was in the position to give us nothing at all.

I told Ollie I'd take him up on the offer of a look at Junior's medical file. I told him to forward it to me and I'd take it to a physician.

49

Ralphie was the only one of the Irregulars who walked into the Merry Widow in hospital blues. For a long time no one spoke to him. The Irregulars can be a judgmental lot—those who would be judged harshly are often the harshest judges of others. They presumed that Ralphie was a doctor and they had spent their lives avoiding doctors or anyone else who might tell them to cut down on their drinking or smoking or various other vices. They also maintained a twisted altruism, caring about the well-being of others despite their self-abuse. They thought it was inappropriate for a doctor to see patients when he was sweating out ten pints from the night before. Those patients might have been their loved ones.

Ralphie was not a doctor, though. He was a nurse. That explained why he'd been a week-on-week-off customer. When the Irregulars found this out they avoided him again, believing he was going to hit on them. Of course, the Merry Widow was officially the last place a gay man would look to cruise, but I guess the Irregulars believed that their good looks and winning personalities would prove irresistible to those of either gender. They thought they *still had it*. At least they did until Ralph showed them a picture of his grandchild, with his beautiful daughter and his knockout wife whose endowments rivalled DDoris's, all the more impressive given that they couldn't be store-bought on a nurse's wages. She had been a nurse too.

I showed the copy of Junior's file to Ralphie. I wasn't looking for a critical reading, just an objective one. I couldn't make out the handwriting.

"I see a lot worse every day," Ralphie said.

Ralphie pored over it, the last five years, and it was mostly mundane stuff.

"I was just interested in the last pages, really," I told him. I was afraid he was going to try to squeeze more than a pint out of the favour.

I suspected that there wouldn't be any entries indicating a cardiac episode in the weeks before the Ol' Redhead and Bones were snuffed. There weren't. There was no mention of amiodarone, beta blockers, and blood thinners. It wasn't just the omissions that set off alarms. The last page was a red-flag entry. A list of symptoms and complaints that would have prompted a right-minded doctor to shut down Junior. *Patient complaining of extreme fatigue, continued weight loss. Glands enlarged. Spleen enlarged. Recommending rest for a period of three months before re-evaluation.* That wasn't the red flag, though. The red flag was the name of the physician who had made the diagnosis. Bones II.

Teams reading this might not have put it together that Bones II, and not the late father, had made the entry. Even if they had been in the know they might not have been suspicious about eastern Ontario's foremost electrocardiologist taking a professional look at Billy Mays Jr. They would have presumed that Bones II was doing a favour for Senior, his former teammate.

But those who thought they were in the know were flying in the dark about the heart meds. The mono had to be cover for something a lot more serious. Hypertrophic cardiomyopathy would fall into that category.

"That's the last entry?"

"Yeah. Nothing before it with beta blockers or anything?"

Ralphie fanned back the pages. "Nothing," he said.

I thanked Ralphie.

He gave me a bit of unsolicited advice. "You know if you're taking Celebrex for Arthur there you shouldn't be drinking," he said. "Stomach bleeding."

50

I called Duke Avildsen. He was glad to get the call. He had been sitting on his mower for a couple of hours. He and his missus lived just beyond the tentacles of suburban sprawl, and their spread was the same one that he had bought with the proceeds of his first summer hockey camp for kids. He had spent the morning grooming the front yard, an expanse that was suitable for a game of Aussie rules football or two. My call spared him another hour or two in the hot sun.

I pulled up Duke's last reports on a bunch of Ontario league draft-eligibles, the second-tier prospects, the ones who were going to be around in the fourth or fifth or nether rounds. Duke didn't bother powering up his computer or looking at any notes. He knew the kids like they had been going to his hockey camp for three consecutive summers.

"Shadow, I might be wrong," he had said too many times to count. "It's just my opinion but at least it's an informed opinion."

That was all you could ask of a scout. Duke knew the limitations. No one could hope to always be right, though a lot who went around thinking that had a lower batting average than Duke did. He put the work in. He didn't just agree with what a scouting director like me would throw out there. He didn't listen to the opinions of other scouts in our department and take shelter under the roof of consensus.

"In that range I guess there are only five kids who turn my crank," he said. He rhymed them off. The first name he threw out there was a tall goaltender who was the backup in Ottawa. In Kingston it was a big defenceman from upstate New York who played like you'd suspect the son of a prison guard would. In St. Catharines it was a pie-faced left winger with marginal size but good hockey sense that had been acquired over three summers at Duke's hockey camp. In Sudbury it was a sometimes sleepy centre who could be good and bad not just game to game, not just shift to shift, but even over the span of a forty-second shift. And in Windsor it was a hard-rock winger who was no better than the fourth most talented forward in the lineup but had a history of making big plays in the biggest games.

"That's all I got, Shadow," Duke said. That has always been Duke's way. Other guys beat it to death and feel obliged to go through dozens of names and catalogue every aspect of their games. Information overload. Not Duke. It's just brass tacks. A hundred and fifty games and he had five names that we could look at when the first hundred or so names had been called out at the podium on the draft floor and posted on the big board.

I trusted Duke more than any other full-timer or part-timer on the staff and almost enough to take him into confidence on Billy Mays Jr., but I held back. I didn't want to involve him. I had to own this. Duke didn't piggyback on anything anyway. Still, I called Duke because I wanted to sound him out about the etiquette and scruples of his former minor-league teammate and long-time friend.

"The Carrot-top Bastard was a good man," Duke said. "Full of shit but honest."

"If Hanratty knew some kid was hurt or a problem, would he hush it up?" I asked.

"Why would he?"

"I don't know why he would. Maybe if he liked the kid and wanted him to get a shot, maybe ..."

"Naw, Shadow, that's a non-starter. If you asked him a question, he'd give you an answer. He wouldn't carry any kid's water. Or any agent's or anyone else's. Wouldn't protect anyone either."

"Would he tell some teams one thing and hold stuff back from another?"

Duke was trying to piece together a line of questioning that had come out of the blue. He could count to four and he knew that Junior was in play with our first pick.

"Red's first loyalty was too close to call," Duke said. "It was either to the game or to his job. He had too many friends and his business was too complicated to get in the position of someone known to play favourites. If he played favourites he knew he could get in a jam. He'd piss off guys and teams in the league that he might need a favour from or have to work with. It would be a mug's game, bound to piss somebody off every time."

"Could someone buy his silence about something?"

This might have thrown Duke for a loop. It was a loaded question. It cast aspersions on the character of another hockey man, one of Duke's contemporaries, one who had just passed over. I had to be direct.

"I'll tell you somethin', Shadow, there is, uh, *was* nothing that you could have bought Red's silence with. It's not that he didn't value money, just that he had all that he needed. If money mattered to him, he could have gone to the pros and made big bucks. He had his chances but he liked the life he had in Peterborough. I thought maybe he'd go when his wife died. For sure she was dead against leaving the small town. But by then he figured that he was too old to be a rookie coach with the big boys, and he was right."

I didn't completely buy the idea that Hanratty didn't care about money, not the way he sidled up to Don Visicale. Still, it would have been no use for Mays to try to buy off the Ol' Redhead and get him to hush up Junior's condition.

"Duke, I appreciate your time. I'm sorry about having to ask these questions about Hanratty. I guess I heard a bad rumour and I wouldn't want it to circulate. We didn't have this conversation."

"What conversation?"

We exchanged our goodbyes, and before I hung up I heard him turn on the ignition of his lawn mower.

51

How long could I sit on all this? Weeks, as it turned out. There was a lag time between the combine and the draft. Practically the whole month of June. I wasn't torn up about it. I knew what I wanted to do and I had a pretty good idea of how I was going to do it. How it had to be done. A killer was walking the streets. A killer was again on the cover of a business magazine the week the draft rolled around.

I occasionally thought about it. Maybe I got a long-distance look in my eyes when I went out to dinner with Sandy or drove a golf cart for her around the course or killed a couple of pints at the Merry Widow watching the playoffs with Sarge or sweated them out in the steam bath at the health club after a workout. I definitely thought about it when I took my piece out of Sarge's lock-up and went with him to the shooting range to work through a few clips, so I kept my eye and not just my licence. I took my piece home with me and kept it under my bed when Sandy was over, within reach on the bedside table when she wasn't. I almost had the goods on a perp who had killed twice and tried for the hat trick. Even with me smoothing him, getting inside his twisted hair-plugged head, William Mays still had more reason to take me out of the game than he had with the Ol' Redhead, Bones II, and Sandy.

Sarge, Sandy, and the others might have thought I was just running on a drained battery after travelling from Portland, Seattle, and Vancouver in the west to Moscow and Omsk in the east. I had lost count of how many changes in time zones I had been through all season. They had that right. I was punchy.

They might have thought I was out of sorts with all the specu-lation about Hunts's job and the L.A. staff. Grant Tomlin had racheted up his act, suggesting on-air that Hunts might not even make it to the draft. "My sources tell me that ownership in L.A. is considering a complete reboot in the front office," Tomlin said on his network hockey-panel gabfest. And it was undoubtedly true, given that Tomlin himself was in our owner's ear on a daily basis. There was plenty of chatter behind the scenes, none of it reassuring. Duke Avildsen told me that Anderson was telling his buddies in the trade that he was looking at real estate in L.A.

I had mixed emotions. I wasn't exactly in love with my job, but I didn't want to lose it and be perceived as a failure again. I sent on a couple of emails to William Mays. I kept the messages short and the words vague. I just wanted to remind him that I hadn't gone away. I imagined the flop sweat. He knew he was going to have to deal with me, though not the way he imagined, nothing like it. Someone else was going to have to deal with me first.

52

I put in a call to Bones II ten days before the draft. I got only as far as his receptionist. I left my name, number, and the message that I wanted to speak to him about Billy Mays's recovery from mono. He got back to me within the hour. Someone with a bum valve was just going to have to sit tight in the waiting room while important business was getting sorted out.

"Ollie Buckhold sent along Billy Mays's medical report and I've spoken to our team doctor," I said. "He told me that you were the doctor who told Billy to shut down his training. That's about the only thing I got clear. Really, I couldn't sort through what our team doctor was saying. Never can. When he says that he's going to put something in layman's terms, he thinks a layman is a second-year med student."

That got a laugh out of Bones II. It also appealed to his sense of superiority. Yeah, he'd play along as if this were an audition for his own afternoon medical-talk show.

"It would be my pleasure to answer any questions you might

have about Billy's condition," he said. "I have patients this afternoon but ..."

"I was wondering if you were going to be at the draft," I said.

It took him off guard. I tried to play it like I made a wild stab at it, like I didn't know that he and William Sr. were former teammates, former roommates, and stress-tested friends.

"I am," he said.

"Can we meet there? I don't need to tell you that our team has an intense interest in Billy, but we really have to cross every *t* and dot every *i*, if you know what I mean. I'd be more comfortable doing that in person."

I tried my best to pass for the guy who fell off the back of the turnip truck. It worked.

"I can do that," he said. He told me the Mayses and their entourage were staying at the Courtyard Marriott. He told me that they arrived on the Wednesday before the Friday-night draft. I told him that I was going to leave a message at the hotel. I hung up and then called the Courtyard posing as Eastern Ontario's Leading Cardiologist and asked to double-check my reservation. What Bones II told me was on the square.

53

I had work to do in the meantime. Madison and the Peterborough police had the eyewitness account of a Caliber speeding from the scene, Ontario plates but no numbers or letters for the licence plate. They didn't have a reason to suspect Mays the Elder on the basis of the information they had, but when questioning him they'd have asked for the name of the vehicle that he had driven to the arena that night. I worked on the assumption that he gave them the name and licence plate of a Jaguar or some other quarter-million on wheels that resided in his seven-car garage. It would have been a perfunctory question, and they'd have been satisfied with and even impressed by the answer. The answer fit the image he cultivated in the business press. They wouldn't have known to ask Junior about Senior's rides to the rink in rentals.

It was a chip shot. I figured with multiple rentals he opted for the same company and as often as not the same location. I figured it would have been "the anti-empathy" if he sent his assistant to look after his transportation needs. I figured he opted for something either close to home or to his offices. If the latter, he would find another opportunity to connect with one of those whom others would call "the little people." I made a few calls and had a few misses posing as the Motivational Guru. I hit the jackpot when I landed an Indian gent who patiently waited out my story at the Avis outfit hard by the food court in the downtown concourse.

"Mr. Mays, how are you?"

"I'm in a bit of trouble that you might be able to help me out with," I said. "I've misplaced a memory stick with some vital business information. It could be easily missed in a standard cleaning of a car, especially after very light use like I had that night. Can you check to see if anything turned up in a car that I rented back on St. Patrick's Day. I think it was a white Caliber. Don't ask me how I remember that."

I told him that I didn't have my Wizard number handy. He asked for my postal code. I had that, thanks to Central Scouting's database where the home addresses of the top draft prospects are posted for organizations looking to get in touch with the players and their families. It struck me that a Caliber wouldn't have been the high-end ride. Maybe the premium cars were all gone. Maybe he was avoiding ostentation as much as he could and that extended as far as his choice in rental cars, but no farther.

"Yes, Mr. Mays, it was a Caliber, white, but I don't see any reports of anything found in the car."

"Could you give me the licence plate number? I just want to check with the lost and found at the head office."

The Indian gent humoured me, though he believed I was just going up a blind alley.

"I'll also put in a request to locate the car for you so it can be checked."

"Please. A memory stick could fall down between the seats.

You'd be more likely to find a dime down there than to see a little black plastic thing when it's in a dark space with dark upholstery."

The Indian gent was sympathetic. Mays had driven a car that matched the one speeding from the scene. I guarantee that he didn't tell the police he drove a Caliber that night. He was going to be caught in a lie. The mileage in and mileage out was going to be the distance between his office and the arena and not a heck of a lot more. And when the forensic crew was through with the interior, blood matching the victims, something more than trace amounts, would show up on the driver's side floor and upholstery.

That was later though. I'd pass on all this information to Madison at the appropriate time. It wasn't the appropriate time yet.

54

I had made up my mind that we couldn't take Billy Mays Jr. I meditated on that thought and its potential consequences for the duration of the 9 A.M. flight from Toronto to L.A. on the Tuesday before the draft. For once I managed to nod off in economy, but don't mistake that for peace of mind and confidence. There was still some heavy lifting to do before the first round of the draft Friday night. DDoris was in my dream, but an announcement from the cockpit woke up me up and I couldn't remember a single detail.

55 _____

When I look at my playing days and my work with L.A., I think of a reading that I did in criminology class in my second and last year at Boston College. The reading was about cultural deviance theory. The theory holds that people in slums and projects act out on their isolation and poverty and that they struggle with and often fail to adapt to middle-class society. They can't handle *normal*. They enjoy trouble. They enjoy acting tough and acting out on angry impulses. They enjoy the sense of being smarter than everyone else in the room. They enjoy thrills. They enjoy hassling cops and any other authority figure. Fighting, drinking, drugs, gambling, rebelling: Those were the fabric of the gang subculture.

I got a B-plus in Crim 200. I felt like I knew a lot of it going in, having grown up as a cop's son. When the prof laid it out, it got me thinking that, well, a lot of that was me. And everyone I played with and against. And everyone else involved in the game. You might think that a player's life is anything but isolated, playing in front of thousands every night. But the fact is, in the game, whether it was playing junior or college or, especially, in the league, everyone is in a bubble, cut off from those who sit in the stands.

When we're in the league we're not average guys with average lives. Our normal is no one else's: What we do to each other on the ice would be criminal in any jurisdiction if it were to take place on the street. Even the cleanest bodycheck would be assault. We glory in fighting. We drink to celebrate. Some do drugs, a lot steroids, but I've known some big weed smokers. A lot of guys gamble up to the line of compulsion and beyond. And we rebel against coaches who push us when we aren't inclined to be pushed, which is always, or against GMs whom we're always suspicious of. A team is just a gang by another name, playing hard, partying hard, living hard. Some harder than most. Some unable to behave differently when they hang their skates up to dry or hang them up for good.

True, we're anything but deprived when we're pulling down millions. And we worked for our money in one sense—all the practices, the workouts, the price paid in games. But we feel like we're stealing it doing what we do. I know guys who made ten times as much as I did and ended up practically homeless because they spent like they were going to make the same money past their playing days. Like there's always a bank to rob.

It's a game in a criminal sense, players playing a game that's run on the owners who are stooges and the fans who are marks to pay the money they do to come to the arena. And we're not deprived of sex. Fact is, you might run out of tape but you'll never run out of ass.

If you played to some half-assed level, you are forever a player. You spent not just your youth but a good chunk of your adult life in the game, and all your values are shaped by the subculture, by peers and the like. A lot of scouts hang around the game because they'd be lost without it, like aging gang-bangers, career criminals who are less comfortable on the street than in the joint. I've never been above it all. Going to the draft in L.A. I was back in the game, and there's some sort of comfort to it. Unlike some, I had been on the outside. And the threat of being on the outside again was very real. When I looked down the Merry Widow's bar at the Irregulars in the days before the draft I thought: *That could be me and soon.* I could have been destined for banishment from the subculture of the pro game.

56

I left a message at the Courtyard Marriott for Bones II on the Wednesday of draft week, two days before the big show. He hadn't checked in yet. I asked the girl at the front desk to hand-deliver a message asking him to call me when he got in. I wasn't going to wait on it. I checked back every hour. Mid-afternoon he was in the house. He was neither friendly nor hostile. I tried to warm him up.

"I appreciate that it's a long flight and a long day and I'm sure Mr. Mays has a great evening planned for you," I said. "Why don't we just put it off until tomorrow? It can wait. It really won't take too much time, and I just want to check with my general manager to make sure that I'm asking the right questions."

He took this as a kind consideration. I was just making time. I was baiting the hook.

The next day I called him. It took a few tries. He slept in. He missed breakfast. I staked out the breakfast buffet at the Courtyard and kept a line of sight on the lobby. He didn't show until 11:30. I made a point of crossing paths with him near the front desk. I told him that I was at the hotel, talking with another prospect and his parents.

"Do you want to sit down now and we can look after this?"

"I wish I could but we have our last staff meeting this after-noon," I told him. "I don't want to get in the way of any plans you might have. Can we do it tomorrow? I don't want to inconven-ience you."

I saw the Mayses exiting the elevator. The boy had been out by the pool, the father sleeping it off. It must have been a hell of a night for the Great Man and his party and, as far as I could tell, it numbered up around three dozen. I beat a retreat before he picked me out of the crowd.

57

Friday. The third Friday of June. It had come down to this. The last stone to turn was Bones II. It had to be done like this. And it had to be done not just last but at the very last. Too soon and all the effort would be wasted.

I sat at the breakfast buffet at the Courtyard from dawn and staked out the guests coming and going, the passing parade of prospects and parents and friends. It's the same scene at every draft. The scouts eyeball the prospects and their mothers, who are usually pretty hot. The scouts use the excuse that you can get a good idea of projecting a kid's height down the line if his mother is tall. The players eyeball each other's sisters, who are definitely and almost exclusively hot. My own draft week at age eighteen when everyone lusted after the number one's sister and my first draft as a scout at forty I noticed the players less than their talented mares.

Friday, though, I looked only for Bones II. I found him early. He came down for breakfast at the buffet just before it closed. My ass was practically numb and my coffee room temperature at that point. I went over, said hello, and told him that if he didn't have plans we could talk at 2 P.M. I asked for his cellphone number and he gave it to me. He said he was expecting a quiet day spent by the pool. He said he and the Mayses had a round of golf planned at Torrey Pines on Saturday.

I took him at his word but I still staked out the hotel. Bones II spent a few hours by the pool eyeballing the other prospects' mothers. He was out there with the Mayses. Poor Junior, he was the colour of a sun-dried tomato. Bones II didn't tell him that one of the pills he was taking for his heart condition, amiodarone, made him photo-sensitive. A sunblock in the hundreds wasn't going to help him. Bones II and Senior just told him to sit in the shade before he came down with heatstroke.

Bones II was well into his daiquiris when he went upstairs for a nap. I called his room on the house phone at 1 P.M. I told him that I was held up and could be there at 2:30 at the earliest. He said it wasn't a problem. I delayed it twice more. He told me just to come up to his room and knock. I'm not sure that he had the strength to get up and I'd have bet against the odds of him making it to Torrey Pines the next day.

I knocked on his door at 3:45. I had fifteen minutes left to get over to our staff meeting. It was going to be fast but it had to be this way.

Bones II had a beer in his hand when he opened the door. As a doctor he should have known this was no way to get rehydrated and beer wasn't going to be strong enough to steady his nerves through my interrogation.

I closed the door behind me. He sprawled on his bed. I didn't bother sitting. I didn't bother easing into the conversation.

"I'm not worried about the mono, but I worry about any kid on heart meds. I'm sure the pharmacy has a record of who prescribed them and when."

"I don't know what you mean," he said.

I reached into my pocket and pulled out a Kleenex that held the pills I'd purloined from Junior's room at his billets. I put them on the night table so he could see them clearly enough through the radiant heat he was giving off.

"I know about the kid passing out and going to the hospital and going to your clinic. That's only the start of what I know. I suspect that it's the father who killed your father and Hanratty, though I'm not sure you're aware of that or suspect as much. For all I know you could be in on it. You don't strike me as that type."

"How did you come to these conclusions?" he asked. He figured being officious could defuse a ticking bomb.

"*How* doesn't matter to you. *How* is going to matter to the police and I figure the College of Physicians, who are going to pull all your papers and your parking privileges too. It all comes down to *what* and you know that this isn't a wild guess. I'm not going to tell you *how* and maybe not even all of *what*. I'm dealing with you on a need-to-know basis."

He couldn't speak. I didn't wait for him.

"I have no interest in taking you down. I can keep things in nice compartments. I'm not going to draft the kid. My team isn't going to draft the kid. But the father is going down and you might consider your options."

He took a big gulp. I thought I would have liked to play poker against him.

"Did you take money from him?" I asked.

"No."

I was relieved that he didn't ask me if I had. I kept going. I had momentum. He was turtling.

"Your father had the results of the tests from the hospital before you did. He knew the kid's heartbeat was irregular.

Either he or the doctors in emergency skedded the tests for him. Your father knew the results. So did you. So did the coach. You gave the kid samples that some drug salesman had left with you. You made out the prescription. You could keep a secret. Your father and the coach couldn't. They were going to tell teams. They were going to make it public. Not like they'd put it out in a press release, just that they'd tell other teams before the draft."

He said nothing. He denied nothing. He registered no indignation. That passed for confession in the circumstances.

"It's not my business to defend you but I'll offer you an out. You're going to be able to claim that a page out of Billy Mays Jr.'s file was missing, that it was taken out. Given that a murderer was handling them, that's not so far-fetched. Maybe you can fudge the timeline. I leave that to you, your lawyer, and the College of Physicians."

I let him take a breath.

"I know he offered you money," I said. "He wouldn't leave anything to friendship if money would close the deal. You have nothing in email correspondence about that, right? Nothing about the murders either."

His defences were shattered.

"There's nothing," he said. His eyes watered. "I never thought he'd kill ... he never said anything like that. And after he killed them, the stakes were all different. I didn't think he'd stop at anything. I was worried about my life. He had the money. He could get things done for him, get a professional rather than do it himself. And who could I go to who wouldn't believe I was in on it?"

"You could have made calls. He bought you with promises or threats. Doesn't matter to me. Maybe you didn't know your friend as well as you thought."

"You have to understand ..."

"I don't have to understand anything," I said.

"No, you have to understand," he said. "He hated Hanratty. Hated him. He said he would have played pro and been a star if Hanratty hadn't benched him and driven him out of junior hockey. His worst nightmare came true when Hanratty drafted his son, but it was going okay the whole time. Hanratty liked the son. He and my father thought they were saving Billy's life. Mays saw it that Hanratty was going to do to his son what he'd done to him twenty-five years before. That's the way he saw it but it wasn't the way it was."

"That explains why he did what he did. So why did you do what you did?"

"I didn't think I was going too far out of bounds. I thought we'd wait and see on Billy. I wouldn't put him at mortal risk, that's for sure. I just didn't want to jeopardize his chances in the draft if it was just a single incident with no chance of repeating."

"Which it wasn't."

"It was an enlargement ..."

"That was going to end his career," I said. I filled in the blank because the clock was ticking and I had to make it back to the meeting.

"Yes, based on what we know now, it was going to end his career," he said. "One hundred percent sure. Just too much risk. We could do follow-up, but I think that would have offered false hope."

"I'll make a bargain with you. You seem like someone I can trust. Mays seemed to think that and he knows you better than me. I won't mention this outside of this room, so long as you never mention to William Mays that we had this conversation. I don't think the police are going to need you to take him down. I can't do anything if he says you're in on it, but you've got time to figure that out and hope. If he knows you were meeting with me you can just tell him we talked about the mono thing."

"Right."

I figured I'd kick him while he was down before I made my exit. "How could you stand by when your own father was murdered?"

He looked away. "It's like all fathers and sons. It's complicated."

Bones II bowed his head and didn't say anything more. He looked pained and self-pitying. His father had supported him but only so far. His father attended to the medical needs of hundreds of players over the years and travelled with the team on nights he didn't have to. He liked the games, the bus rides, the beer, the cigars, and the company of the Ol' Redhead more than the time he spent with his son and the rest of the family. Bones was a better doctor than a father. When his son made it as far as the Peterborough team, he came up just short of his aspirations and his father's best friend's minimum standards.

Bones II became a much better doctor than his father in every way but one. Bones II would try to keep a secret when truth-telling was the right thing to do. He was a guy who, like me, would skip number 24. Which is okay, maybe ideal if you're a player or a PI, but not what you look for in a doctor.

I left the room.

58

Hockey Time is fifteen minutes early. Hockey Time isn't a negotiable option. It's a drop-dead proposition. Eight isn't 8:01. If the bus is leaving at eight, at 8:01 it's a speck on the horizon. The first pick of the draft was at 8 P.M. that Friday night. We were going to have our last war-room meeting in the late afternoon. We'd go over scenarios. What we might do in the event of Hunts making a deal on the floor, a deal that landed us a second first-round pick, probably in the twenties. It was unlikely to unfold that way but we had to be prepared for it. Hunts sent out the message that we'd meet in the lobby at 4 P.M. It was Double Super Hockey Time. I hustled out of the tense but brief session with Bones II and made it into the lobby with my laptop and notes at 3:59. I was the last one to arrive by twenty minutes.

We were staying at the Marriott like most of the clubs, but we couldn't book a room there for our last pre-draft meeting. Other teams had beaten us to every conference room in every time slot. We cabbed to the team's offices in the arena in twos and threes, fourteen of us on the staff and four of our part-time bird dogs who were sleeping two to a room. The part-timers had flown to L.A. on their own nickel with the hope that Hunts would see fit to bring them in full time. The poor deluded souls, they imagined that Hunts had a scouting budget to play with.

"After the meeting, we have to talk," I told Hunts in the cab ride over. "Five minutes. Just you and me."

I could see the pressure getting to Hunts, as out of the single request he sensed some sort of creeping conspiracy. "If you have a job lined up, tell me now," Hunts said, pissed off. "If you've talked to another team, let me know now and you don't have to go out on the floor tonight. You can turn around and walk back to the hotel."

"It's not anything like that, for fuck sake," I said.

I glanced back. The other guys on the staff were looking at us. Their antennae were twitching involuntarily, like they did any time it seemed that change was in the air. Change would have been opportunity for them to move up. Or change would have been reason to look elsewhere, as if I had been job hunting because I knew Hunts was going to be pink-slipped.

"All I need is five minutes before we go out on the floor," I said.

"What can take five minutes that you can't say in front of these guys? What do you wanna say that none of these guys can contribute to?"

This wasn't the place to start arguing the point. I drew on history.

"One guy once came to me, knocking on my door at 4 A.M. of the worst morning of his life, and I didn't ask him why he didn't take it up with the team."

Hunts didn't recognize himself immediately and we'd joke about it later. If I had to make it seem like I was in trouble, so be it. If I had to do that to stop him from putting his job on the line, so be it.

He sighed. My private audience with my best friend was booked, though he wasn't happy about it.

HUNTS PUT IN a request for a snack tray and coffee to be brought into the largest conference room in the team's offices. It might have sat ten comfortably, twelve in a crunch. We had to roll in chairs from surrounding offices. Crowded doesn't start to describe it. I couldn't have swivelled without my chair hitting another guy's legs. When someone spoke in the back of the room and everyone turned, it was like bumper cars.

The discussion sputtered to a mundane start. I stood at the erasable board. I drew up a vertical list, numbers one to thirty and beside them the teams that were picking in that slot in the first round. We went through the first three picks with lightning speed.

1 Galbraith
2 Dailey
3 Meyers

Nothing much to discuss. Back in mid-winter I liked Mays over Meyers and I would have fought for the point. Not on the third Friday of June, though. Other guys in the room debated the order, but I stayed out of it even though I was supposed to be managing it. They could have spent an hour talking about it but Hunts shut it down.

"Okay, if I knew we were going to sit around and toast marshmallows all day long, we coulda walked over to the park and started a campfire," Hunts said. "Shadow, put four up there. That's why we're here. Mays. We're all on board with that."

I tried my best to keep a poker face when I filled in the name in ink as pink as the Wonder Boy's cheeks.

4 Mays

I kept my back turned on the group and stared at the board. I pretended to be deep in thought while discussion ensued. I listened to them going back and forth. They knew that Hunts liked Mays. Liked him a lot. They were falling over themselves, trying to show that they liked him a lot, as much as Hunts, who might give them a promotion or at least spare them from the axe if he had to chop the scouting budget. They didn't discuss Mays so much as bid him up as if it were a cattle auction.

"Upside all-star."

"Upside franchise player, trophy winner."

"Potentially the best player to come out of the draft."

They kept at it for five minutes. Hunts took the back seat. I tried to be inconspicuous and would have liked to hide behind the lonely rubber plant by the window, but I wasn't about to get away easy.

"Shadow, you saw him more than the rest of us. He was your assignment. What do you have to say?"

I had a lot to say, but this wasn't the time or place.

I sat down and opened my computer. I went to the team's database. I called up my files. I counted the dates.

"Twelve views this season. He was the best player on the ice ten times. He was the best player on the Canadian team at the summer 18s ... best in his birth year. He's smart ... wins the league award for academics. He interviewed well at the combine. He did well in personal interviews. Spotless record off the ice ..."

"What next? You gonna tell us that he's a member of the glee club? What he has for breakfast? Favourite movie? Are you going to read from the team's media guide or tell us what you think of this kid?"

Hunts was a runt among goaltenders. He's maybe five foot ten. He found ways to compensate. He walked around the dressing room on his tiptoes to give the illusion of being at least a passable size. In the net he made any guy who skated too close to his crease look up his navel. His trademark wasn't a fast glove, a kick save, a sprawl across the net. What he did with his stick was criminal. One hard slash across the back of the knees took the skates out from a trespasser and usually left him writhing on the ice. Hunts led all goaltenders in penalty minutes because of a wicked stick and a fast mouth. Here in the dressing room he didn't have a stick, but he ran his mouth like he would have on the ice. He was out to humble me since I didn't come out with a strong opinion about Mays and because he suspected that I might have been talking to another team about a job, a violation of my contract, and, worse, betrayal of a friendship. "All that points to us taking Mays," I said without looking up.

I didn't lie. I just held back as much as I could.

"Well, thank you for that. The amateur scouting director has spoken. Thank you."

I tried to not get bothered but Hunts's yap got under my skin like a hypodermic needle. Deep breath. I reminded myself that it would all come out in good time.

I stood up and went back to the erasable board.

5

"Sorensen," I said.

"Not gonna come to that," Hunts said. "It's a four-deep draft. If Mays is gone at four we're taking one of those top three guys on the board. It's not that complicated, Shade."

He had never called me Shade, not even when we first met.

I hoped that the mood would change. It didn't. Hunts belittled me at every turn and the rest of the staff lapped it up. All the established scouts thought they had a shot at what looked like my soon-to-be-former post.

I sucked it up but it was a long ninety minutes until we wound down to a cluster of guys we expected to see when our third pick,

81

rolled around.

I logged each of the names in as we went. Our list had eighty-seven names on it. I would print it out and get it copied for each guy who'd be sitting at our table Friday night and Saturday. I wasn't about to send it as an email because, well, who knows? One of them might let it leak out. One of them might lose his computer, leaving it in a cab or on a bar or something. Someone from another organization might pinch it. It has been known to happen. It's bound to happen when you're working against guys who spent their entire lives playing with their elbows up, charter members of the same subculture.

THE OTHERS FILED out of the room with what they thought were knowing backwards glances over their shoulders. They figured that whatever it was that was going down was bad for me and good for them. Probably very bad for me and very good for their job prospects. Ultimate *schadenfreude*.

"So, Shade, what's this all about? You've got something to tell me ..."

"I had to do it this way."

"So who is it?"

"Mays."

"We've been through this. If the first three picks go the way it should—it will—then we're taking Mays. You were a little less sure of that in our meeting an hour ago but thanks for chipping in. Let's cut the shit. Who is it? Who is it you're going to work for? Not that I can blame you. No, because you're like me. You have no idea if your job is going to be here July first. It doesn't look that way, does it? Why wait? You ..."

He kept going on. He was wound up and unravelling like a ball of string. One recrimination after another. He had nothing to go on but his gut instincts, this time all wrong, and he was casting me as Judas, betraying the team and, worse, him.

"Back the fuck off. I'm not trying to protect my job. I'm trying to protect yours," I told him.

Left unstated was that by protecting his job I was protecting mine, but no matter.

"It's Mays," I said. "We can't take him."

Hunts rolled his eyes.

"It's done. We're taking him if he's there. If you had something to say you had a chance to say it in the meeting. You didn't have to wait till now."

"I couldn't say it in the meeting. I had to wait. I want only you to know. I have to do it this way. It's Mays. He's never going to play a game in the league."

"Maybe not this year, though I see him stepping right into the lineup in the fall."

"I'll bet my testicles that he won't play a single game in the league. Ever. He can't. It's medical."

"The shoulder has been checked," Hunts said impatiently, packing up his computer and notes, getting ready to head out the door.

"It's not his shoulder. It's his heart."

"What the kid has no problems with is his heart."

"You should ask a cardiologist for a second opinion."

Hunts stopped packing up. He couldn't get off the idea that I was questioning the kid figuratively rather than literally. He took a breath and tried to make sense of it all.

"The only reason I'm telling you this now is that I only found out the other day. I thought something was up ... something wasn't right about this all along, and I couldn't put it together."

Hunts leaned back in his chair. He was still skeptical.

"The kid didn't do his testing at the combine but nothing showed up on his physical. He got a green light."

"'Cept that his resting heart rate was in the low forties ..."

"Which means that he's as fit as an Ethiopian marathoner."

Hunts was proud of the reference, even though he couldn't have found Ethiopia on a map.

"I don't know any marathoners who take beta blockers before their combine physicals."

Hunts didn't say anything, but we had known each other almost twenty years, so he didn't have to. His look said: How the fuck do you know that?

"Something bugged me right from the point when Hanratty and Doc shut him down from off-ice training. His shoulder was on schedule in rehab, but even if it wasn't, why couldn't he ride the stationary bike? Had to have nothing to do with his shoulder. Had to be something else was up."

Hunts didn't say anything.

"The mono thing bugged me," I said. It was a messy, complicated deal, but this seemed to be a decent entry point. "They shut him down before they put out the word that he had mono. A week before. I didn't believe it."

"That's all covered in the medical reports from his agent."

"Yeah, it's on there that it's mono, but doesn't it strike you as strange that those reports are from Bones II?"

"Bones the father's not around to do the physical."

"But the old man wasn't his doctor of record. He had a GP in Toronto, the guy with the complete medical history. But he gets his physical from Bones II."

"Who just happens to be a big doctor, bigger than his father was," Hunts said. He sighed impatiently. "So we're going to pass up a possible franchise player—no, a likely franchise player—because you have suspicions."

"I got into the medicine cabinet at the billets' house," I said. "I saw the pills. The kid's on drugs to regulate his heart rate. I talked to a cardiologist, gave him the names and dosages of the pills, and he told me that they could keep him in regular rhythm for a while, enough to get through his physical at the combine—never mind that Bones II is overseeing the physicals at the combine. I don't know exactly how bad it is that this kid is taking heart meds. That they're not coming clean about it tells me that it's most likely to be a big deal."

Hunts leaned back in his seat.

"Jeezus."

"There's more. There's a lot more."

I told Hunts how William Mays had walked out of the Ol' Redhead's office with medical files that he disposed of. How he had tried to get at Sandy and probably planned to snuff her. How there was plenty of reason to suspect that he had broken into Sandy's office.

Hunts drank it in.

"You know all this how?"

Item by item. The break-in at Sandy's office. Mays assaulting Sandy. The beat-down and unmasking after the chase scene.

"If William Mays jumped Sandy, why wasn't he charged?"

"Because I didn't want him charged."

"He attacks your fuckin' girlfriend and you don't want him charged?"

"He's going to get his day in court. I don't just believe it, I know it. If the attack on Sandy is part of it, great. He's going to go away for the murders of Hanratty and Bones ..."

"What? You're fuckin' kidding me?"

"... so the assault on Sandy is something that I want to keep buried. I don't have everything on him, but I know where the police can get everything. But I wanted to wait until after the draft."

"What's the draft got to do with it?"

"It's about what we know and what others don't."

Hunts puzzled over this for a minute. I didn't wait for him to catch up.

"You asked me to sit on Billy Mays. I did. The more I sat on him, the more suspicious it all seemed. Some things didn't add up. Then a lot of things didn't add up, too many to be a coincidence. And then the more I sat on him, the clearer it seemed. They were conspiring to keep some sort of medical issue out of sight. A major medical issue. Not a normal sort of injury, because even if this kid was out a season it wouldn't fry millions. This had to be that big."

Hunts was taking it in. He was going from didn't-want-to-know to had-to-know-more. I still hadn't given him enough to trust the dope.

"Look, we might be done no matter what goes down," I said. "We could be dead men already. Fearless Leader might already have a handshake with Grant Tomlin or someone else for your job, and that means my job is fried like the breakfast buffet's bacon. We need to do something big to save our asses and I don't see any way of moving up. We've got to move off the fourth pick or we have to take someone other than Mays if he hasn't gone."

"It's worse than you think," Hunts said.

"Howz it get worse than this? We're in a dead heat with Getting Audited While You're Having Root Canal right now."

"No, I was out to dinner Wednesday night," he said. "Japanese place, high end ..."

"A boy from Morden, what did they have, trout sushi?"

"You might not be making jokes if you saw what I saw. I saw the guy who signs our cheques—maybe our last cheques—out having dinner with the kid and his father. Seems like Galvin wants Mays's old man to do some motivational speaking or something. He wants all the employees in his corporation to read his books. I told them that we were looking to take Billy Mays at number four. Galvin even invited the old man to come up to his box before the lights go up tonight. The father told him that he's gonna drop in but that he has to sit with his son and their family and friends at eight. For all I know he's in there right now."

"Okay, we've just inched ahead of Tax Work at the Dentist's Office."

"We're gonna get killed," he said, his head bowed down. Thank God there wasn't a bottle in the room or all those clean and sober years would have gone out the window. "We're gonna get buried by the reporters, by Grant Fuckin' Tomlin. He might be sitting as the GM at our table at the start of the second round the way we're going to get trashed. This is one helluva spot we're in. What are we gonna do?"

It was bad for all of us but me in particular. I had a stabbing feeling in my back: William Mays burying me to Galvin.

I had an idea. It wasn't going to guarantee our ongoing gainful employment. We could hope that it would buy us a few days' grace. I was never what you'd describe as a finesse player, but this time I showed a sleight of hand that would make Gretz green with envy.

59 _____

A season in scouting leaves you on your own for hundreds of hours at a time and with thousands, no make that tens of thousands, of miles behind you. You work unnoticed if not quite undercover. Fans in the stands know your team and might even know your name, but they don't recognize you. You work if not in the dark then with the house lights down. You're peripheral to the action. You're part of a team but always apart from it. You're low-profile. You're anonymous.

And then there's the draft, the last act of the league's season. Bright lights. Teams sitting at their tables on the arena floor. Television cameramen snaking through the narrow aisles between the tables. Some nights you feel like you're making a contribution to your team, like you're *making* it. A lot of nights you don't, knowing that the report won't factor in any decision and might even go completely unread. And then there's the draft, the weird spectacle where the famous GMs and big names are flanked by hockey's working stiffs, guys like me. It's not exactly our turn to shine. It's the one time that we're out in the daylight and held accountable.

The first three picks of the draft went as we mapped it out on the erasable board in the war room hours earlier. Vancouver selected Galbraith, the hometown hero. He was on billboards outside the team's arena before he had played a game or even signed a contract. Oakley was scooped by Minny. Meyers was going to Colorado. The head scout in Denver was an old Quebec league guy. If it had been close between Meyers and Mays at number three, then local knowledge tipped the balance.

I had said nothing over that stretch and just neatly ran a black magic marker through the names atop the list in front of me at our table. I tried to distract myself by thinking deep thoughts. *I'm in the afternoon of life like everyone on the floor of the draft. Like them, I'm just trying to believe that what I do is significant and not just a pitiful appendage to life's morning.*

Hunts had no time for deep thoughts. He had spent the last half-hour before the draft started and the first half-hour on the arena floor in a dead scramble. None of the teams were interested in letting us move into the top three slots. Hunts offered bundles of picks. First and second didn't get it done. First, second, and third didn't get it done. Even first, second, and next year's second didn't. No one was budging. Hunts then scrambled from table to table trying to trade down, trying to get someone to give us a useful player for the fourth overall. No dice.

I could tell he was steaming. He was steaming about the hand he'd been dealt: A lot of GMs could count on the support of their owners. It just happened that those GMs were with winning teams and their owners stayed out of hockey ops, one of those chicken-and-egg propositions with regard to cause and effect. He was steaming at me: Even if I had let him in on everything at breakfast I would have given him a better chance to talk to teams and float trades out there. He was thinking that I could have told him more as the stuff unfolded. He might have been right. Still, I had to close the circle with Bones II.

After Calgary's management team walked off the stage with their pick at number three, Meyers, the commissioner gave a wooden reading to the customary line:

"The fourth pick of the first round belongs to Los Angeles. Los Angeles, you're on the clock."

All our fans in their L.A. sweaters cheered.

Hunts was on the clock and in a flop sweat. It was 8:30 P.M. I called our runner over to our table. A runner is one of those kids, ten or twelve years old, who wears a team sweater that dangles down to his knees and runs notes and messages and paperwork from one table to another on the draft floor. It might be a note that has to be run from a team's table to the league overseers, to let them know that a trade is going to be announced. The runners are like pages in Parliament or Congress. I had always wondered how much those kids understood about the importance of the stuff they held in their grubby little hands. In Ottawa or Washington the stakes in those envelopes might be billions of dollars and lives. Here in L.A. it was just millions and our jobs.

I was hoping that our trusted runner would be a kid heading to a military school, a kid who would soon be heading off to science camp, or a kid who was spending every waking hour either playing hockey or committing to memory the names of every player in the league. No such luck. Our kid did not instill a lot of confidence. The twelve-year-old assigned to our table looked like he might skateboard from one table to another. His greasy hair fell in front of his eyes and down to his shoulders. He was less likely to address us as "sir" than "dude."

I handed the kid an envelope and he took off on a dead run.

He climbed over the boards and ran up a flight of stairs to the concourse; ran through an obstacle course of fans carrying hotdogs, popcorn, and beers; and made it to the elevator that went to the luxury suites. He went up to the 600 level, ran past a security guard who recognized him, and, flagging a little, knocked on the door of the owners' suite, which opened. He brushed past a bunch of D-list freeloaders and had to duck under a few pairs of silicone breasts to the front-row throne where our owner sat. He handed him the envelope and said, "Here, Dad."

At 6 P.M. I had walked the preadolescent slacker through what I wanted him to do. I had walked through the steeplechase course. I had slipped the security guards up in the 600 level a couple of double sawbucks to make sure he had safe, unimpeded passage. And I had driven home the message to the kid that he had to hand the envelope to his father personally, not to his third-and-counting stepmother, not to any of his geek elite. To his father only. And with the side that said URGENT—EMERGENCY facing up. I had told the kid to be insistent that his father get onto it right then and there.

Our owner opened the envelope. It carried a message that we couldn't have delivered sooner and wouldn't have trusted he'd read on his email. He might not have answered his cell. We needed the equivalent of draft-floor registered mail.

> Mr. Galvin,
>
>   Our scouting dept., headed by Brad Shade, has found out that Billy Mays Jr., the player we would have selected at number four, has major medical issues. Not just a shoulder injury, which is well known, but a problem that threatens his career and makes him too risky to take anywhere in the first round. We will be criticized by the media when we don't pick him. I want to let you know about this in advance. I would have told you about this

earlier, but Brad has spent the last few days confirming this and
we had to wait until this last hour to let you in on it.

Hunt

The kid ducked out momentarily as I'd instructed and dialed me on his cellphone. I had programmed in my number.

"Okay," he said, breathlessly.

"You did it?"

"I did. Gave him the envelope. He read URGENT and he opened it."

"Okay. Stay there. Wait."

At that point I nodded and we started to head up to the stage.

60

"This is way outside the box. A terrible pick for L.A. I have no idea what Hunt is thinking with that pick. Billy Mays Jr. isn't just going to be a great player, but he's a kid with star quality. He's not just a player who might have put Los Angeles into the league elite two or three years from now, but he'd probably get this team a profile in a competitive sports market where the team struggles to sell tickets. How you pass up a talent like that ..."

Grant Tomlin was in high dudgeon and thrilled. We looked up at the Jumbotron and could see him jumping out of his seat on the network's set, pounding the desk. His diatribe would have played out on the owner's wide screen up in the box but he was shouting loud enough to be heard unamplified all the way up in the rafters. He was shovelling dirt onto Hunts's casket and, by extension, mine.

"... Gord, you got to wonder about who's running the show with that team ..."

Hunts and I exchanged looks. Hunts had bought into my story 99 and 44/100 percent sure of the dope on Billy Mays Jr.

Tomlin's verbal beat-down was enough to make the .56 percent leave him trembling. The disbelieving looks of everyone at the L.A. table couldn't have helped. Even they were sure Hunts was going to call out Mays's name when he stood at the mike.

"... Gord, there are teams that don't have this Swedish kid in the top ten ..."

We were back at the L.A. table and, yes, Stefan Sorensen, Stockholm's own Andrew Ridgely, was sitting between Hunts and me, looking stunned. Sorensen looked uncomfortable in his L.A. sweater—it was a generic one, no name across the back, and we were keeping one that had Mays stitched above the number one in a box out of view. Poor Sorensen. I looked at him and thought he'd look so much better in a Choose Life T-shirt. At that point my phone rang again. It was the voice of our errand boy, our runner, a kid who was never asked to be patient.

"Can I come down, now?"

"Stay there," I told him. If it had been another kid, I could have paid him to carry out the task and been confident he'd follow through. How do you buy the commitment of a twelve-year-old who carries a platinum card? Thankfully the back end of his duties were not quite as time-sensitive.

New York was on the clock.

"... Gord, I'll be shocked, shocked if New York goes with anyone other than Billy Mays Jr. I have it on good authority that they were trying to move up into the top four to secure a chance to take him ..."

This was in direct conflict with the facts. Hunts had spent fifteen minutes at the New York table pitching a trade of our pick, number four, for New York's first, number five, and their second, number thirty-five. Just a small consideration. And I had overheard Anderson make his case to pull the trigger on the trade. The conversation on the flopped picks went nowhere.

Number thirty-five was a non-starter. New York's hard-assed GM didn't even offer number sixty-five. He must have been in cigar withdrawal to let a sweetheart deal like that slip by. He hadn't even offered a pick from next year's draft—sort of like putting the deal on a line of credit. It wouldn't have flown anyway. Hunts wasn't about to make a trade for a pick that would be exercised by his successor as L.A.'s GM.

The New York staff followed draft etiquette. They waited until our staff had made it back to our table before heading up to the stage. When they did go, though, it was in something close to a dead sprint. They couldn't believe their luck. In the first round general managers usually announce the first picks, a little face time for some healthy egos, a chance to remind their owners who's in charge. On this occasion, however, the New York GM didn't exercise his honours. Frankly, he never thought much of the draft and never had seen Billy Mays Jr. He must have been still stinging from a small embarrassment from the year before when, standing at the podium, he had looked at the mike and forgotten the name of the kid they'd end up selecting. This time he had delegated the task to the guy who'd given him the face-saving cue: Anderson.

"We would like to thank Los Angeles for putting on such a great event this year and for their generosity ..."

Normally that pre-pick patter is supposed to repel booing, but Anderson wasn't delivering the line to the fans but rather us sitting at the L.A. table. We were directly in front of the podium. He smirked at me and seemed to laugh at our pick, who by his reckoning had no future as a hockey player but possibly one as a male model.

"... New York is pleased and proud to select from Peterborough of the Ontario league Billy Mays Jr."

At that point almost an entire section of seats, maybe upwards of two hundred, went to their feet and cheered in full throat. Theirs was the largest delegation at this convention. Mays was dead centre, befitting the nucleus of the gathering. His father was on one side of him, DDoris and Ollie Buckhold on the other. The father was smiling with his usual self-satisfaction. DDoris wrapped Ollie in a hug that was more meaningful than her son, her ex-husband, her husband of the moment, and everyone in the business could have known.

It was handshakes, hugs, and air kisses all around. Mays the Elder had brought along a troupe large enough to stage a Billy Jr. edition of A&E's *Biography*. His atom, peewee, and bantam coaches were among them. His teammates from his minor midget team were in one row, from the Peterborough juniors in another, though Markov couldn't attend because of an expired visa.

Billy survived the gauntlet of handshakes, high fives, hugs, and kisses from those whose plane tickets and tabs were being picked up by William Sr. and Buckhold. Onstage, Anderson and the New York execs awaited his arrival. The applause didn't let up when he got on the stage and ran a second more select gauntlet of well-wishers, those who were going to soon be telling reporters that they had landed a franchise player, a natural from a great family, a young player made of all the right stuff. For Anderson and Co. this was, they believed, a Pick They Could Dine Out On. On the Jumbotron, Grant Tomlin was in rapture.

I had prepped a message on my BlackBerry. I had risked repetitive-stress syndrome in cobbling it together an hour earlier that day. My right thumb was throbbing. It read:

Maddy,

Go to the Avis rental desk in the basement of the Bay at Yonge and Bloor. You'll find that William Mays Sr. rented a car on the night of the Hanratty murder, a Caliber that matches the one seen speeding from the arena. I suspect that there'd be splattered blood and maybe some dust that survived several vacuumings and would match the cinder block. I'm sure that Mays told you that he was driving his Mercedes or another out of his fleet that night, but the parking lot attendant didn't remember any car that would have matched his. And the attendant would have remembered any high-end car from his rounds checking tickets.

Mays killed Hanratty and the doctor to cover up the fact that his son had a medical condition that would prevent him from playing as a pro. I suspect that it was even payback for Hanratty cutting short Mays's own career. You'll find that the old doctor's medical filing cabinet will have files on all the Peterborough players, with the exception of Billy Mays Jr. If you look at the security video from the night of (approximately 7 P.M.), you'll see that Mays left the coach's office carrying a file that matches those in the doctor's cabinet, but later that night he didn't have it. That shows in other videos. It washes with my recollection too. Before the game he used the file to write out his name, #, and email for me, and after the game he gave me a handshake and a hug, empty-handed. (Trust me on that one: I felt sorta uncomfortable with this rushed bromance.) I have reason to suspect that the doctor's son knew about the cover-up, or the plans to cover up anyway. He's likely made a large deposit recently that can be tracked back to William Mays Sr. I think you might be able to get him to flip on Mays with a bit of sweating on a conspiracy-murder rap.

Billy Mays Jr. shed his suit jacket and donned a New York sweater for the first and I suspected just about the last time.

I hit Send.

IT LANDED in Madison's personal account seconds later. I didn't think it would be a good idea to have sent it to him through the official police lines. I didn't want to go in the front door and have to answer a bunch of questions. Or have Madison have to either ask or answer them himself.

I bcc'd Harley Hackenbush. No harm throwing a bit of a scoop to the guy sinking in the newsroom. I used to read him in *The Hockey News*. I still had that yellowing signed copy of *Tough Guys of Hockey* in a box with my textbooks from B.C. It was a signature he could spend his life trying and failing to re-create.

Anderson led Billy Mays to the New York table. Like I said, our table was next to New York's and I had my back turned to it. Anderson brushed the back of my chair. I ignored him even though Hunts flashed me a look. I turned around. Mays recognized me but didn't have time to acknowledge it. Again, he was caught up in a swirl of congratulations. New York's media-relations guy was giving him the details of a promotional trip to Manhattan, where he could meet the media and do videos for the team and the league.

I turned around and gave Anderson a nudge. "Andy, right there is a real heart-and-soul player," I said and winked. Anderson went from smug to puzzled in a split second. It all had seemed easy just a couple of minutes before. The thought was only now penetrating the many layers of conceit: It seemed too easy. It's never that easy. I could read the question on his scarred grill: Why had Hunts come to the New York table looking to flog the number four pick? We knew something he didn't.

He had company, of course. Hunts and I knew something that no one else at our table did. No one else in the league. For that matter, no one in law enforcement either, unless Madison had already opened his email.

I called Skater Boy up in the owner's box.

"Okay, give the second one to him."

"Okay."

The kid handed his father the second envelope.

> Mr. Galvin,
>
> Per my first message, we also know that William Mays Sr. is being investigated by police for the murder of the Peterborough coach and the team doctor in connection with a conspiracy to cover up his son's condition.
>
> Hunt

"Per" was my idea.

61

We didn't celebrate after the last pick of the first round Friday night and the adjournment until Saturday morning. Hunts's plan was to bring the scouting staff back to his suite for a couple of beers to steady our nerves and for a post-mortem on the twenty-nine other picks in the first round. Hunts had set up an erasable board in the living room and I stood by it listing the thirty names as they were called in the left-hand column and the top twenty as-yet-unclaimed players on our list on the right side. Hunts was mostly talking to himself at the start. Not a mumble, not a murmured laugh, nothing from the rest of the gathering.

Duke Avildsen was unelected but spoke for the group.

"What just happened?"

"We found out something," Hunts said. "If we're right, and I believe we're right, we saved ourselves a wasted pick and a lot of grief and maybe, just maybe, our jobs. That's all I have to say about it. It will come out eventually. Let's just say that I can't say."

I was facing the erasable board with my back turned to Hunts and the scouts. I did my best to stay deadpan and Hunts did his best to conduct the meeting, but after twenty-five minutes he declared it a night. He called for all of us to report back to his suite at 7 A.M. Effectively a curfew called by a guy whose early mornings were just one way he kept his life on the rails.

62

I had never worried about Hunts falling off the wagon, but when we went our separate ways that night, I thought that he might need a quart to settle his nerves. I had a notion to go out on patrol on the Strip and duck my head into his old haunts from his wet days. Many have lapsed for less. Hunts managed to stay in the pocket that Friday night, but Saturday morning he still had a hangover. It wasn't the sweats or anything like that. It was Hunts's 56/100th Percent Uncertainty that was banging like a bass drum in rhythm with the vein on his temple. The vein swelled when his jaw was clenched hard, like it had been for a week after his last drink and like it was when he started to get a read on the fall-out from our choosing Sorensen over Mays.

Hunts was a piñata for the league's chattering classes. The *Times* top sports columnist was no fan of the game. Since I went to L.A. as a rookie I had never seen him in the flesh. Supposedly he timed his visits to our games to coincide with full solar eclipses. That didn't stop him from weighing in on our GM. For such occasions he saved His Premium Outrage and Vitriol.

Hunt inherited a position and has never shaken the interim tag.
Nor should he. His mishandling of his team's first-round pick,
a consensus dropped ball, has surely guaranteed his ticket out of
town ...

The column cited many unnamed executives and scouts calling into question Hunts's call on Sorensen. The columnist didn't have any sources in the league. He did have three zealous interns who worked the floor at the draft and sent files to him and called him at his home in Newport Beach. I even suspected that one or two of the unnamed scouts were members of our own staff—one of the interns stopped me for comment and I tried to talk up Sorensen without saying anything about Mays. My quotes ended up being not quite racy enough to make the column. The one expert who was willing to attach his name to an opinion about our first-round pick was, yes, Grant Tomlin.

"I've said all along that I thought Mays was no worse than the second-best player in the draft. I can't even start to comprehend what L.A. was doing with Sorensen. He wasn't even good enough to play for the Swedish under-18 team ten months ago. Has he improved? Yes. Is he Billy Mays Jr.? Not even close. First-round draft picks are valuable assets. You can't just waste them. L.A.'s poor draft record is a major reason why they've struggled. Until they get that right, this franchise is adrift and it falls at the feet of Hunt."

63

I got a text message from Lanny.

The gurls at the gym say you blew the pick. What happened?

I texted back.

Tell them 2 put it in writing and u save it 2 show them later.

64

The second day of the draft started at 11 A.M. Saturday. We were on the clock with our second-round pick when my phone vibrated. Incoming call, 705 area code. I recognized it as Detective Madison's number. I messaged him. *Back 2 U ASAP.* We ended up taking a little kid out of the Quebec league, a smart, skilled kid, a very nice skater, but (and you knew there would be a but) undersized. He wasn't physically mature. His father was a decent size, so I held out some hope that he'd grow a bit. In the third round we took a lanky goaltender from just down the road from Morden, Hunts's hometown. In the fourth, at Duke Avildsen's urging, we took Markov.

"Can't see the point of taking some eager untalented kid over him, and besides, the Mays kid liked him," Duke said. All true. A roll of the dice, but then everything is a roll of the dice on day two.

After round four I figured I couldn't keep Maddy waiting any longer. I went for what looked like a bathroom break. I went below the stands and out a side door to get better reception and privacy. I took a deep breath. There were going to be questions.

"Maddy, Brad Shade here."

"Interesting message," he said.

"It's all good."

"Is that all there is?"

"There's something more, but I'll have to come in to talk to you about it."

Dead air.

"I'm heading back tomorrow afternoon."

More dead air.

"I can move my flight up to the red-eye, I guess."

We ended up having a long, involved conversation. I told him a lot of things. What he needed to know. I left some things out. What he was better off not knowing. What I was better off with him not knowing.

65

It was the second week of July. I was sitting in the Merry Widow, nursing one, waiting for Nick to finish changing a keg so that I could get an update on our baseball roto league standings. Polo was at the bar. He didn't pick a team. He couldn't find enough Czech players.

Hunts messaged me: *Have u seen it?*

I messaged back. *Yeah. One for the good guys.*

It had been all over the late-night news and sportscasts. The boys picked up Senior and he was going to appear in court in an hour or so to be formally charged with the murder of the Ol' Redhead and Bones. The morning paper had it splashed across the front page. A headshot of the Beloved Mentor of Men before that shot that split his head in two. A pic of Mays from a charity event in Peterborough alongside his son.

"... junior hockey star Billy Mays Jr., a first-round draft pick of New York ..."

The newspaper had only the sketchiest details. From the outside no one could have made sense of it—the father of a future millionaire killing the coach who had made his son. He seemed to have every reason to thank him rather than kill him. He should have felt a debt, not held a grudge. On the surface it made no sense to anyone except the detectives in Peterborough, Hunts, and me.

I messaged again before Hunts could reply. *Dominos falling. Give it a few days.*

Hunts knew those dominos about as well as I did. William Mays Sr. was dead to rights on a double murder. Bones II was going to be implicated. He wouldn't be charged with the murders but he'd have his ticket punched as an accessory and he'd make a deal, giving the cops Mays's motive, giving the Ontario College of Physicians his shingle back. Bones II's deal would be made at the expense of his once-promising medical career.

Of course, there'd be implications on the hockey end, too. New York's management had tried to make a splash by quickly signing Billy Mays Jr. to a contract and then putting him on tour on Broadway, trying to squeeze all the pub they could in the wake of a losing season. Senior even managed to bang the drum, getting some ink in the *Times*, doing a couple of book signings in midtown Manhattan. Pretty soon the New York GM would be on the phone to the commissioner, to the lawyers, to try to void the contract of the Kid Formerly Known as the Franchise's Saviour.

To say it was going to be complicated doesn't start to cover it. The league had run the combine and provided teams with Junior's bogus medicals as written up by Bones II. The insurance company that underwrote Mays's contract wasn't going to pay out because of a pre-existing condition not disclosed by the player or team or league. New York's corporate ownership was perturbed, to say the least, that the New York tabloids were painting the team's management and scouting department as a bunch of boneheads.

The papers spared the front office the full Agent Orange Carpet-Bombing only because so much of their attention was devoted to the gawdawful basketball team, a 60-loss sideshow complete with a team president at the centre of a sexual harassment case and a coach whose divorce and a full bench of infidelities played out daily on Page Six of the *Post*. New York's GM was pissed because the team had wasted a draft pick—in that slot scouts are expected to deliver a first-line player who's good for a thousand games in the league. Anderson and his buddies were being paid not just to sort out the talented from the mediocre but also to sort out the game-readys from the damaged goods. No extenuating circumstances could explain away their failure.

There'd be dark speculation that Ollie Buckhold was in on it too, speculation that was unfounded. Still, his rep took a tarnishing. And thereafter, teams weren't going to take medical reports on his players at face value.

It wasn't all bad news. London whizzed Pembleton but a couple of Peterborough alums convinced the board of directors that he'd be a perfect assistant coach for Bobby Reagan, who was installed as the bench boss. It might not have seemed fair, Pembleton with about seven hundred wins working for a guy who was in his first coaching job at any level. Reagan, though, was one of the Ol' Redhead's most famous and best-liked alums and a fixture on the scene in Peterpatch. The job was staying Inside the Tent Pitched by the Greatest Coach in Junior History. Reagan could be sold to the good citizens of Peterborough, though everyone on the inside knew that it would be Pembleton doing the heavy lifting. It was a good situation for Pembleton: not quite head coaching money, but some of the weight was taken off his shoulders. And Harry Bush, the overmatched assistant to the Legend Taken from Us Too Soon, had enrolled in AA and managed to convince Pembleton to get with the program. The next time I saw him, Pembleton was chain-chewing Nicorettes.

Pembleton would not have been Giuseppe Visicale's hire, but the Hockey Godfather's bid to acquire the Peterborough team fell a bit short. The mayor and a couple of board members grew spines. Visicale could get in on the arena, a money-maker, but not the team. Vis Hockey Enterprises set its sights on the franchise in Ottawa, which actually had long-untapped potential at the gate. It would also offer a chance for the Don to start snapping up kids' hockey teams in eastern Ontario. He was petitioned by directors of the Quebec league to buy in but declined to make any bids on available franchises. "That league is just too dirty," he told them.

66

A week after William Mays was arrested, Sandy and I sat down for breakfast. Egg-white omelette for her. French toast for me. She was quiet. I could tell something was on her mind.

"You knew, didn't you?" she said. An accusation dressed up as a question.

I chose to dodge. "I had reason to suspect," I said, knowing that was true enough not to trip a lie detector or her professionally honed bullshit detector.

"What reason?"

"I want to say gut feeling but that's such a cliché," I said. "The thing that bugged me from the start was the father talking up what a great coach Hanratty was. I knew he didn't believe that, not for a second, not the way Hanratty shot down his career twenty-five years before …"

I was going to skate around the fact that I chased Mays down in the parking lot, ripped off his mask, beat him to a pulp, and then didn't call the police to have him charged with assaulting her. I know. Greasy as the home fries on my plate, but in this line of work you gotta be.

"Do you think he was just going to let the boy sign a contract and take the money and then not play? Or do you think he'd actually let his son risk dying to play?"

I punched some chipotle ketchup onto my home fries.

"I know he wasn't going to give the money back, no matter what," I said. "Still, the money wasn't a motive. The Mayses hardly have use for that much more. I think Senior was going to let Junior play and run the risk of stroking out on the ice, maybe. Maybe just for a while, maybe longer than that. Just think how much the father loved the spotlight—so many of the parents do, but Senior here was the worst. He was practically needy. He was going to live vicariously through his son—even if it might kill the kid.

"You're the psychologist, not me, but I know players and how they think. Every scout is trying to get inside the head of the kid he's looking at—it's a psych game too. So here was a guy who could have been a player—to his mind anyway. Hanratty screwed him out of a career, just killed it, again at least to Senior's thinking. He wanted revenge. The son is the revenge at one level. When Hanratty and Bones found out about the heart deal, it looked to Mays like Hanratty was going to do the same thing to his family again—kill a career."

Sandy went silent.

"Why do you ask?" I said.

"Let's drop it," she said. "And you've got ketchup on your face."

67

Sandy's car was in the shop, and she wanted me to pick her up from her office Friday and take her out for dinner. It was August, hockey's doldrums, so work didn't provide me any excuses, not that I was looking for one. By all accounts and my self-image I'm no romantic, but Sandy's demands were close to the league minimum, really. A dinner, maybe two a week, a movie here and there, a drive out to the beach, a bit of life like everybody else, as if we weren't a guy who'd heard the cheers and a girl who passes Kleenex to kids telling her their woes.

I texted her from the curb. I wasn't about to pull into the parking lot, especially at three dollars for a half-hour.

1 last patient gimme 15, she texted back.

I idled outside. The construction crew was on a break. I watched a stiff in a suit carrying a briefcase and trying to hold on to his dignity as he rushed to catch a train out to the suburbs. I watched a gum-chewing secretary who had spent her working day fending off her boss's advances and was going to spend the night leaning against a bar, looking to hook a handsome and,

she hoped, flush guy. I watched a bicycle courier chase down a
cabbie who cut him off, a street sweeper checking his watch, a
hot-dog vendor sweltering behind the grill. Life's Rich Pageant.
It occurred to me that I did a lot of watching. That watching is
my living. That maybe I'm watching instead of living. I twisted
my Cup ring around my finger and rubbed it with my thumb.

Tick-tock. I reminded myself not to seem impatient when
Sandy eventually made it out.

I looked at the door. She walked out. Holding the door for
her was her 1 *last patient*, Billy Mays Jr.

She couldn't tell me that the Former Wunderkind was going
to her because he got to know her a little with the grief counselling in Peterborough. No, she *really* couldn't. It only made sense,
though. Now it was grief counselling of a different sort—his
hockey career ended before it really started, his father off to
jail. It seemed so unfair to Young What-Might-Have-Been but
that's the game. Every game, I suppose.

I figured he'd figure it out. He was a smart kid, very smart. His
life had been turned inside out and splashed across the papers
and all over television. It had been only a few weeks but supposedly there was a movie in the works. Yeah, he'd be torn up, but he
could put together the pieces with Sandy's help.

I watched Mays the Younger wave goodbye to Sandy and
head off to the subway. He didn't spot me behind the tinted
windshield and I didn't blow the horn or anything. I was one
of his yesterdays and he had to get on with his tomorrows. He
would never know that I put away his father. He would never
know that I might have saved his life. I wanted him not to know.
I wanted him to have a second shot at innocence.

Sandy didn't notice me watching Mays, or at least didn't let
on that she noticed. She opened the door and sat down beside
me, tilted her head back haughtily.

"Home, James," My Dancing Partner said.

I slipped it into gear. I pulled away.

My thoughts went to Junior. My workup on him was more comprehensive than Sandy's or anyone else's. Scouts always look for sons of players. Junior was one. Some of the game is imparted by the men in their lives. Say what you want about the life lessons Senior imparted, he made sure Junior had the best possible hockey education. Genetics, you just had to look at Billy Mays Jr. to see he had all it took, save a bum ticker.

Sandy would be concerned about Billy's future. In Crim 200 we did the short workup on theories about the criminal make-up. One theory, pretty much accepted, is that there's a genetic component. A son of a criminal is far more likely to be a criminal than the average kid, and not just because of shared circumstances. There's something there right down in the genetic coding, a criminal gene. We did a few case studies, some readings, a paper or two. Sandy's work would have been a lot more detailed. I'm sure she would be concerned about Junior's possible predisposition to be a criminal someday.

That wasn't the case, though. No reason for her concern, and no criminal gene in Billy's DNA. Yeah, M.T. Smith lost his father early, struck down by cardiac arrest late in his fourth decade, but M.T. never had a blot on his record stiffer than a speeding ticket. One real beef and he wouldn't have been eligible for his realtor's licence. Yeah, M.T. and DDoris have their names engraved on a trophy at the Toronto Lawn Tennis Club: 1991 mixed doubles. Their photo is still in the trophy case. They couldn't defend the next year as she was with child, a boy who took her husband's name and, naturally, played her boyfriend's game.

ACKNOWLEDGMENTS

I'd like to thank my editor at Penguin Books Canada, Nick Garrison, whose boundless enthusiasm, energy, and faith made this book possible. I'd like to thank Penguin Canada CEO Mike Bryan for not simply saving a spot on the slush pile for a manuscript from a fiction writer with a career total of one published short story. I'd like to thank Sandra Tooze, Stephen Myers, the rest of the Penguin staff, and copy editor Marcia Gallego.

As always, this wouldn't have happened if not for my agent, Rick Broadhead, who has gone to the wall for me so many times. Others made big contributions by reading my rough drafts: Jessica Johnson, John Brydon-Harris, Mike Sands, Damien Cox, Dr. David Newman, and my partner, Susan Bourette.

Finally, I have to acknowledge the many scouts and hockey men I've met in my work on the beat over the years. None of them is Brad Shade, but I hope if they read *The Code* they'll recognize him. And I hope they don't mistake me for Harley Hackenbush.